PROFESSOR IN PERIL

Called upon to perform a positive identification of a Soviet scholar who wishes to defect to the West, bookish and dignified James Glowrey attends an academic conference in Rio de Janeiro. In this sultry paradise, he is immediately thrust into an underworld of mobsters, gamblers, and beautiful women, one of whom he wins in a risky game of chance. But danger follows them from Brazil to the United States and finally back to Oxford, where the ultimate intellectual challenge awaits him, as well as a supreme test of courage.

PROFESSOR IN PERIL

Anthony Lejeune

ATLANTIC LARGE PRINT

Chivers Press, Bath, England.
Curley Publishing, Inc.,
South Yarmouth, Mass., USA.

Library of Congress Cataloging in Publication Data

Lejeune, Anthony.
  Professor in peril / Anthony Lejeune.
    p.   cm.—(Atlantic large print)
  ISBN 1-55504-973-7 (lg. print)
  1. Large type books.   I. Title.
  [PR6062.E465P76 1989]
  823'.914—dc20   89-32460
                                                        CIP

British Library Cataloguing in Publication Data

Lejeune, Anthony
  Professor in peril.
  I. Title
  823'.914[F]

  ISBN 0-7451-9556-3
  ISBN 0-7451-9568-7 pbk

This Large Print edition is published by Chivers Press, England, and
Curley Publishing, Inc, U.S.A. 1989

Published in the British Commonwealth by arrangement with Macmillan
London Limited and in the U.S.A. with Doubleday & Company Inc

U.K. Hardback ISBN 0 7451 9556 3
U.K. Softback ISBN 0 7451 9568 7
U.S.A. Softback ISBN 1 55504 973 7

To Mac and Carroll Ball,
dear friends and true Charlestonians,
in whose house on King Street
some of this book was written.

NOTES TO THE READER

The previous adventures of Dr. Gabriel, Richard Clayburn and Jeremy Mitchell-Pearce, and the origin of the Fishers, were described in a book called *Strange and Private War*, published by Macmillan in 1986. How Sir Arthur Blaise came to be head of his peculiar department was told in other books long ago.

The present story, about Professor James Glowrey and Cressida Lee, stands nevertheless entirely on its own. Professor Glowrey owes allegiance to no organization and no department.

The two wonderful sentences from the old black people, quoted on page 232, are real, taken from childhood recollections of South Carolina. Whose recollections? Alas, I no longer know from what book I copied them. If I did, I would offer my thanks and acknowledgements.

A.L.

PROFESSOR IN PERIL

CHAPTER ONE

A WALK IN THE PARK

The man on the bench beside the gate was watching us; I know that now, although I didn't at the time or for a long while afterwards. He was inconspicuous enough, middle-aged, a bit plump, wearing a rather ill-fitting dark suit. He was reading a magazine and never looked up at us; or, if he did, I didn't notice.

I remember him only because the whole scene is still so vivid to me. Perhaps some of the details are imaginary. A great deal flowed from that moment; it changed my life. But retrospective importance surely can't conjure up things which were not registered at the time. Or conceivably it can, if all our memories continue to exist, stored away, latent, waiting for a hypnotist or the mysterious power of our own minds to resurrect them.

Anyway, rightly or wrongly I believe I can remember everything about that morning with total clarity.

Kensington Gardens had never looked better. The air seemed washed by earlier rain, and the sun was now shining to give the promise of a perfect June day. There were

1

quite a lot of people around: tourists with guidebooks, mothers pushing prams—even one properly starched nanny; scruffy young persons entwined and nibbling each other or addling their diminutive brains with pop music played through headphones. An idiotic jogger panted past. And my two dogs flushed some Arabs. The Arab children would have talked to the dogs, but the grown-ups cowered. 'Take them away, take them away,' cried one.

The dogs are perfectly harmless, Aberdeen terriers, Angus and Hamish, but of course they'll chase whatever scurries, whether pigeons or squirrels or people. Although I call them 'my' dogs, they belong to the woman—a friend rather than a landlady—in whose house I had a pied-à-terre. I should have liked to keep dogs of my own, but it's difficult for bachelors, particularly if, like me, they spend most of the year in an Oxford college.

I had come down from Oxford the day before, ostensibly to do some work in the British Museum, really to get away from the Commemoration Balls. Not that I disapprove of dances and parties, you understand. Rather the contrary. However, I felt like the philosopher in Yeats's poem 'Sailing to Byzantium':

That is no country for old men. The
    young

2

In one another's arms, birds in the trees
—Those dying generations—at their
    song . . .

The reference is appropriate, since Byzantine studies are my field. But don't, please, picture me as decrepit. I was forty-three, if you want to know.

So there I was in the park, taking Angus and Hamish for a walk or being taken for a walk by them. With some difficulty I recalled the dogs from their pursuit of Arabs and squirrels, fastened leads to their tartan collars and began urging them homewards through the gate near Kensington Palace. A car was parked outside, a rather ancient limousine, with two men standing beside it. Seeing me, they moved forward.

I recognized the younger one. His name was Richard Clayburn. He had been an undergraduate at my college shortly after I became a Fellow. I'd met him once or twice since, at Gaudies or when he was dining as a guest at High Table, and I'd read his articles and even one of his books. He was, to the best of my knowledge, a travel writer. I was soon to learn that my knowledge, on that score, was inadequate.

The other man was small, elderly, wizened, but with very sharp eyes. He wore a black overcoat even though it was summer.

'Hello, James,' said Richard. 'What jolly

3

dogs!'

'I'm not sure that "jolly" is the word,' I said. 'They're dour, as Scottish dogs should be.'

'Oh, I'm sure they're not.' He knelt and put out his hand to them. They approached, sniffing cautiously. 'By the way,' he said, looking up, 'I don't think you've met Dr. Gabriel. And this,' he added, completing the introduction, 'is Professor Glowrey of my old college.'

As Gabriel and I shook hands, I had a distinct feeling that he already knew who I was, that they had been waiting for me.

'And what brings you here this fine morning?' I said.

'You,' said Gabriel.

'We've been to your house,' explained Richard. 'A nice woman told us we might find you here.' The dogs were now licking his fingers. Without their approval I might have been sterner.

'Really,' I said. 'How peculiar. Why do you want me?'

'I rang the college first,' said Richard. 'They gave me your London address.'

'It's no secret.'

'Perhaps,' said Gabriel, 'we might walk a little in the park.'

'I don't suppose the dogs will mind going a bit further,' said Richard.

'I'm sure they'll be delighted,' I said. 'The

4

question is, will I? However, if you want to walk, we'll walk.'

So we strolled back the way I'd come, passing the neat flowerbeds and the unkempt young and the tourists and the Arabs and the mothers with their prams. Did the man from the bench get up and follow us? I have the impression that he did; but that probably is imagination.

'Do you,' asked Gabriel, 'remember meeting a man called Surov?'

'I. P. Surov? Russian classical scholar? I know his work, of course.'

'Yes, but do you remember meeting him?'

'Now you mention it, yes, I do. At a conference in Budapest about five years ago. But only very casually.'

'Still, you met him.'

'So?'

Richard intervened. 'There's something we should tell you first. Dr. Gabriel and I are involved in what you might call an occasional enterprise which, among other benevolences (as we like to think), helps people across frontiers. Refugees—defectors—however you want to describe them. It goes back quite a long while, to before my time, to when Gabriel was helping Jews out of Germany.'

'The Fishers,' murmured Gabriel. 'We were fishers of men.'

'Sounds amusing,' I said.

'Not always,' said Richard, 'but we believe

5

it's a job worth doing.'

'And you can help us,' said Gabriel. 'At least we hope you can.'

'Indeed? How?'

'There is a degree of secrecy about this. You will regard it as confidential?'

'By all means—if you wish.'

'Surov,' said Gabriel. 'He wants to defect.'

'Good. But what has that to do with me?'

'He isn't just a classical scholar. He's a cypher expert. Rather an important one, I gather.'

'It's the textual criticism,' I suggested. 'Deducing, or guessing, emendations. Bletchley found that kind of talent useful during the war. Mind you, in my opinion, it's better for code-breaking than for Greek plays. Try to make sense of the text as we've got it, is my rule. If humanly possible.'

'Not my field,' said Gabriel. 'But the point is that Russians with the kind of knowledge which Surov must possess are not usually allowed out of the Soviet Union.'

'He's not being *allowed* out, is he? I gather he wants to escape and you're trying to help him.' As I said it, I felt—as though I were standing to one side, listening—that our conversation was becoming a trifle bizarre. The dogs, I remember, having sighted a squirrel, were pulling at their leads. I hauled them back. I didn't realize, of course that we were approaching, for me, a personal

6

Rubicon; and yet I was aware, already, that something strange was touching my life. Perhaps it was Gabriel's personality; he was by no means an insignificant little man.

'He is being allowed out. For a few days. To another conference. This side of the Iron Curtain.'

'And that,' said Richard, 'is where we hoped you might come in.'

'Would you be free,' asked Gabriel, 'in three weeks' time, to make a little journey?'

'Now hold on,' I protested. 'Stop beating around the bush. But first let me tell you: I don't like journeys; I've no desire to get mixed up in this sort of thing; and, since I met this man Surov only once, for a few hours, several years ago, I don't see what use I could be to you anyway.'

'You met him only once,' said Gabriel, 'but no one else in this country seems to have met him at all. No one we can find. And what we need to know is whether the man who presents himself actually is Surov. Do you think you would recognize him?'

'I might. But why shouldn't he be Surov, if that's who he says he is?'

'Maybe no reason. It's probably quite all right. But we've learned to be cautious; and, as I said, I'm a bit surprised that a man in Surov's position should be allowed to travel in the West.'

'All this may sound rather melodramatic—'

put in Richard.

'It does.'

'—but we do have reason for care. We've walked into traps before.'

'And how about the Foreign Office? Do they know anything about this plan? Or are you going to cause an international incident?'

Gabriel smiled grimly. 'It wouldn't be the first time. Governments don't like us and we don't like governments. But, as a matter of fact, the Foreign Office does know; at least, a certain department of the Foreign Office, in which I have an old friend. Surov asked that we should make the contact. He doesn't trust them. He wanted us to negotiate on his behalf.'

'So he's not just bringing a knowledge of classical texts?'

'No. Other things, which my friend will be glad to receive.'

'And can't your friend identify Surov?'

'Not for sure. There's only a bad photograph.'

'It's probably no worse than my memory.'

'Perhaps. But you could supplement your memory. You're a distinguished classical scholar. You could talk to him about his own subject. Wouldn't you know if he was a fake?'

'Plenty of fraudulent academics go undiscovered a great deal nearer to home; fawned on by some of my colleagues.'

'But not by you,' said Richard.

'No, not by me. And why, pray, should I undertake this task?'

'As a kindness,' said Gabriel. 'Patriotism? For a reasonable fee, if you want one.'

'For fun,' said Richard.

'Ah, now that's a better argument. You haven't told me where this conference is going to be.'

'Rio de Janeiro,' said Gabriel. 'A beautiful place.'

'Hm,' I grunted. And thought. The truth is that I was restless. The prospect of the summer vacation filled me with no joy. I don't believe in holidays, but nor had I much enthusiasm for the research on which I was, rather desultorily, engaged. There was certainly no hurry about it. There was nowhere I wanted to go, no one I particularly wanted to see. I had no serious engagements until a college meeting in September.

'Well, I suppose I might,' I said grudgingly. The Rubicon was crossed. 'But if I'm really going to do this—and I've not yet definitely said I will—I shall need to know a lot more. About Surov. And about this fishing affair of yours.'

'Of course,' agreed Gabriel.

'Could you come to dinner tomorrow night?' asked Richard. 'We could brief you then.'

'All right. Where?'

'My flat.' He smiled sheepishly. 'I married

9

a wife not long ago.'

'Yes. So I saw in the College Record. Congratulations. Marriage, I believe, is generally supposed to be a matter for congratulation.'

'Oh, it is. You should try it.' He scribbled on a bit of paper. 'Here's the address. Eight o'clock?'

'Eight o'clock.'

'See you then.' Richard stooped to pat the dogs, who were making their boredom obvious.

Gabriel gave a slight bow. 'Goodbye for the present, then, Professor Glowrey. I am most grateful to you.'

And they were gone, out through the gate of the park to their car. I stood watching them, while the dogs panted and whined. My feelings, as far as I can remember, were chiefly of amusement; amusement at how suddenly things can change, and at myself for accepting so readily—if I had accepted, and it seemed I had—such a peculiar proposal.

★   ★   ★

Richard's flat was in Belgravia. I walked from Sloane Square tube station. The evening was clear and cool. Outside the pubs young men in blazers and girls in summer frocks stood, glasses in hand, chattering noisily. The houses, with their white pillars and balconies, were utterly and elegantly characteristic of that part of London. Most of them nowadays, like the one where Richard lived, were divided into flats. His name was on a card next to the third in a column of five bell-buttons. I pressed it. A woman's voice answered on the entry-phone. I announced myself, she told me to walk up two flights of stairs, and the door clicked open.

I had, as I told Richard, vaguely noticed his marriage, not to anyone I knew but to a girl who had been at Oxford a few years after him and who had, as I recalled, been fashionable in her day. He was standing in the doorway to welcome me, and she emerged from the kitchen into a little hall. 'Darling,' he said, 'this is James Glowrey. My wife, Diana.' She was a good-looking woman; fair hair, well-cut features; dressed simply and, I imagined, expensively in blue. Her handshake was firm.

As we went through into the sitting room, two men stood up. One was Gabriel, the other, immaculately suited in light-grey Prince of Wales check, might have been a little older than at first glance he seemed, which would have been in his early- to mid-thirties. He had a quizzical air, which was superficially youthful and flippant but masked something shrewd.

'Dr. Gabriel you know,' said Richard. 'This is our associate, Jeremy

Mitchell-Pearce. Now, what will you have to drink?'

The answer, of course, was sherry, this being, in my view, the only proper drink before dinner. Spirits are an insult to one's hostess, since they anaesthetize the taste-buds. I had good hopes of dinner. Richard's wife was unmistakably efficient, and the table at the far end of the room gleamed invitingly with silver and glass. Glasses, indeed, in promising profusion.

We talked of nothing in particular until Diana lit the candles and summoned us to the table. The food and wine lived up fully to my expectations. Light conversation is not, perhaps, my strong suit, nor, I fancy, was it Gabriel's; but Jeremy sparkled. I found him, truth to tell, a little irritating. Richard and Diana were excellent hosts. I'm always rather touched when the young are nice to me; not, in fact, that Richard is very much my junior, but it felt as though they both were.

Outside the open windows, the sky above the chimneyed roofs of Belgravia changed from duck-egg blue to purple. It was quiet; there's not a great deal of traffic in those streets at night. Richard, I thought (letting my attention wander while Jeremy told a long story), was to be envied, starting on married life in such agreeable circumstances. Always assuming that one wanted to be married. But if one did, this girl must surely be a sound candidate; adequately pretty and sensible, too.

She went out to fetch the coffee, and he produced a decanter of port. Without asking, he poured brandy instead for Gabriel. It was obvious that these four people knew each other very well, curiously matched though in some ways they were. Not a word had been said so far about the purpose of our meeting, and I had studiously refrained from raising the topic or asking about the mysterious enterprises in which they were, I presumed, jointly engaged. I gathered, from his anecdotes, that Jeremy had once been in the army—a very smart regiment, I felt sure—and I'd learned that Diana was involved, or had been involved before her marriage, in running an art gallery; but I had discovered nothing more pertinent. Some of the talk, inevitably, was about Oxford. Gabriel said very little, but I formed a distinct impression that he was summing me up. Well, if he wanted to play conversational poker, let him. I was quite good at that game, too.

At last, when the coffee had been poured and the port circulated, Richard said, 'Do you think, reluctantly, we should get down to business?'

'"However entrancing it is to wander unchecked through a garden of bright images,"' quoted Jeremy, '"are we not

13

enticing your mind from another subject of almost equal importance?"'

'I'm glad someone still reads Kai Lung,' I said, staking my claim to competitive literacy. My opinion of Jeremy Mitchell-Pearce changed slightly, or at least swung looser at its moorings.

'Shall I run through the main points?' suggested Gabriel. 'Those things which Professor Glowrey ought to know.' He had a slight accent, German, I supposed, and his voice was soft but there was an undertone of authority. Not authority in the military sense, rather more as one speaks of an academic authority; the confidence born of knowledge or experience or faith.

'One,' he said, holding up his forefinger. 'As we told you' (he was looking at me), 'we have a little organization, started by me long ago, by me and a friend'—he paused for a second, his mind apparently slipping back to a far past—'which we call the Fishers. I needn't trouble you with many details. We believe that what we do is useful, and I don't think we do anything which you would find objectionable. Well, not often.' He smiled. 'Sometimes it is maybe a bit illegal, but usually not in this country and certainly not on this occasion. However, I must be fair and tell you that we have enemies. The people we try to help are all escaping from something. A few months ago a very determined effort was made to destroy us. More than one person was killed. I think that's over now, but it could happen again.'

'Sooner or later it will,' said Jeremy.

Diana shivered. 'I hope not.'

'Perhaps,' said Gabriel. 'But that need not concern Professor Glowrey. If he agrees, very kindly, to do what we are asking, he will be involved with us, with the work of the Fishers, for only a short while. Barely a touch. He will need to meet our colleague in Rio and talk to Surov. That's all. There should be no danger for him.'

'I'm glad to hear it,' I said drily. At that point I didn't really take his mention of danger seriously. The idea was too remote, too anomalous, in that quiet London room, towards the end of an eminently civilized dinner party. As things turned out, Gabriel's reassuring prediction was wildly wrong, although—to do him justice—his analysis was right.

He continued, raising two fingers. 'Second: Surov. Surov wants our help to defect. He wants us to negotiate the terms of his asylum. He trusts us, apparently, more than he trusts the British Government. All right. I can imagine he might have heard of us. I can imagine he might think it safer to make the first contact through us. That kind of thing has happened before. But we must be sure he's genuine; that he is who he says he is and

15

wants what he says he wants. Richard, have you the photograph?'

'Yes.' Opening his wallet, Richard extracted a small glossy print. It was an amateur photograph, perhaps a clandestine one. It might have been taken at a party; there was a blur of other people in the background. The man in the foreground was stocky, bald, with a round, cheerful face and slightly slanting eyes.

'Is that the man you met?' asked Gabriel.

'I think so,' I replied. 'At least it could be. I'm not sure after so long.'

Gabriel nodded. 'That's as much as we could expect.'

'Where did you get this picture?'

'From a friend in the Foreign Office. The one I was telling you about.'

I passed the photograph back to Richard. 'How did Surov get in touch with you?' I asked.

'The Fishers are not a vast organization with agents everywhere. Don't imagine that. But we do have friends. Some behind the Iron Curtain. I'd rather not tell you anything too precise. It's safer for us and for you. I learned about security in a hard school.'

'Of course. I understand. But the message, in whatever form it reached you, said that Surov means to defect during this conference in Rio?'

'Yes. We shall provide a safe house and

arrange onward transmission to London. Again, none of that need concern you.'

'And have you fixed political asylum for him?'

'Not exactly. That may depend on what he has to offer. But he can be sure of a welcome.'

'Is it—would it be—my job to tell him?'

'No, no. We shall have our man there. All you need do, when you talk to Surov, is satisfy yourself of his identity.'

'Am I supposed to know about the defection? Do I tell him that I come from you?'

'If you wish. Whatever seems convenient.'

'The conference, I presume, is the Schliemann Society Conference on Classical Epigraphy and Textual Criticism?'

'How did you know that?'

'It was no great feat of detection. There aren't all that many international classical conferences, and, to the best of my knowledge, there's only one being held this year in Latin America.'

Gabriel looked at me rather as I had looked at Jeremy when he quoted that sentence from Kai Lung. 'Ah. Is it an important conference, the sort which Surov might reasonably wish to attend?'

'Oh yes. Most respectable. The Schliemann Society meets in a different country every year. The locations are chosen more as being suitable for a jamboree than from any

17

scholarly connection.

'I looked it up,' I said. 'The conference begins at the end of the week after next.'

'Will you go?' asked Gabriel.

'If you pay my fare. First class.'

'We'll do more than that. I mentioned a fee—'

'I don't want a fee. You can send me a case of port and a case of claret when I get back. Decent port and decent claret.'

'Speaking of which,' said Jeremy, 'the poor man's dying of thirst. Shove that decanter round, will you, Diana?'

Gabriel held up three fingers. 'Good. Now, number three. Practical considerations. This is how I suggest that we proceed . . .'

The party broke up at around half past twelve. Jeremy gave me a lift back to Kensington in his car, a magnificent old sports model; a Morgan, I think. There may have been someone watching the house when we came out. It seems to me now, remembering the man on the park bench, quite likely. But, if so, I didn't see him. We were in a cheerful mood. Carefree.

CHAPTER TWO

'ALL THE WORLD IS WILD AND STRANGE'

I flew to Brazil ten days later. It's a long haul, but I never mind that; one has time to think. Think is about all one's allowed to do on an aeroplane. The constant inedible meals and snacks, the peddling of duty-free but over-priced alcohol and tobacco, the 'in-flight movie,' the hot towels and cool drinks, the forms to fill in and the announcements from the captain ensure that passengers get a minimum of rest. And the air hostesses are no longer worth looking at. However, I'm quite good at drifting and dreaming. So I closed my eyes and took stock.

It was mildly surprising, still, to find myself there, flying across the ocean. I'd been becoming set in my ways lately. Indeed, some of my acquaintances say I've been set in my ways—and my ideas—since I was twenty, or earlier. And why not? A satisfactory routine is not a bad formula for a contented life; there is much to be said for an ordinary day. As for ideas, only a fool keeps changing them, the way silly women keep changing the shape of their dresses.

They change their skies but not their minds

19

who rush across the sea, said the poet Horace. And the state of one's mind is more important to one's happiness than the state of the sky. Why, really, had I agreed so easily to Dr. Gabriel's suggestion? The answer, I suppose, lay in my mind. I had become at least mildly discontented, for no cause I could exactly define. Looking back on it now, I'm tempted to wonder if our lives may not be shaped by influences, factors, patterns—call them what you will—quite beyond our perception. You can call them 'chance': but as Voltaire said, chance is the known result of unknown causes. A little superstition in such matters seems to me prudent (perhaps this is my Highland ancestors speaking); I have a healthy respect for unknown gods.

However, since (despite my Highland ancestry) I cannot, I'm glad to say, foresee the future, my speculations, as I sat in that aeroplane, were less profound. I thought that, having fulfilled Gabriel's mission, which shouldn't take more than a couple of days, I might go to Peru and look at the Inca ruins, or perhaps down to Chile, where a government so universally reviled must clearly have some merits, which would be interesting to observe. I thought a little about Surov, but I could only just remember him. He was a competent scholar, but not a particularly original one; not somebody with whom I yearned to have academic discussions. I thought rather more about Gabriel and Richard and the Fishers. Gabriel had impresed me; in him, I suspected, there were complexities worth plumbing. And there was obviously a side to Richard Clayburn which I hadn't guessed. I was not, I dare to say, altogether an innocent in such matters. Oxford dons, in our uncivilized century, have been frequently involved with worldly affairs; I've heard strange stories, after dinner, in the common room of my own college.

So I dreamt the flight away, and I was quite sorry when the changed note of the engines revealed that we had begun our descent.

As the plane tilted, a crescent-edged carpet of lights slid beneath us. I caught a glimpse of the illuminated Christ-figure on its mountain-top. However sophisticated a traveller one may be, there remains something ineffably mysterious and exciting about coming down into a foreign city at night. Although I had been in Rio before, the topography is difficult and I could summon only a vague impression of the beaches and of the mountains pressing in on the city, with squalid clusters of shacks clinging to them, so near to and yet such worlds away from the great international hotels. I knew that, despite its name, Rio has no river and that it is indeed a place of extraordinary beauty, comparable with Cape Town or San

21

Francisco. Later in the year it would be intolerably hot, but now it should be quite agreeable. By the time I left London the British summer had reverted to normal and it was raining. English people, though not I, were accustomed to take summer holidays in order to escape the rain. If all else failed, I could regard this curious trip in that simple light.

The plane touched down with the barest jump and judder. After the usual irritating delay, during which we stood, waiting, clutching our cabin luggage, we were allowed through the door, and instantly the blanket of tropic warmth enfolded us. The Brazilian immigration officer, who appeared to speak very little English, stamped my passport and waved me on with careless rapidity, and, for once, my well-worn canvas suitcase was among the first on the carousel. I hauled it off, passed equally without trouble through customs, looked around, and was immediately approached by a slim olive-skinned man with greased hair and a little black moustache.

'Professor Glowrey?' he said.

'Yes.' I wondered how he had recognized me so confidently. Possibly my tweed hat. No one else was wearing a tweed hat.

'I am Ramirez,' he said. 'Welcome to Brazil.' The accent was American but he seemed to speak quite good English. He took my case and led me out to a battered motor car; the battering, I soon decided, was attributable more to his method of driving than to the antiquity of the vehicle. As we sped towards the centre of the city, he talked, often raising his hands alarmingly from the wheel in order to gesticulate more vigorously.

'I put you in a nice hotel,' he said. 'Very nice hotel. Facing the beach. This conference you go to is in big hotel. Not far. Surov stays there, but I thought better you didn't.'

'You've met him?' I asked.

'No. He came yesterday and he called a number like he was told to. Not mine. Until we are sure, we are being very careful. No contact. Not direct. But we don't have too much time. The conference, it lasts one week.'

'I know. And it starts tomorrow. I'll identify him and talk to him as soon as I can, and then I'll tell you yes or no; this is or isn't the man I met before. And that's my job done.'

Ramirez smiled and gestured expansively. He had a gold tooth. 'After that you enjoy Rio. Or maybe you enjoy the conference?'

'I doubt that.'

'But you are a man of much learning. My friend Jeremy tells me so. You know my friend Jeremy?'

'I met him in London.'

'What a man! A man, like they say, to go

23

with you into the jungle.'

'I did rather get that impression.'

'But you are not a man for jungles. You are a man for books. I read many books. Your Mr. Harold Robbins. And James Bond. You read them?'

'I'm familiar with them.'

'What you like to see in Rio? I show you round. Girls on beach? Boys on beach? Or maybe genuine special-for-tourists Macumba ceremony?' He laughed.

'Let's wait until I've done the job. And I imagine you'll have arrangements to make.'

'I make arrangements. No problem.'

He was right about the hotel. It was quite small, facing across the wide Avenida Atlantica to Copacabana Beach. The staff at the reception desk were polite, the rooms clean and cheerful. In front, on a slightly raised miniature terrace, tables were set out, each bearing its own glass lantern with a candle inside. By Latin standards the evening was young, but about half the tables were occupied, and not, I thought, by tourists; a good sign.

'The manager here,' said Ramirez, 'he is friend of mine. Good man. Safe place. But better maybe you and I are not seen together too much. So you come home to my apartment. We dine there.'

Again we drove through streets that registered only as a confusion of lights and darkness, with glimpses of the sea below, as we wound quite steeply upwards; and always above, though from different angles, Christ the Redeemer, arms outstretched, on Mount Corcovado. Modern concrete gave way to what seemed much older stone buildings with wooden shutters and wrought-iron balconies. And the streets were quieter; we had left behind the unending procession of tourists and indeed natives—Cariocas, one was supposed to call them—walking up and down, to see and be seen, to gossip and chatter and flirt the long warm hours away.

We drew up outside a tall house, shadowy in the dim street lighting. My recollection is of peeling paint and rusting iron, a deserted lobby, a lift that ascended reluctantly and noisily, another tiny hallway with two doors. Ramirez, inserting his key, whistled—three rising notes—to announce his arrival. That the woman who greeted us should have been attractive, in an ample Latin way, was no surprise. The uxoriousness of Ramirez, evident immediately and throughout the evening, was.

Having embraced her, he said, 'Luisa, my love, my flower, here is my new friend, the Profesor Glowrey. Professor, here is my beautiful wife, the mother of my children.'

Luisa curtsied before shaking hands. Ramirez poured me a drink, and then went through to another room, where his two children were apparently waiting for him to say good night. While Luisa, who spoke only a few words of English, prepared the dinner, I looked around the apartment, which was cluttered with bits and pieces, cheap china ornaments, plastic toys left on the floor, paperback books, Brazilian women's magazines, a garish picture of the Virgin; by no means gracious living, but a home in which real people lived.

The dinner which followed wasn't too bad; the wine, if undistinguished, was plentiful. Luisa tried to make up, by attentiveness and smiles, for her lack of English. Ramirez told stories and laughed and made fun of the Cariocas. After dinner we looked at television, at a programme which he said was one of Luisa's favourites. He gave me a running translation. It featured an investigative reporter whose function, as far as I could understand it, was to bring together in the studio people who had the strongest possible reasons to dislike each other. The more violent the confrontation, the more entertaining the spectacle was deemed to be. If they came to blows, Ramirez said, the evening was considered a particular success. Tonight no blows were struck, for which Ramirez courteously apologized. But we saw a weeping woman accuse a man—a jilted lover, I gathered—of having put her baby in the oven, a man whose house had been machine-gunned in a quarrel over some small debt, and, for light relief, a dentist facing a whole row of patients whose false teeth didn't fit.

'Why do these villains agree to appear on the programme?' I asked.

'For money,' chuckled Ramirez. 'Much money. One time we had somebody kill himself right there in the studio. That was magnificent.'

He and Luisa sat side by side on an uncomfortable-looking sofa, his arm around her shoulders. Several glasses of fiery brandy completed the evening. She curtsied again when saying goodbye, and, at about one o'clock, Ramirez—or Pedro, as I had now learned to call him—drove me back to the hotel. Not until we were in the car did he make any further mention of our business. Then he said, 'Tomorrow it will be best you get a taxi to the conference. Not far. Five, ten minutes. When you have seen our friend, you give me a call. Like you say, just yes or no. After, I fix everything.'

'Gabriel gave me your telephone number,' I said, digging in my pocket for the small address book I carry. 'Is this the right one to use?'

'It's my office. Import, export. You know—everything.' He waved his hands airily. 'My secretary, she answer the telephone. You leave messages. But I give

27

you my home number too. If Luisa answer, you just tell her your name. She understand. I call back. You write the number.'

I wrote it. He dropped me at the door of my hotel. The tables on the little terrace and the sidewalk of the Avenida seemed as busy as ever. The stars shone brightly in a velvet sky above a dark sea, lined at the edge with the phosphorescence of the waves. I shook hands with Pedro which is what he seemed to expect.

'That was a most enjoyable evening,' I said, and actually meant it. 'Please convey my thanks to Luisa. I hope I shall see her again while I'm here.'

'Of course. Next time we celebrate.' And with a flourish he zoomed away.

I fell asleep at once, with no opportunity to think forward or back; and, anyway, nothing had happened yet to suggest that what lay ahead was going to be more difficult or far-reaching than I had expected. Before leaving London I had looked up all of Surov's articles that I could find in the classical journals. If by any chance the man I was about to meet was not the genuine Surov, he would nevertheless have equipped himself with at least a superficially plausible amount of knowledge on Surov's subject; but I had worked out lines of conversation which would, I hoped and believed, rapidly distinguish a genuine scholar from an impostor who had merely absorbed a briefing.

The sun was already quite hot when I awoke, and already on the beach deeply bronzed young men were throwing medicine balls at each other. I wanted to be at the conference for the signing-in session, so that I could pick out Surov—or false-Surov—as soon as possible.

As Pedro had told me, the journey to the huge American hotel, all gleaming white concrete and tinted glass and air-conditioning, was short. A notice-board in the lobby offered several conferences, all tediously commercial except for the Schliemann Society's, which, it informed us, was being held on the third floor in the Bolivar Room.

In an outer room, under-lit and quite chilly, two dark-haired girls sat at a table, dispensing plastic folders and name-tags. Through open double-doors I could see the conference room: a dais, a lectern, rows of hard chairs. Some of my colleagues—some of everybody's colleagues—spend much of their lives attending conferences, where they listen, or doze through, lengthy papers being read to them, which they could read for themselves (in the improbable contingency of their wishing to do so) in a quarter of the time. Presumably they enjoy it. I don't.

Nor did my heart leap at the sight of several familiar faces. There was a Cambridge don whose ignorance is exceeded only by his vanity, and a French professor whom I once engaged and, I'm happy to say, routed in acrimonious debate, and an American whose Germanically detailed learning would be more acceptable if he refrained from communicating it in such undigested gobbets. One or two others whom I recognized were harmless, but not the sort I would choose for drinking companions, even when tasting the Pierian spring.

The girl at the table checked my name on her list and gave me a name-tag to pin on my coat. I promptly put it into my pocket. Why should one go around, labelled, announcing one's identity to people whose acquaintance one may have no desire to make? However, on this occasion the system proved helpful. The badges were laid out on the table, in front of the two girls, in alphabetical order, and among them, sure enough, was one bearing the name 'Dr. I. P. Surov.' Retreating to a chair against the wall a few feet away, I opened my folder and made a show of studying the papers.

Two Oxonians appeared: a female historian, of unattractive aspect but, I had to admit, scholastically excellent, and a left-wing don from Balliol. I buried myself deeper in the wodge of duplicated material. Fortunately they were too busy talking to notice me. Among the papers I found a complete list of those attending the conference, with nationalities in brackets after their names. Surov was not the only Russian; there were two others, unknown to me.

Even as I was reading their names, they emerged from the lift. There was no mistaking them. Surov I recognized at once, although whether from the photograph or from memory would be hard to say; but the stocky figure, the bald head, the Slavic features were what I had been expecting. One of his companions was a small man with a grey wispy beard. The other was large and much younger; his eyes darted around the room. I could quite believe that he was a secret policeman. Their suits were ill-fitting in a way distinct from a badly cut Western suit. I rebuked my tailor recently for not understanding what a tweed suit is about; the essence, the theme (as Churchill said of an unsatisfactory pudding) had escaped him. But far more than just a theme had escaped the manufacturer—one could scarcely call him a tailor—of these suits. However, one mustn't hold a man's clothes against him. (Not excessively. These Russians had the excuse of having come from Russia. The Balliol don had come from Oxford. There could be no excuse for his suit.) Surov was talking animatedly to his companions. I was reminded again that I had thought him, when we met before (if it was indeed the same

31

man), quite agreeable.

I let them collect their folders and badges—Surov was duly given the one I had been watching—and then followed them into the conference room. No one had greeted them or approached them. The room was filling up, but more people were standing and conversing than sitting. Surov's party strolled down the right-hand side towards the front. Tacking to avoid the Cambridge don, I went briskly down the centre aisle and turned towards them; hesitated, looked at Surov and then approached with my hand extended.

'It's Dr. Surov, isn't it?' I said. 'Do you remember me? Glowrey. Oxford.'

'But naturally,' he said, taking my hand in his podgy paw. His grip was firm. 'Who in our field does not know the work of Professor Glowrey?' So he knew that I was a professor. But he could have read that on the conference list, which he would, no doubt, have studied in advance.

'We met somewhere,' I said. 'Another conference perhaps . . . ?'

'Perhaps. It is a very hard life we lead. We must come to these dreadful places.' He laughed jovially. 'You know my friends, Professor Ilyin?'—the one with the beard; 'and Dr. Korbanov?'—the younger one with the searching eyes. They bowed from their positions farther along the row of chairs.

People were now beginning to take their

seats, and the chairman of the first session, a Brazilian, had mounted the low dais, followed by the President of the Society, an American from Yale, whose work I knew but whom I'd never met. The Russians sat down. I took the chair next to Surov.

Before I could open another line of conversation, the chairman was tapping a microphone on the lectern to test it. The chatter died down. After a few sentences of flowery welcome, the chairman introduced the President, who was to give the opening address, called, according to the agenda, 'Sermons in Stones.' Truth to tell, it was quite an elegant oration; I sat through it, only mildly restive.

Next came a paper on the latest methods of rendering worn inscriptions legible. It told me more than I wished to know.

Lunch followed, a buffet in an adjoining room. I couldn't altogether avoid my acquaintances, but, having slid from one group to another, exchanging a civil word, I rejoined the Russians. The gambits I had planned were, in the nature of the case, quite rarefied; I could test Surov or false-Surov (and, after watching him all morning from the corner of my eye, I was no nearer being sure which he was) only by pursuing topics too remote and improbable for any impostor to have swotted them up. I intended, for example, to raise the question of Thracian cavalry tactics and the peculiar diamond formation which they employed when charging. This had only the most devious connection with Surov's expertise, but something in one of his articles led me to believe that he was, in fact, familiar with the obscure text from which we derive that piece of information. However, it isn't the easiest of subjects to raise casually, even at a conference of classical scholars. Nor were the other possible lines of attack which I had prepared.

The lunch hour was drawing to a close and so far I had achieved nothing. Every attempt had been frustrated, either because Surov had led the conversation away on a tangent or because we had been interrupted. And I was aware, all the time, of Korbanov watching and listening. My job was clearly going to be more difficult than I had realized. I needed to get Surov by himself for at least half an hour.

I looked at my watch. 'We'll be going back in a minute,' I said. 'You know, I think I'll cut this afternoon's session. I'm still pretty tired from the journey, and it will be more polite if I sleep in my hotel room rather than during our colleague's paper.'

'Sleep is natural,' said Surov. 'More natural than listening to lectures.'

'What are you doing for dinner tonight?'

'We three dine together in our hotel. Things to discuss. Then I expect we sleep too. Early bed.' He smiled disarmingly, put his hands together beside his head and mimed the action of sinking on to a pillow.

There was nothing for it but to show a card. Korbanov had turned away for a moment, to hear something Ilyin said. I dropped my voice a little. 'Actually I've come to Brazil not just for the conference but for the fishing. I'd like to discuss that with you.'

Our eyes met. 'Ah,' he said, 'that's different. Tara's Hall. Eleven o'clock.' Turning away, he immediately joined in the conversation with Korbanov and Ilyin.

I picked up my folder, and, as the others began drifting back into the conference room, I slipped out of the other door and escaped. Surov had spoken so softly that I wasn't sure I'd caught the name correctly. But that was what it sounded like: 'Tara's Hall.' I could hardly ask him to repeat it.

The sun was very hot outside, and I was glad to get back to the cool of my own room. Glad, too, to be away from the conference. I've often said that my decision, made in the Fourth Form at school, to be a classical scholar rather than go on the Modern or Science side was one of the few in my life that I have never for a moment regretted. I love the ancient world, its sense of proportion, the Roman discipline, the Greek hatred of monsters. I love old books and old libraries. But I do not love the company of my professional colleagues, who take their

35

subjects at once too seriously and too lightly: too seriously in their zeal for unimportant technicalities, and too lightly in that they don't really listen to the authors. Xenophon would feel much more at home among the young Guards officers and with the hunting and fishing conversation at Pratt's Club in London than in the company of modern scholars. Those couples walking, entwined, beside the ocean were far closer in spirit to Catullus and Sappho than the dons assembled in an air-conditioned conference room.

Appearances, of course, deceive. Young hearts may beat beneath wizened exteriors. The driest scholar may once have heard the nightingales, may hear them still despite his pedantry.

I was much more intrigued by the problem of Surov than by the problems of epigraphy. The Fishers, I realized, had hooked me too. I was taking now the first step away, or perhaps it was already the second step, from the everyday path, the safely trodden track.

A stone's throw out on either hand
From that well-ordered road we tread,
And all the world is wild and
     strange . . .

No one had lured me, no one had tricked me. I knew what I was doing. I lay on my bed, looking at the ceiling. I picked up the

36

telephone.

I dialled Pedro's office number. He was there, perhaps waiting for my call. I told him what had happened and what I thought Surov had said to me. 'Does that make any sense to you?' I asked. 'Tara's Hall?'

'Oh yes.' He paused. 'You will go there?'

'If you tell me where and what it is.'

'Tara's Hall is a night-club. And a place for gambling. And other things. Very smart, very crooked. The man who owns it is called Fernando O'Malley. Surov likes to gamble. That I learned from our friends. So I told him to go last night to Tara's Hall; just to play a little, nothing more. He could say he had asked the porter at the hotel where was good place to gamble. And maybe go again tonight. So it will seem normal. No one will be surprised if he go there later.'

'And you want him there?'

'At Tara's Hall things can be made to happen.'

'This man O'Malley is a friend of our friends?'

'Senhor O'Malley is a friend only of himself. But his help is for sale.'

'I see. And where is it?'

'Ask the desk clerk at your hotel. He will get you a car. He knows Tara's Hall. Best that I should not be seen there. But I will arrange. When you arrive, say, "Senhor O'Malley is expecting me."'

'And he will be? How much does he know?'

'Nothing yet. Not from me. But I have used him and his men before. Who knows how much he knows? Too much, maybe. But he will make sure you and Surov can talk. I fix now. Good luck, Professor.'

CHAPTER THREE

THAT SMALL DANGEROUS ROOM

English names are chic in Rio; which presumably includes Irish names. The words 'Tara's Hall' were written in italicized red neon above the door, followed by a green harp. A doorman in a green uniform stood outside. Light glowed through curtains. It looked an expensive establishment.

When I'd mentioned Tara's Hall to the desk clerk at the hotel, he responded with a professional blend of impassivity and a delicately raised eyebrow. 'I'm told that it's an interesting place,' I said.

'Interesting, senhor? I believe so.'

'Do you know Mr. O'Malley, who runs it?'

'By reputation, senhor.'

'Good reputation or bad reputation?'

'That depends what you want.'

I grunted, and sat down to wait for the taxi.

We drove through a tunnel, and then along brightly illuminated streets; and now here I was. As I paid the driver, I had been aware of the doorman scrutinizing me. But he said nothing, merely pulled open the curtained glass door. The vestibule was small and elegant, with low lights and two leather-padded (or, more likely, plastic-padded) doors opening off it. A young man in a dinner-jacket sat behind a reception desk. He looked up.

'Mr. O'Malley is expecting me,' I said. 'Professor Glowrey.'

'Oh yes,' he said, glancing at a file in front of him. He lifted an ivory telephone and said a few words in Portuguese. 'Someone will be with you in just a moment, Professor.'

The 'someone,' who emerged from the right-hand door, was a thug in a dinner-jacket, which he probably called a tuxedo. In describing him, and indeed instantly placing him in my own mind, as a thug, I was responding, of course, to a stereotype; but stereotypes are accepted because they do generally—not always, but generally—represent a truth. Anyway, this man was a thug if I've ever seen one, burly and wary.

'This way,' he said.

Beyond the door was a little hall, with cloakrooms on the left and a hat-check girl behind a counter on the right. We passed through and into a restaurant. It was half-full: just two or three couples gyrating on a postage-stamp dance-floor. The music was soft, the room bathed in a warm pink glow; the impression was of luxury. We skirted the podium, on which the half-dozen bandsmen sat, and went through another door, hardly visible in the cream-and-gold painted wall. We were in a corridor with several doors, and with another corridor leading off it; the building was a warren. We turned a corner, and in front of us was a double-door. Inside hung a red velvet curtain. The thug held it aside for me to enter.

In somebody's memoirs—Gronow's, I think—there is a description of the inner room at Crockford's, the most famous gambling-house of all, where so many Regency aristocrats were ruined. 'I shall never forget that small dangerous room,' he said, and I can echo his words. The room was indeed quite small, and dark, but the darkness was inviting, comforting rather than chilling. It was a room calculated to make one feel at ease, which was part of the danger. On the far side was a bar, back-lit, from which a girl in a very short skirt carried drinks on a silver tray. There were a couple of bar stools and, in the far corner, two armchairs; none of them in use. The occupants, perhaps fifteen or twenty people in all, men and women, were seated in two groups. At a table on the

40

left, they were playing roulette. The table in front of me, with a silk-shaded light above, was ringed by people playing cards. Recollecting them now, I can see black-coated male backs, the bare shoulders of women, jewels round their throats, and two faces.

The man directly opposite me was dealing. He was middle-aged, probably nearer fifty than forty, with a round face, eyebrows that seemed to turn up at the ends, and the quizzical air of a mischievous—in retrospect I would say wicked—leprechaun. Beside him but a little behind, as though to dissociate herself from the game, sat a girl.

The beauty of women is a strange thing, partly objective—how else could there be film stars or beauty contests?—but also intensely personal. What determines, very early in life, that we shall prefer, say, Joan Crawford to Marilyn Monroe, or whatever more modern examples you wish to take? It's not that one of them looks like our mother or the girl next door or even unlike the girl next door. The roots of aesthetic preference are more profound and mysterious, and they affect our whole life. There is no greater power in the world than beauty. Paris gave Aphrodite the prize, and so do we all.

Homer never describes Helen, except to say that she had white arms. He simply tells how, when she walked on the walls of Troy, the old men looked at her and said, 'No wonder. No wonder the Greeks and Trojans should have fought so long for such a woman.' Let me copy Homer's wise restraint. I will only say, about the girl on whom I first set eyes that night, that the soft lines of her face struck me almost like a physical blow. Objective beauty or subjective? Objective to the extent that no one could deny this was a beautiful woman, subjective in the sense that hers was the kind of beauty which I had always imagined. A rare, rare thing. She was much younger than the man. Much younger than me.

Passing the cards to his neighbour, he rose and came to me, smiling, his hand extended. 'Professor Glowrey, is it? My name's Fernando O'Malley, if you can believe such a thing. You're very welcome.' His Irish brogue, I thought, was too ostentatious to be entirely plausible.

'A mutual friend suggested—'

'I know, I know. No names, no pack-drill; that's O'Malley's rule. And you're wanting to have a little talk in private with another friend. He's not here yet but no doubt he'll be coming. Are you a gambling man, Professor?'

'Not really,' I said.

'And very wise too. It's a weakness of mine, as you can see. You won't join us at the table, then; but you'll take a drink, surely, while you're waiting, and I'll ask Cressida to entertain you.' He signalled to the girl, who was still sitting, watching us.

She wore an evening dress of deep crimson, smooth and simply cut, like her black hair.

'My dear,' said O'Malley, taking her hand proprietorially, 'allow me to present Professor Glowrey. This is Cressida Lee, all things to all men but mainly to me. Provided she's a good girl.' She winced, just for a second; he had squeezed her hand, if I was not mistaken, harder than affection would, or should, have dictated. 'Cressy, take care of the professor.'

'It'll be my pleasure,' she said. 'Shall we sit over here? Are you new to Rio, Professor Glowrey?' She led the way to the armchairs in the corner. The girl from the bar was already waiting with two glasses of champagne.

'I'm learning about Rio,' I said. 'But I don't think you're Brazilian.'

'More Scarlett O'Hara than Carmen Miranda. Does my little ole Southern accent show?'

'To the trained ear.' I'm not easily tongue-tied but I didn't quite know how to pursue the conversation. Cressida Lee, however, as I soon discovered, was never at a loss for words.

'It's years since I left but I guess the accent sticks. Now where do you come from?'

'England. Scotland, originally.'

'And what do you profess?'

'Classics. Greek and Latin.'

'Oh my. You look too human. On second

43

thought, maybe you don't; you look stern.'

'Do I? I'm sorry.'

'No need to be. It's rather attractive. But what brings you to Tara's Hall? I wouldn't have thought this was your sort of place. Sorry, I'm not supposed to ask questions. He doesn't like it.' She nodded towards O'Malley.

'I came to meet someone,' I said.

She looked at me. (*Each glance of the eye so bright and black* . . . But actually her eyes were blue.) 'Yes, people do come here to meet people. And to gamble, of course. You don't want to try your luck?'

'Not at cards or roulette. It annoys me more to lose than it pleases me to win. But tell me about Tara's Hall. Are there other gaming rooms? Is this just the *salle privée*?'

'It used to be a casino, under another name. Then for a while the Brazilian Government made gambling illegal. Fernando bought it and turned it into a night-club. But he gives the customers what they want—as long as they're rich enough to pay. That was before my time. I came down here to sing.'

'With the band?'

'A solo turn. My name and picture outside. But, truth to tell, I'm not a very good singer.'

'You still do it, though?'

'No. I have other talents.' She paused, and I could think of nothing to say. Then we both started to speak simultaneously. We laughed, and deferred to each other. Eventually I said, 'I was only going to ask about Mr. O'Malley. Is he really an Irishman or a Brazilian or what?'

'I believe his father was Irish and his mother Brazilian. But he's lived here all his life. He knows everyone in Rio and everything that goes on.'

'Fernando O'Malley. It sounds like an old music-hall song: "I'm the only Jewish Scotsman in the Irish Fusiliers."'

'Perhaps I should add it to my repertoire. But I wouldn't dare sing it. He laughs a lot but he doesn't have much of a sense of humour about himself. Don't tell him I said that.'

'Of course not.'

'I talk too much. I know I do.' Impulsively she leaned forward and, for a moment, put her hand on mine. 'Professor Glowrey, I think I'm going to like you. I wonder why. Be careful of Fernando. You're not used to people like him.'

'Perhaps not. But why—' The door opened and Surov came in. I must have stiffened.

She said, 'Is that the man you're going to meet?'

'Yes.' I'd better let Surov make the first move, I thought. He looked around the room, saw me and gave a small waving gesture. O'Malley had risen to greet his new guest. He brought Surov over. 'Do you want a

45

private room,' he asked, 'or will this do?'

'I'm happy here,' said Surov, 'if the professor is satisfied.'

'Certainly.'

'We shan't disturb you,' said O'Malley. 'Cressy, our friends want to be alone.'

'It's been nice talking with you,' said Cressida Lee. She went back to the table with O'Malley.

'Now we talk,' said Surov. We sat down in the two armchairs. Nobody was paying attention to us; the gamblers were concentrating on their gaming. 'You said you were here for the fishing,' he invited.

'You too, I believe.'

'For the conference, Professor. But I could bear to leave it.'

'I can understand that. The arrangements aren't up to me. Actually, I was hoping for a scholarly conversation with you.'

He glanced at me quizzically. 'We are scholars. Why not?'

'I was very interested,' I said, 'in an article of yours—translated—in *The Journal of Hellenic Studies* . . .' And I launched into my prepared routine. From simple matters I led the conversation into progressively more sophisticated byways. He followed well. And sometimes led. Was he leading me away from points he couldn't deal with? After twenty minutes I really didn't know. He was a genuine classical scholar: there could be no question about that. But was he the genuine Surov? Probably, was all I could say. If no doubt had been raised, I should have had no doubt.

Eventually he called a halt to the conversation. 'How pleasant it is,' he said, 'to have professional talk with a colleague. But after a day at that conference we should enjoy, perhaps, a little diversion. Shall we try our luck?' He nodded at the table where O'Malley was again presiding, with Cressida Lee beside and slightly behind him.

'Not me,' I said. 'I don't enjoy games of chance. Do you find yourself lucky at them?'

'That was just an expression. Luck is not the point. The laws of chance are laws like any other, but many people do not understand them. I enjoy the calculation.'

'I can see you might. I've always gathered that Russians travelling abroad were pretty short of foreign currency. Isn't that a problem?'

He smiled. 'It's true but not a problem. I come with very few cruzeiros. I leave with more. I am law-abiding. I observe the laws—of chance. Of course, it depends how long the game continues. For how long do you think I should calculate, Professor Glowrey?'

'I don't know,' I said. 'That's not my business. But I suspect not very long.'

'We don't have very long, do we? Our

conference is not as endless as it seems. Professor Glowrey'—he lowered his voice a fraction—'if we are to go fishing, I should like you to take me. You, not a stranger.'

'I told you, that isn't my business.'

'You must make it so. I know that you are who you say you are. Our little conversation tonight has shown me that. I came to your friends because I thought I could trust them. I think I could trust you. A stranger could be anyone.' He rose to his feet. 'Now I shall try—not my luck, my calculation.'

I stood up too. 'I'll tell my friends what you say.'

He sketched a formal bow. 'We shall meet again soon. I hope. Remind them that I do not come empty-handed.'

He strolled over to the table, leaned down and whispered to O'Malley. O'Malley spoke curtly to Cressida, who gave Surov her chair. She turned to me. 'All right?' she said.

'Yes. I suppose so.'

'Another drink?'

I shook my head. 'I must go.'

'Shall we see you here again?'

'Perhaps.'

She raised a slim forefinger and touched my chin. 'Do come. You and I have only just started.'

That flirtatious gesture would, in almost any other circumstances, have been the chief thing in my mind as I sat in the cab, the lights

48

of Rio flowing past, on my way back to the hotel; but Surov's reversal of my own ploy predominated. Everything that happened was drawing me further into this affair, which was not what I had intended—but was it any cause for alarm? Was there any reason why I shouldn't act as go-between, if that was what Surov wanted? I could refuse, but it was a dull idea, anyway, to leave the story unfinished. All that would be required, probably, was that I should pass on to Surov whatever arrangements Pedro might make; perhaps at the conference, perhaps on another visit to Tara's Hall. And if at Tara's Hall, I might see Cressida Lee again. Then I did feel, vividly in my imagination, the light touch of her finger . . .

As soon as I was in my room, I sat on the bed and telephoned Pedro. He answered at the second ring. I told him I was eighty per cent satisfied of Surov's authenticity; that I had done all I could; in that sense, my job was over but Surov had asked for me to be his contact.

'Do you want me to?' I said. 'Would that be helpful?'

'I think so,' said Pedro slowly. 'Yes, why not? If anyone is watching, better they see you than someone else. You are both professors. It's natural you talk.'

'Very well. What next?'

'I tell you. Maybe tomorrow. Maybe next

day. Maybe day after. I arrange.'

'So I wait to hear from you?'

'Yes, you wait. But, meanwhile, you keep an eye on our big fish.'

'At the conference?'

'At the conference, sure. But maybe you do something else for me. He will keep going to Tara's Hall. I tell him that. Make a pattern, become familiar person there. Maybe you go too. See who talks to him, who watches him maybe. You will do that for me?'

'If you like. Every evening?'

'Tomorrow evening you tell him all okay. We contact him soon. Then, yes, maybe one, maybe two more evenings. I fix with O'Malley. Afterwards, we relax, we celebrate.'

'I sincerely hope so,' I said.

Lying on my bed, waiting for sleep, with the sounds of laughter and bustle still wafting through the open window from below, I kept seeing that small dangerous room and three faces—Surov, O'Malley and Cressida Lee.

*　　*　　*

Dutifully I attended the conference next day; a twofold duty, as I now perceived it, to establish a normal academic reason for my presence in Rio and to keep an eye on Surov. I wondered if Pedro was having him watched and followed when he left the hotel. Inside,

50

Ilyin and Korbanov stuck close to him; but I could imagine they might well have found it difficult, plausibly, to insist on joining his nocturnal escapades. I couldn't picture them in Tara's Hall.

The conference plodded on. We were regaled with a paper on 'Major Cruces in Minor Poets.' My attention wandered. Surov earnestly took notes. At luncheon I was cornered by the female don from Oxford. Her name was Emily Bryant. She had straight straw-coloured hair and unflattering spectacles and wore a crumpled linen suit.

'Well, are you enjoying it?' she asked. 'I don't think I've ever seen you at one of these conferences before.'

'No,' I said. 'That is, yes, I am quite enjoying it, but no, I don't usually go to conferences. I just decided this year that I could combine the pretence of work with a holiday.'

'I don't regard it as a holiday. It seems to me a duty to keep up with international scholarship. But I hope to have a day free at the end of the conference. It would be wrong to see nothing but the inside of the hotel.'

'It would indeed. You should go on the town, Miss Bryant.'

'That's not easy for an unaccompanied woman.'

And I was filled with shame. The unfairness of the world is nowhere more bitterly evident than in the distribution of good looks among women. Emily Bryant would doubtless have looked like Cressida Lee if she could, and, if she had, I would have said, 'Let me show you the town, Miss Bryant.' But she didn't and I couldn't.

I meditated on this sad subject during the afternoon's paper on the preservation and restoration of papyrus fragments, until I dozed.

★   ★   ★

At nine o'clock that evening, after bathing and shaving for the second time in a day (something I hardly ever do), putting on a favourite tie and inspecting myself in the glass (with satisfaction as to my apparel, less so with regard to my distinctly lived-in features), I summoned a taxi and set out, again, for Tara's Hall. Again I told the man at the desk that Mr. O'Malley was expecting me. This time he merely indicated the door and said, 'Please go through.'

Skirting the dance-floor, I found the door to the inner warren. It was easy enough to find, since the thug who had escorted me on the previous night was leaning against the wall beside it. He said nothing, but pushed the door open. Right and left down the corridors I went, meeting no one, until I came to the double-doors. It was eerily silent

52

in those passages, one's footsteps muffled by the carpet, the sound of the dance-band faint and dwindling, no sound from the rooms one was passing; and yet I felt, as one feels at night in wild country, that, although I neither saw nor heard a living thing, eyes might be watching me.

I wondered if I should knock but decided against it. I opened the right-hand door and parted the velvet curtains. The effect was like raising the curtain onto a stage. There in front of me was the little room, peopled as before, with the murmur of conversation, the click of the roulette wheel. And there was O'Malley. And there was Cressida. No Surov yet.

O'Malley looked up at me. 'If it isn't the professor,' he said. 'Come in, Professor, have a drink. You do drink? Even professors drink?'

'Thank you,' I said.

'Cressy, amuse him. You're not amusing me.'

She stood up: and the two of them—O'Malley with a glass in front of him and the cards in his hand, Cressida much changed from the day before—might have been figures in a Victorian *genre* painting, so clearly did they tell a story. When I say that Cressida was much changed, I am perhaps exaggerating. Her magic, for me, was undiminished, perhaps enhanced even, by a loss of sparkle and its replacement by something more subtle. She might have been crying or she might be angry, or both. The shadow on her cheek could have been a bruise.

There was nothing subtle about what was wrong with O'Malley. He was drunk. 'Do you like Cressy?' he said. 'You can have her. What'll you give me for her?'

I walked round the table and started to say something to her, I really don't know what. 'Answer me, you bloody professor,' he said. 'I made you an offer. Or, rather, you make me an offer. I'm waiting.'

The man on his left put a restraining hand on his sleeve, but he shook it off. 'To hell with you. To hell with the lot of you. Are we playing cards or aren't we?'

'I'm sorry about that,' said Cressida softly to me.

'I think you're the one who's owed an apology,' I said.

She smiled faintly. 'Owed? I don't know what I'm owed. Perhaps I'm just getting what I deserved.'

'Are you all right?'

'Oh yes, I'm all right. Let's sit.'

We took the same two chairs in the corner, and the mini-skirted girl brought champagne. I looked at Cressida over the top of my glass. It was a bruise on her cheek.

'What shall we talk about?' she said. 'I'm

supposed to be amusing you.'

'Mr. O'Malley,' I observed, 'appears rather out of sorts.'

'You could put it that way.' O'Malley was slapping the cards down as though angry. 'We won't talk about him. Are you enjoying yourself in Rio?'

The conversation didn't exactly flow. There were things I should have liked to say and do, but couldn't, and I had no reason to suppose she wanted to talk to me at all. So we talked of nothing much.

Then Surov came. Cressida made as though to leave us, but I said, 'Don't go.'

Surov raised an eyebrow at me. I shook my head. 'Nothing yet,' I said.

'Then perhaps I'll play,' he said. Turning away from us, he took an empty place at the table. Cressida and I watched him in silence. It was not a happy game. O'Malley was, by turns, morose and aggressive. Shortly afterwards, two of the other players left. O'Malley, I gathered, was playing badly, which hardly surprised me, and Surov won. But it was an uncomfortable victory. Dangerous, even. As soon as he decently could, Surov rose.

'Sadly,' he said, 'I must go. There is reading I must do for tomorrow.'

'"Reading,"' snarled O'Malley. 'So you're a reading man, are you? You look like one. You take our money and run away. I could tell my men to keep you here.'

'I'm sure you could,' replied Surov, 'but I trust you will not. As for me, I do not take your money. I do not collect what I have won. Good night.' And he was gone through the curtained doorway.

'Russian bastard,' said O'Malley.

There were three vacant chairs now. He swung round to me. Cressida stiffened. 'What about you,' he said, 'if you can tear yourself away from that bitch of mine?'

'I'm not a card-player,' I said, containing myself.

'Scared? Or too ignorant? You don't know how to play cards. Well, come here'—he crooked his finger—'and I'll make it easy. A simple little bet. Something you'll understand. Cressy, get me a clean pack.'

Without a word she brought a sealed pack of cards from behind the bar and put it on the table in front of him. I had risen to my feet. 'We'll cut three times,' he said. 'Best of three. You can understand that, can't you?'

What I should have done, I suppose, was follow Surov. O'Malley would not have moved. I could have caught Surov up and arranged a different rendezvous for the following night. But I was too angry and I'm too combative. 'How much?' I said.

'Oh, not money. I don't think you're in my class. We'll play for something worthless. We'll play for Miss high-and-mighty Cressida

Lee over there.' She was standing stock-still. 'The only thing is,' he continued, 'does she go to the winner or the loser?' He laughed. 'What do you say about that?'

'I say you're drunk.'

'Drunk, am I? Of course I'm drunk. Why shouldn't I be drunk? But I'm not so drunk I can't cut a pack of cards. All right. If you win, you can have her, and good riddance. If I win, I'll take her. And then she knows what to expect. Don't you, Cressy?' The glance he threw at her was frighteningly malicious.

'Don't be absurd—' I began.

'Do it,' said Cressida.

'You heard the lady,' O'Malley taunted. 'She says do it.'

'Go on. Please,' said Cressida.

There was no movement in the room. The roulette players had stopped and were watching us. I looked at her and I looked at him. 'All right.'

'Any side bets?' he said to the room in general. No one responded. 'Shuffle them,' he said. Cressida stepped forward and, with an expressionless face, dextrously shuffled the pack. She was clearly used to handling cards. Then she stood back.

'Will you cut first?' I think I still hesitated. 'No? Then I will.'

The card he turned up was the eight of clubs. 'Not good, not bad,' he said.

Cressida replaced the cards and shuffled

again; this was, I realized, a familiar routine. Taking a deep breath and aware of everyone's gaze on me, I leaned forward and cut. The nine of diamonds. 'A nose ahead,' remarked O'Malley. 'Let's try again.'

Again Cressida shuffled. 'Now no cheating, my dear,' he said, 'just so you can stay with me.' The pack was alone in a pool of light on the green baize. He weaved his hand teasingly above it, then cut. He scowled. It was the five of clubs.

Another shuffle, and, optimistically, I cut. The four of spades.

'Oho,' he said, 'then it's all to play for.' He snapped his fingers, and, while Cressida shuffled, the girl beside the bar filled his glass with whisky. Sitting back in his chair, he said, 'Isn't this a darling game? For you and me, of course, it's only a trivial matter. But I'll wager Cressy's finding it exciting. Aren't you, Cressy?'

The stillness in the room was almost tangible. 'What a miserable sober-sided lot you are!' he said. 'Will no one enter into the spirit of the thing? Would anyone like to buy the next card from me? Look what you'd be getting. Shall we auction her?' No one spoke. 'Ah, you're a disgrace to Tara's Hall.'

'Suppose I bid for your card,' I said. 'What will you take for it?'

O'Malley roared with laughter. 'You want to bet against yourself, do you? Oh no,

58

there'd be no sport in that. Come to think of it, I've a fancy now to win this game myself. So let's be testing the luck of the Irish.'

With a quick gesture, he cut. Starkly, there lay the king of diamonds. A wordless rustle flickered over the room. 'That's a fine sight,' he said.

Cressida shuffled for the last time. She was very pale, but her hand was steady. I felt trapped; but, of course, it was she who was in the trap and I could do nothing to help her. O'Malley's eyes were fixed mockingly on me. 'Won't you sit down?' he said. 'You're looking a wee bit worried.'

In fact I was quite shaky. If only to delay that final cut, I took the chair which Surov had vacated. I had a wild thought that I might overturn the table, and flee with Cressida before anyone could stop us. But that, I knew, was a fantasy. We should never get out of the building, perhaps not out of the room. The shuffle completed, she had stepped back again from the table. After all, she wasn't my responsibility. What did I know about her or about her relationship with O'Malley? If I grabbed her wrist and pulled her towards the door, she might not even come . . .

'We're waiting,' said O'Malley.

Slowly I reached out to the pack, put my fingers around it. The slight protrusion I felt could have been imagination; no, not imagination, it was just that Cressida, for all her apparent calmness, had this time not stacked the cards quite so neatly. With a real physical effort, as though the pasteboard had become heavy, I lifted and turned them. And we were looking at the ace of hearts.

CHAPTER FOUR

'I'M YOUR RESPONSIBILITY NOW'

'We'll be going now,' said Cressida. I realized she was standing very close behind me. As I rose, she took my arm and pulled me towards the door. Everyone in the room must have been watching us but I was aware only of O'Malley. He had been looking down at the cards on the table; now, slowly, he looked up. He didn't speak. Nor did anyone else. What O'Malley might have said was written on his face. Willingly I followed Cressida.

Just as we reached the velvet curtains, he said: 'Going, is it? There'll be nowhere for you to go in this town, you stuck-up whore . . .'

Cressida turned back, walked over to him and hit him as hard as she could across the face. It took him by surprise. There was a bead of blood on his lower lip where her ring had cut him. He sat, staring at her. The whole room seemed to be holding its breath.

Now she was beside me again, urging me through the curtains, and through the door, and into the corridor. 'Quickly,' she said.

Her fingers on my arm were tight. She let go, and walked so fast ahead of me that she was almost running. She passed the door leading to the restaurant, from behind which I could hear the band playing a samba, and hurried on a few more feet to the end of the corridor, where she turned right, glancing behind her as she did so. She wasn't looking at me, she was looking beyond me to see if anyone was following. Nobody was; but she clearly expected, and her expectation set my nerves on edge, that at any moment there might be a pursuit.

Beyond the turn, the corridor led to a short flight of stairs. Down we scurried. The floor now was uncarpeted; bare concrete. Cressida's evening shoes clacked hollowly. Light came from an unshaded bulb. In the corner was a pile of rubbish: cardboard boxes, empty cans; and a broom leaning against the wall. The green-painted door facing us—the paint was flaking away—had a heavy metal bar across, of the kind you see on the exit door from cinemas. Cressida pushed, and with a clang it opened. Never had fresh air felt more welcome; the warm breath of a tropical night. We emerged into a dark, deserted side-street. The door swung shut behind us.

61

Cressida hesitated warily. 'Keep in the shadows,' she said.

'Do you think he'll try to bring you back?' I asked.

'You'd better believe it.'

We crossed the road, slipping between parked cars into the protective shadow of tall unlighted buildings. The road sloped up towards lights and traffic. Cautiously we emerged into the wider street. The front of Tara's Hall, with the doorman outside, was about fifty yards away on the left, separated from us by a couple of shops. We turned right.

It wasn't a busy street, but there were people and cars, and the doorman at Tara's Hall was opening the door for a pair of new arrivals who had just alighted from a taxi.

They were literally knocked aside by the three men who burst out of the club. One was the familiar thug in a dinner-jacket; the others came from the same mould. Ferociously they surveyed the street, and I had no doubt what they were looking for. Cressida gave a little gasp. Before we could move, one of them spotted us. She ran, and I was pounding after her, and the three of them were running in pursuit.

Passers-by stared, but showed no disposition to interfere. I barged into someone but staggered on, his angry expostulation fading behind me. A quick glance showed the three men strung out, the first one—lighter built than the others— gaining on us. Cressida's long dress hampered her. I caught her arm. The nearest of our pursuers was now less than twenty yards behind.

We reached the kerb of another side-street. As we plunged across, one car almost hit me and another slowed us down for a moment. There were fewer pedestrians here. In vain I looked wildly round for any kind of refuge or even something I could use for a weapon. I'm quite heavily built and not unfit, and I boxed at school, but I wasn't foolish enough to believe that I had much chance against even one professional strong-arm man, let alone three. However, desperation must be served. Perhaps I could deal with the first one before the other two caught up. Perhaps, seeing us actually being assaulted, some passer-by would come to our help. Anyway I'd rather be facing him. I turned.

He was very close. And something gleamed in his right hand. It was a knife.

That blade was suddenly the focus of my world. I couldn't run again. He was too close, and I didn't dare expose my back to him. There wasn't even time to be afraid. I kicked, and caught him on or near the knee. He stumbled. I grabbed for his wrist. He was off balance or he would surely have stabbed me; instead of which, I got both hands on his forearm and whirled him around. We fell on to the pavement together, rolling and grappling. Then he cried out. Cressida had struck him on the head with the heel of her shoe. She hit him again, and he went feeble in my grip.

I rolled away from him and was stumbling to my feet when the other two thugs arrived. One had a knife, the other held something small and black which I took to be a cosh. We hadn't a hope. I don't think I should even have got a swing at them before being struck down.

But it didn't happen. Two other men appeared from nowhere. They were simply there. I've no clear picture of them; it was all too quick and confused. They acted as a team, each taking one of our pursuers. And you couldn't call it a fight. My impression is simply of fierce blows, which sent the two thugs crashing to the ground. A kick below the chin of one who was still moving ensured that neither would resume the attack. Then, barely glancing at Cressida and me, our two blessed rescuers (although their behaviour had scarcely been angelic) departed as abruptly as they had come.

They just walked away, across the road, between parked cars and out of sight. A few concerned citizens of Rio stood gaping. I remember a fat woman with her hand to her mouth and a man visibly dithering.

'Are you hurt?' asked Cressida, helping me to my feet.

'No. Surprisingly.' I was bruised and shaken, but, as I recovered my breath and began brushing some of the dirt from my clothes, strangely exhilarated. Three men lay sprawled on the ground at our feet, quite possibly dead or seriously injured. The fat woman had started clamouring hysterically. There was still no policeman in sight, and, although I should have welcomed one a few minutes before, I had a distinct feeling that Brazil is not a country where I wanted to be involved with the police if it could be avoided.

'We'd better remove ourselves,' I said.

'Let me put my shoe back on.' Cressida's voice was a little unsteady, but only a little. The shoe was still in her hand. I noticed how sharp the heel was. Balancing herself against me, she slipped it on. 'All right,' she said. 'Come on. I think I know where we can get a taxi.'

That remark, so commonplace, so banal, made me laugh, and she smiled too. There was no need to ask which way. We were certainly not going back past Tara's Hall. She led me farther down the street, the woman's clamour fading behind us, and then into a side-street which went sharply downhill. We walked briskly. No one followed.

'Who do you think they were,' asked

Cressida, 'the men who rescued us?'

'I'm not sure. They may have been friends of friends of mine.'

'Whoever they were, thank God for them. But it was very strange, wasn't it, the way they went off like that?'

'It was rather.'

We walked on in silence, until we emerged into a small paved square with an equestrian statue in the middle and, on the far side, a hotel, outside which stood a couple of taxis, their drivers dozing at the wheel. I'd stopped looking over my shoulder and listening for footfalls, but only now could I fully believe we'd got away.

The driver of the front cab emerged reluctantly from sleep as I opened the rear door. I gave him the name of my hotel, because I couldn't think where else to go.

'I was afraid you wouldn't understand about the shaved card,' said Cressida, relaxing beside me.

'I didn't. What shaved card?'

'The one you cut. The ace of hearts.'

'I still don't understand.'

She sighed with exasperation at my unwordliness. 'I slipped it in, you silly. From a shaved pack we keep behind the bar. The cards are slightly tapered, so that if you turn one of them around it feels different. Couldn't you feel it? I hoped it would be just enough to guide you.'

'Actually it did. Well, obviously it did, though I wasn't aware of it. I thought it was just one card sticking out a bit. You're handy with cards.'

'Part of my job. If O'Malley hadn't been so drunk, he'd have guessed. Perhaps he did guess after we'd gone, and that's why he sent those goons after us. No, he'd have sent them anyway. He was so mad at me. And at you now, I'm afraid.'

'That doesn't matter,' I said. 'I shan't be here long. But what are you going to do?'

'Oh, I'm your responsibility now. You won me, don't you remember?'

I stared at her. Illumined by the passing lights, her face was serene. I wasn't absolutely sure that she was joking.

'It was a fixed game,' I said, keeping the tone less than serious.

'Yes,' she agreed, 'but it's like the Chinese. When they save someone's life, they're responsible for that person ever afterwards. You're stuck with me.'

'We'll see about that,' I said.

'I'll need some clothes. We'll get them in the morning. I'm afraid I don't have any money. Are you rich?'

'No, I'm not rich.'

'I wouldn't ask—I mean, I don't want to be a burden to you—but I can't very well go back for my things, or anywhere O'Malley might find me.'

67

'I suppose not. I expect we can fit you out. But—'

'You did offer to buy his card,' she said softly. 'That might have been very expensive.'

Before this embarrassing conversation could proceed further, the taxi drew up outside my hotel. 'I'll see if we can get you a room for tonight anyway,' I said as we entered.

Neither my dishevelled appearance nor Cressida's lack of luggage raised so much as an inquiring eyebrow from the man at the reception desk. There was indeed a single room available. He gave me the key, which I handed to Cressida.

'Please,' she said, and her voice was suddenly more childlike than teasing, 'may I come to your room for a bit? I don't much feel like being alone.'

So we went upstairs, and she sat quietly in the chair while I washed and tidied myself. 'Now,' I said, 'if you'll excuse me, I must make a telephone call.'

'Do you want me to go?' she asked.

Good security practice would have made me say yes, but I hadn't the heart. 'No, it's all right. You can avert your ears.'

'I'm used to doing that.'

I called Pedro, and again I was lucky; I got him at once. I could hear the television in the background. 'Trouble,' I said. 'Trouble with your friend O'Malley.'

'Not exactly my friend. He is everybody's friend—and nobody's.'

'He's not mine.'

Pedro listened without interrupting. When I had finished, he said, 'You are right. That is trouble. I do not think O'Malley is a forgiving man. The girl, where is she now?'

'With me.'

'I feared so. Were you followed? Is it possible O'Malley knows where you are?'

'I doubt it. Not after those three were dealt with. Was it your men who came so opportunely? Were you very kindly keeping an eye on me?'

'No, not my people. Maybe they should have been. I didn't figure you for a man who would get into trouble over a woman.'

'H'm. I don't know that I should put it quite like that. I wonder who they were, then. However—what now?'

'You can't go back to Tara's Hall. And not me either, maybe. I must make a new plan. I come to you tomorrow morning. Nine o'clock.'

'All right. I'm sorry to have muddled things for you.'

'There is always something,' he said. 'In this world—never simple. Good night.'

True enough, I thought as I replaced the telephone. So who had they been, the two men who had probably saved my life? I doubted if I should even recognize them again. Could it be that Dr. Gabriel and the Fishers believed in making doubly sure; that, without Pedro's knowledge, they had been watching my performance?

Cressida interrupted. 'My, you look thoughtful. But I suppose professors should be thoughtful. It's their business.'

I sat on the bed. 'We've a good deal to be thoughtful about, wouldn't you say?'

She smiled. 'I'll just leave the thinking to you.'

'Young woman, I will not accept responsibility for your life.'

'Now you're cross. Please don't be cross.'

And the truth was, I couldn't be. 'We'll talk about it in the morning,' I said. 'I can lend you a pair of pyjamas, but not a toothbrush.'

'What a funny old-fashioned thing you are.'

'Out,' I said, thrusting my spare pyjamas into her hands and propelling her towards the door. Not that I was tired of her company, but I didn't want, I didn't dare invite, further complications at the moment; and I needed a few minutes' peace and quiet in which to take stock. Peace and quiet, I suspected, were not easily found in Cressida's vicinity.

When she'd gone, I stood by the window, gazing out at the sea. I'd interfered in what wasn't my business and had the narrowest of escapes, but, running through the sequence

70

of events, I didn't see that I could have acted differently. And where there was no choice, there could be nothing to regret. Indeed, to be honest, I was quite pleased with myself. The debit side was that, just when the problem of Surov had been, if not solved, at least settled, our intended meeting place had become impossible and my role as go-between was rendered more difficult. In addition, if O'Malley was really thirsting for vengeance. Rio might now be a dangerous city for me. I could leave at once, tomorrow, but, if Pedro—or Surov—still wanted me, I surely had an obligation to see the job through. And Cressida, did I have an obligation to her? No, dammit, I didn't. Not a moral obligation exactly. However . . .

I was still pondering these questions in bed when I turned out the light and sleep washed over me.

★   ★   ★

I was woken by a tap at the door. The travelling-clock on my bedside table said seven-thirty, not an hour when I'm accustomed to receiving visitors—or doing anything else, if I can avoid it. But I was wide awake immediately. A sense of danger came with recollection of the previous night's adventures. Surprisingly, perhaps foolishly, it was more exciting than frightening.

'Wait a minute,' I called. I slipped out of bed and put on a dressing-gown, which made me feel less vulnerable. 'Who is it?'

'Pedro.'

I let him in. He was wearing a lightweight blue suit and smelled of after-shave lotion.

'I thought we should talk early,' he said.

'It's early,' I agreed.

'We must finish up this business quickly. O'Malley knows too much, if he wants to make trouble. He could tell Kallinin.'

'Who's Kallinin?'

'He is KGB Resident. O'Malley could tell him that Surov has been meeting with us. Then—poof!' He flung his hands wide.

'Is that likely? He has nothing against Surov.'

'But he has something against you, my friend—from what you tell me last night. And because of you, against me. So maybe he wants to poke a stick in our plans. Is the girl still here?'

'I presume so. In bed, I imagine.'

He looked at my blameless bed.

'She has a room along the corridor,' I said with some asperity.

'O'Malley does not like that people should take things away from him. Maybe, though, he looks for her and does not think of Surov. But if he looks for her, he looks for you. And if he looks for you, he comes to me.'

My exhilaration was distinctly waning. 'I'm

very sorry,' I said. 'I'm afraid I have rather let you in for it.'

He shrugged. 'I can deal with O'Malley when you are gone. He's a man one can trade with. I hope. But first we must get Surov away. I will arrange. But it cannot be until tomorrow.'

'Is there anything I can do to help?'

'Yes. Too risky now for me to get in touch with him directly. Best that you should do it at the conference. Can you talk to him so no one hears? Or give him a message somehow?'

'I'll try.'

'Please, my friend, succeed. Tell him not to go again to Tara's Hall. And tell him that he must be ready to go with you tomorrow morning. From the conference.'

'Suppose O'Malley does contact this KGB man, Kallinin. Wouldn't they whisk Surov away at once—today? Can we afford to wait twenty-four hours?'

'Maybe not. Is risky both ways. But less risky, I think, to make proper arrangements. Once he comes, I get him out of town altogether. Maybe Kallinin would not move so quick. Maybe he watch and wait.'

'That's a lot of maybes.'

He smiled, showing his gold tooth. 'We play the odds, no? Kallinin is a cautious man. I think he would watch. Maybe he doesn't quite believe O'Malley. Maybe he suspects funny busines.'

73

'Well, it's your decision. What are we going to do about the girl, about Cressida?'

He cocked his head on one side. 'You wouldn't let me take her back to O'Malley? That might save much trouble. No, I suppose not. But she must not involve you again.'

'We'd better ask her what she wants to do.' I picked up the telephone and asked—with some difficulty in making myself understood—for Cressida's room. It rang so long unanswered that I began to think, with dull and unreasonable depression, that she'd gone; unreasonable, because that would have simplified matters considerably.

Then her soft voice spoke. 'Whoever you are, do you know what time it is? The middle of the night.'

'It's me,' I said. 'I trust no one else knows you're here. Can you come along to my room?'

'You sound cross again. Last night you didn't want me.'

'We need to talk,' I said. 'Now.'

'Yes, sir. Whatever you say, sir. May I wash my face and brush my hair first?'

'As soon as you can, please.' I firmly replaced the receiver.

'She is very beautiful, I believe,' said Pedro. 'I have heard of her. She has been with O'Malley maybe six months. She was a singer.'

'So she told me.'

She came almost at once. I opened the door to her knock. 'Hi!' she said. She was wearing my pyjamas and nothing else, the trousers rolled up at the bottom, the sleeves flapping over her hands. But she had brushed her hair—and put on lipstick. 'To hear is to obey,' she said, marching confidently into the room. 'Oh, we have guests.'

A formal introduction, in the circumstances, appeared faintly ludicrous, but what else could I say? 'This is Pedro Ramirez. Pedro, Miss Lee.'

He bowed in a courtly manner. She giggled. 'Pardon my costume,' she said. 'I wasn't allowed time to change.'

Extracting from the wardrobe the light overcoat which I had been wearing when I arrived, I dropped it around her shoulders; not that she really needed it for warmth. Snuggling into it, she sat in the chair. Pedro leaned against the wall, eyeing her curiously. I sat on the bed.

'We need to know your plans,' I said. 'Pedro and I are going to be busy, but if there's anything we can do to help . . . I'll cash a traveller's cheque and give you some money. You'll want clothes.'

'Miss Lee should maybe not go shopping today,' said Pedro. 'Not good if O'Malley finds her.'

'Not good at all,' she agreed.

'We don't want him coming to this hotel,'

Pedro explained. 'Better she is not seen. My wife Luisa, she will bring clothes.'

'That would be extremely kind,' I said. 'So, Cressida—'

'Call me Cressy. It's friendlier.'

'Cressida, we must ask you to stay here for twenty-four hours. In fact, probably until tomorrow night. Afterwards, if you want to leave Rio, which I should think might be best, we'll get you a plane ticket. Pedro, I'm sure, will see that you're all right.'

'What about you? Won't you see that I'm all right?'

'Of course. But I shall be leaving myself.'

'Running away from your responsibilities?'

'Think about it during the day,' I said, 'and tell me this evening where you want to go.'

'All right. I'll think.'

Pedro pushed himself from the wall. 'I go now. There are many arrangements. Luisa will come soon. Best maybe that she spend the day here.'

'Is she my size?' asked Cressida.

'No,' he said, measuring her with an experienced glance. 'My Luisa is a little more—plump.'

'She can buy you something,' I said, rising to fetch my wallet.

'Of course,' said Pedro, waving aside my offer. 'Our pleasure. She will come here first and you tell her what you like.'

76

'You can be thinking about that too,' I said.

'Don't be so damned patronizing,' said Cressida, flaring up; then was immediately remorseful. 'I'm sorry. You're both very generous.'

After a moment of embarrassment I said, 'I ought to get dressed. I want to be at the conference before it begins.'

Cressida went back to her room quite meekly. Having arranged with Pedro that we should talk again later, I sent for breakfast. The tray arrived as I was tying my tie. There was a clear half-hour before I needed to set out for the other hotel. I breakfasted in a leisurely and contemplative manner, sitting beside the window, through which a small breeze blew, stirring the curtains.

When I reached the conference, only a few participants had yet arrived. A routine having been established, the atmosphere had become more informal. People wandered into the hall, looked for friends and sat gossiping.

Surov entered, flanked as usual by Ilyin and Korbanov. I made no attempt to approach them, taking a seat instead near the door into the adjacent room. Emily Bryant came and sat next to me. I responded as politely as I could to her earnest conversation but I wasn't really listening. My original idea had been to write my message to Surov and slip it to him during the day, perhaps between the sheets of one of those duplicated papers; or perhaps I could write it on the agenda paper and contrive to exchange mine for his; but, on second thoughts, committing it to paper at all seemed too dangerous, particularly with Ilyin and Korbanov watching him like hawks.

The opening item scheduled for that morning's session was uninvitingly called 'Agricultural Simile in the Minor Greek Poets': and it fully lived down to my expectation.

During the coffee-break, having excused myself from Miss Bryant, I manoeuvred through the crush until I was near Surov, but there was really no chance of an unobtrusive word. Ilyin and Korbanov blocked me on one side, and Surov was talking to the Balliol don. After ten minutes, frustrated, I went back to my seat.

Lunch-time, and we adjourned again to the buffet laid out on a long white-clothed table in the adjoining room. While the crowd was still surging through the door I steered across Surov's bow and collided with him, dropping my folder on the floor, where the papers spilled out.

'So sorry,' he said, and we stooped simultaneously to collect the scattered papers. People were talking and laughing around us. I spoke softly, just loud enough for him to hear when our heads were close. 'Don't go back to

Tara's Hall. Be ready tomorrow. Here.'

He smiled as we stood up, handing me his batch of papers. 'Thank you,' I said. He nodded to me—'Professor'—and moved off to join the other two Russians.

Duty done, I had lunch, conversing, idly but I trust amiably, with colleagues. I should have preferred to go straight back to my own hotel afterwards, but I thought it was wiser to attend the afternoon session. If Ilyin or Korbanov really were watching over Surov, I didn't want them to have any reason for considering me. My momentary collision with Surov on our way into lunch had surely not looked suspicious, but, if I left the conference so soon afterwards, it was just possible that someone might wonder.

As the speaker droned on, I shut my eyes in order to concentrate, not, I'm afraid, on the scholarly subject he was expounding, but on what the future might hold. The applause woke me. Questions followed, and in the interval before the final session of the afternoon I was able to slip away.

By now I'd acquired a certain wariness. Between the taxi and my hotel door I looked sharply around, and again as I entered the small lobby. I'm not sure just what I expected, or was afraid, I might see. Mainly, I suppose, somebody from Tara's Hall, come for Cressida—or for me. Anyway, I saw nothing to provoke alarm bells. I was even

79

slightly cautious when I opened the door of my room; but there was no one there and no sign of disturbance.

I called Pedro. 'It's all set,' I told him. 'I was able to pass your message without anyone else hearing.'

'Good. And me, I have been making the arrangements. Listen carefully, please. This is what we do tomorrow. There is a break in the conference during the morning? What time?'

'Eleven-fifteen.'

'You must get Surov out of the room. Best if no one notices, but I do not think they would try to stop you in any case, not with so many peoples there. Go down to the lobby but not out through the main doors. Turn right, down that passage where are shops. You have seen it, maybe? Go along and you come to side-entrance. Side-entrance of hotel. Still many peoples moving about. Then a short path to open gate. Outside I will be waiting.

'We will have a closed van. Blue, with words 'J. C. Valente, Limitada' on the side. It will be near the gate, near as possible. I will not be driving. Best maybe that I should not be seen. I will get driver, good safe man. I will be in the back. You and Surov get in the back with me, pretty quick, and off we go. Then I take you both to safe house. Not for long. I get you both away tomorrow night—but in different directions maybe. Better you should leave too. A pity we have no time for celebration. I will arrange your travel, if you tell me where you wish to go. Back to London maybe?'

'No, I thought I might go on to Peru or Chile, have a bit of a holiday.'

'Better you make it Chile. I think maybe O'Malley has friends in Peru.'

'That's a good reason. We should do something for Cressida.'

'If you wish. Ask where she would go and I will make arrangements for her too. Luisa is still with her. Best I thought that Miss Lee should not be left alone, wandering about.'

'I'll go and find her, and call you again later.'

I brushed my hair, straightened my tie and went along to Cressida's room. She and Luisa were watching television, some gameshow; I heard the sound of it—the inane audience laughter—as I knocked on the door. Cressida was wearing a white linen trouser-suit with a red cashmere pullover under the jacket. Her make-up was immaculate now; she seemed to have a gloss that shone; she was Technicolor in a sepia room.

Luisa rose and curtsied. Cressida sat and smiled. 'Have you had a nice day?' she said.

'Moderately. I see Luisa got you some clothes.'

'Yes, wasn't it darling of her? Do you like

them?'

'Very much. Do you speak Portuguese?'

'Enough to get by.'

'Please thank her for me, and tell her that I will look after you now. She must be wanting to get home.'

How accurate Cressida's Portuguese may have been, I don't know; but she approached it, as she approached most things, with lively confidence. Luisa clearly understood and gushed in return; then, with more smiling and gesticulating and after expressions of mutual regard, took her leave.

'Now,' said Cressida, 'you're going to look after me. Can't we go out? I've been stuck here all day.'

'You're safer here, if O'Malley's really looking for you. About that—do you want to leave Rio?'

She shrugged. 'I don't have anything to stay for. And I can't stay indoors for ever.'

'Can't you go home? Where is home?'

'Charleston, South Carolina. That's where I was born and raised. But there's no one there who matters. No reason to go back. What are you going to do? Are you staying in Rio?'

'No, I shall be leaving tomorrow. I'm going to Chile. But, before I go, I want to be sure that you're all right. I do accept that much responsibility, though God knows why I should.'

'Because you're a gentleman, who won't abandon a lady in distress. Can I come to Chile with you?'

'Certainly not. I mean, what for? It would be most unsuitable . . .'

She laughed aloud. 'We can still have separate rooms. Come on, Professor, you mustn't leave your winnings behind. Seriously, I've nowhere else to go and nothing to live on, and you're quite right, I do need to get away from Rio. I'll be no trouble. I'll be quiet as a little mouse. And then we can talk about my future.'

It would be untrue to say that the idea of taking Cressida with me had never crossed my mind, but I'd thought of it only as a fantasy—what fun it would be; and suddenly I was confronted with the wildly improbable fact that she might really come, that she wanted to come. I had only to say yes. I wasn't so blinded as not to know that there were many sound reasons for declining her offer. This was not the sort of girl whom a respectable middle-aged Oxford professor should lightly pick up on his travels. One knew of colleagues whose personal and professional lives had been wrecked over women much less dangerous than Cressida Lee. When I'd called it unsuitable, that was an understatement; and I had always been a cautious man, a canny Scotsman. She and I had nothing in common. I should be bored by her within a week. She was probably bored with me already, but saw me, for the moment, as a meal-ticket. The idea was absurd. I must firmly say no.

'All right,' I said, 'if you really want to.' And I could hardly believe I'd said it.

She jumped up and kissed me, and then, of course, I was really lost.

She would have liked to go to a restaurant for dinner, but there was no point, I insisted, on taking needless risks now. We could dine in the hotel; but I agreed, as the early dusk thickened, that we might have a walk along the beach.

The crowd, which all day long packed the sand, had mostly gone. A few belated figures were collecting their sports equipment or wandering up with towels across their shoulders, and at intervals along the curving margin where the concrete esplanade fenced in the beach were pin-points of flickering light from candles on the little altars which the Macumba men erected. One of these Macumba men, an elderly black man with grey hair, extinguished his candle, packed up his portable equipment, climbed on to the esplanade and walked off, while a dog barked angrily at his heels.

'That's rather sinister,' I said.

'Do you think dogs *know*?' asked Cressida.

'I do. I'm a great believer in dogs.'

So we did have something in common. 'It's

a strange mixture of religions, this Macumba.'

'New Year's Eve is the great time, when the whole of Rio comes down to the beach, and they all throw lilies into the sea. They're propitiating a goddess. But I don't laugh at them. One shouldn't.'

'"For gods are kittle cattle,"' I quoted, '"and a wise man honours them all."'

She looked up at me curiously. 'Where I come from,' she said, 'in the Deep South, there are traces of voodoo still. It's mostly gone now, but when I was a little girl, there was an old black woman who used to tell me stories. And in the woods, and on the sea islands, you sometimes hear about hants and hexes. It can be quite frightening.'

'Tell me about Charleston.'

'It's very small and boring. You might enjoy it; it's full of old things.'

'And you don't want to go back? You've no family at all?'

'Oh, I expect I'll go back eventually. Charlestonians usually do. And you, Professor, do you have a family?'

'I've a sister in Edinburgh. She's married to a doctor.'

'No wife?'

'No wife.'

'Not ever?'

'Never the right girl.'

'Oh, do you believe in that—soul-mates? Is

that rational, Professor?'

'There are limits to rationality.'

'I can't go on calling you "Professor." What's your Christian name?'

'James.'

'You wouldn't call me "Cressy," so I suppose I mustn't call you "Jim."'

'I'd rather you didn't. No one does.'

'No one calls me "Cressida" except you. I rather like it.'

'Do you realize that the fickle Cressida of *Troilus and Cressida* is really the same person as gentle Briseis in *The Iliad*, the name having been corrupted or, rather, confused with Chryseis—'

'Professor dear, I don't understand a word you're saying.'

We walked by the sea until the stars were fully out and the lights of Rio blazed back at them and the illuminated Christ-figure, arms spread in blessing, looked down on us. Then we returned to the hotel, where I telephoned Pedro, who said he would book two seats, for tomorrow evening, on a flight to Santiago. He scrupulously made no comment, except to say that it would be best if Cressida came with me in the morning. 'My van will hold one more,' he observed drily.

Cressida and I dined together in the small restaurant of the hotel, which was half-empty. The food and wine were very good, or perhaps that was an illusion. It was a happy evening.

*   *   *

Cressida came to my room for breakfast, and we finalized our plans. Should we check out? Should we take our baggage? The safest thing, we decided (although we had really no reason to suppose anybody was watching us or the hotel), would be not to make our impending departure obvious. Pedro could collect our things and pay our bills later in the day; but, just in case this was, for any reason, impossible, we would take with us a single bag containing the necessaries for life-support. The rest we would pack and leave in our rooms.

The taxi I'd ordered came on time. Cressida, as I should have expected, had equipped herself yesterday with considerably more than the one ensemble. This morning she wore a loose, but cunningly tailored, coat and skirt of cream linen. Our joint provisions were in a green canvas grip. As the taxi bucketed up the street I was tense but quite pleasurably so.

The multiple glass windows of the conference hotel gleamed in the sunshine. I'd warned Cressida that she would have to kick her heels in the lobby or walk in the hotel gardens. She had said that she would prefer to come now, with me, rather than wait for an hour in her room and take a second taxi later. 'You could come into the conference,' I said, 'but I really don't think you'd enjoy it, and you would be rather conspicuous.'

'You mean,' she said, widening her eyes with disingenuous astonishment, 'that I don't look like a lady professor?'

And she certainly didn't. But in the lobby, guarding the canvas grip, she was comparatively inconspicuous, although there was no one else nearly as pretty. Having equipped her with a clutch of fashion magazines from the bookstall, I said, 'Be on your toes at eleven-fifteen. See you then,' and went up in the elevator to the third floor. I was mildly uneasy at leaving her, but, provided she stayed in the public parts of that big hotel, I couldn't believe she was in any serious danger. If anything untoward happens, come and find me, I'd told her.

The numbers attending the conference had distinctly thinned. Emily Bryant came but not the Balliol don. I was on tenterhooks until Surov appeared. I couldn't help being afraid—although, again, there was no reason to suppose it—that Surov's colleagues might have guessed his intention and removed him. But it wasn't so. Surov entered the room, together with Ilyin and Korbanov, just before the first session began at ten o'clock.

Deliberately keeping well away from him, I chose a seat near to the main doors leading back into the ante-room and thence to the elevators. The subject of the morning's lecture, delivered by a voluble Italian, was billed as 'Variant Readings in Greek Papyri.' The last minutes ticked away, while the chairman coaxed a final question or two from the sluggish audience.

The hands of the clock on the wall had nearly reached a quarter past eleven when he said, 'Well, if there are no more questions . . .'

Firm decisive action, I'd already decided, was the thing. As the movement towards coffee began, I cut into the crowd and halted Surov. 'May I have a word with you?' I said. 'It's about a point you raised in your article on the Constitution of Thrace.' As I said it, my hand was on his elbow, steering him away. He said something in Russian, over his shoulder, to Korbanov and Ilyin, presumably to the effect that he would join them in a minute. They stared at us but could hardly follow. Deep in conversation, Surov and I strolled up the centre aisle.

Like water through a funnel, most of our colleagues were being washed through the side-door into the room where coffee was waiting, Korbanov and Ilyin among them. Surov and I reached the door to the ante-room. We quickened our pace. Rather than wait, I had intended to take the stairs; but the indicator above one of the elevators showed a lift coming down. I jabbed the button, and the door slid open almost at once. The lift was empty. We went down in silence.

I was tense, inevitably, keyed up for something to go wrong. Surov, dressed in a silver-grey suit with a red tie, seemed calm. The lift door opened at the ground floor. A woman with a miniature poodle on a lead was waiting. As we emerged into the lobby, Cressida, rising from an imitation-leather sofa where she had been sitting, the magazines on her knee, picked up the canvas grip and swiftly joined us.

'All right?' she said.

'All right.' I didn't bother with introductions; this wasn't a time for social niceties.

I'd made sure, when we arrived earlier, that I did know the shop-lined passage to which Pedro had referred, and that it was a clear run. The length to the glass door at the end was perhaps two hundred feet, deep carpeted, the shops—one a jeweller's, another selling expensive knitwear—brightly lit. There was no commissionaire guarding the side-entrance. A sudden thought occurred to me: suppose the door was locked? I should have checked.

Surov had politely taken the grip from Cressida. We must walk. We mustn't attract attention. But I was a couple of steps ahead. I pushed the glass door. It opened.

Outside was a strip of garden: palm trees, a gravel path, red flowers. And, beyond, the road. Suppose the van wasn't there? But it was. A blue van with the name 'J. C. Valente' painted in gold on the side. The gravel crunched beneath our feet. In the driver's seat of the van I could see a figure lounging, looking bored, smoking a small cigar. There was no gate from the garden; the path debouched straight onto the sidewalk. The twin-doors at the back of the van were slightly open.

'Our carriage awaits,' I said.

'In we go then,' said Cressida. It was actually she who opened the door.

We were looking down the barrel of what seemed a very large pistol. 'Top of the morning to you,' said Fernando O'Malley.

CHAPTER FIVE

FEARFUL JOURNEY

It was dark and there was a roaring in my ears when I woke—or at least struggled back to a form of consciousness. I had no idea where I was. Oxford? No, not Oxford. I'd been somewhere else. The mind, that wonderful instrument, began releasing pictures. Rio . . . Surov . . . Cressida . . . O'Malley . . .

91

'Top of the morning,' he'd said, pointing a gun at me. Then I remembered it all. Another man had appeared behind us, also with a gun, the muzzle just visible beneath the jacket slung across his arm. And the driver had come round from the front of the van. 'Step into my parlour,' said O'Malley.

We were forced into the back of the van, up a single step. I did wonder, for a moment, whether we should make a break, simply run, gambling that O'Malley wouldn't really start shooting in broad daylight on an open street. But he was a gambler, not me; if he was bluffing, the bluff succeeded. The odds weren't acceptable. He was too dangerous a man; there was no knowing what he might be willing to do. I followed Cressida, whose face had gone white but who walked, head high, like an aristocrat to the guillotine, up into the van. Surov followed me.

O'Malley, seated on a large cardboard box, motioned us in with his pistol. 'Take a seat. It'll have to be the floor, I'm afraid.' The other man with a gun came in too, shutting the doors of the van behind him. A single bulb in the roof bathed us in a dim yellow light. The engine started, and we were moving.

O'Malley just sat, grinning at us. The other man stood, feet apart, balancing against the closed doors; his gun, an automatic, now unconcealed, covering us.

Surov had brought Cressida's canvas grip. It was on the floor between O'Malley and me. 'You're prepared for a journey,' he remarked, nodding towards it. 'That's good, because I've a journey in mind for you.'

How had he come to be waiting for us? Might Pedro have betrayed us? I couldn't believe so—unless, which was a horrible thought, under torture.

'Where's Ramirez?' I asked.

'I didn't think we wanted him along, so we gave him a little knock on the head. He'll live, I dare say. But don't be expecting him to rescue you. We shan't be waiting around for that.'

'He'll know it was you. And he has friends.'

'Of course he'll know it was me. But that's all he knows. And if you want to play those games, Professor, I have friends too. Rather more than he has, I fancy. One of them, one little dicky-bird, whispered to me about this van. So don't be worrying your head over me. Just relax and enjoy the trip.'

The van stopped. We couldn't have gone very far; simply around a couple of corners. I heard the door being opened, and had a brief hope that we might have been stopped, for some reason, by the police. But it wasn't the police. It was the driver. He mounted into the van and closed the door again.

'Now,' said O'Malley more sharply. 'The

three of you, turn over and lie on your faces.'

'I should have killed you,' said Cressida savagely. 'I had enough chances. And enough reason.'

'Didn't you, though?' agreed O'Malley. 'But, you see, no woman's killed me yet. Turn over.'

Having no choice, we obeyed. The driver stepped across, to me first and then the other two, pulled our hands behind our backs and tied them with what felt like electrical flex.

'I want you to be comfortable,' said O'Malley. He knelt beside me, took hold quite gently of my left wrist, pushing up the sleeve, and I felt a prick. 'Sweet dreams,' said O'Malley, before the blackness engulfed me.

*   *   *

It was still black, but my eyes were open. Was I dead, or very ill, or—my God!—blind? But I didn't feel unwell, just a little muzzy, and now I could discern cracks of light. My hands were still tied behind me, and I was sitting with my knees up under my chin. I tried to straighten my legs and they immediately struck a wall. I turned my head and there was rough wood against my cheek. The cracks of light suddenly made sense. I was in a box, a wooden crate. And the roaring sound also made sense. I was in an aeroplane.

Whether because my movement had been

perceived or merely by coincidence, I don't know, but I heard voices, the crate was shaken, there came a brief splintering sound and the whole side of it fell away. I was hauled unceremoniously out on to the floor of the plane. The second gunman (as I'd named him to myself) and a man I hadn't seen before were prizing open another crate. They pulled poor Cressida out, her hair dishevelled, her cream coat and skirt marred with dark smears. She seemed only half-conscious. The men opened a third crate and extracted Surov. He was certainly awake, watching them.

We were in the back, the cargo area, of quite a small plane. Through a wire-mesh barrier, pierced by a door, I could see passenger seats and, in front, the back of the pilot's head. Only one other seat was occupied—by O'Malley. He had twisted round, looking at us.

He rose and came through the door in the mesh screen. 'You're awake?' he said. 'And how's my Cressy?' Her eyes focused on him as he knelt beside her, and you could see full consciousness—realization—welling back. 'You'll be all right,' he said. 'I want you all to be feeling fine.'

He gave an order, and the two men propped each of us up against the wall of the plane. My arms were numb. The second gunman produced a knife, which sent my

95

heart into my mouth; but he used it to cut the flex holdng my wrists. Gradually sensation returned, as I worked them to get the circulation flowing. O'Malley poured coffee from a Thermos into a paper cup and offered it to me. There was no point in refusing sustenance. I drank. Cressida, however, turned her head away. Surov drank.

'As I said,' burbled O'Malley, 'I want you to be comfortable, and you wouldn't be comfortable travelling in an old crate now, would you? But I always think the best way to get through a long journey is to sleep. And there's nothing like a nice warm drink before bedtime. Cressy, my dear, you really must try this coffee.'

Crouching beside her, he forced her head back and was trying to pour the coffee between her lips. I was going to protest. I was going to do something. But a great lethargy held me, and I was confused, and the sound of the engine filled my ears, and the blackness came up again, and I slept.

* * *

When I next woke, I was still in the aircraft, with Cressida slumped beside me, Surov beyond her. I tried to pull myself upright but felt something drag my arm. Looking down, I saw that my right wrist was handcuffed to a stanchion. I slumped back and drifted away again.

For quite a while I continued in this floating state, waking and sleeping. I'm pretty sure that I was given more to drink, perhaps to eat as well, and I can vaguely remember Cressida stirring and saying something. But dreams and reality were all mixed up. O'Malley's face grinned at me. And the engines throbbed steadily.

I suppose he kept me drugged, kept all three of us drugged, so I had no idea how long the flight lasted. Several hours certainly, probably many hours. Then the engines changed their note, and I was aware of rolling sideways, until my arm pulled against the handcuffs. O'Malley had gone forward and was sitting beside the pilot. The other two men were seated up there as well, but one was slewed round in his seat, watching us. If that was a precaution, it wasn't necessary. I felt much too weak and lethargic to move, even if there was any move I could have made.

The plane was landing. It bumped along a runway. Surov was awake too. Cressida seemed still to be asleep, but, as I looked at her, her eyelids flickered.

The motion stopped, the engines cut off, leaving only the ghost of their roaring in my ears. O'Malley unfastened his seat-belt, stood up and stretched; then gestured in our direction. Obeying him, the two men came through the mesh door towards us. At the same time, a wide door in the side of the aircraft opened, letting in a flood of sunlight.

They unlocked my handcuffs first, and hoisted me to my feet. O'Malley had followed them. 'Welcome to my country estate,' he said. 'Now you will be sensible, won't you, and not cause any trouble? You really couldn't get away. And why should you want to? You'll all be my guests for dinner tonight. We can have a nice long talk then.' He chuckled, went forward and presumably left the plane through the pilot's door.

A man in blue overalls appeared in our door, and the head of another rose behind him. My mind had begun to clear, although I felt very shaky on my feet. O'Malley was right, of course; there was no point in resistance at this stage. I let myself be handed over to the men in the doorway. Behind me Cressida was being released.

The sunlight was dazzling. I swayed and caught hold of the rail at the top of the ramp. The man in overalls, swarthy and unshaven, steadied me. Deliberately I took my time, breathing deeply, accustoming my eyes to the light. The first thing I realized was the sun's position. It was low. So we'd been flying all day. Assuming it was the same day. Could we have landed, refuelled, and flown on through a night and another day without my knowing? I couldn't be sure even of that. It didn't seem probable but nor was it impossible.

We had landed on a grass airstrip. On one side, to my right, open country—yellow grass and sporadic bleached trees—sloped down towards thicker and greener vegetation in the distance; beyond which forest stretched away as far as I could see. On my left were mountains, not very high but rising sharply in a cascade of inhospitable rock. Two spurs came down almost to the two ends of the airstrip; and between them, hugged by the rocks, was a line of wooden buildings, some of which were plainly warehouses but, beyond, a couple of one-storey structures with windows and veranda in front, presumably living quarters. There were several figures moving about.

At the bottom of the ramp a Jeep was waiting. A man in an open-necked shirt and wearing dark glasses sat behind the wheel. Rather unsteadily I made my way down, and, since it was clearly expected of me, climbed into the back. Surov, with one of our escorts, or captors, followed closely. The other emerged, supporting Cressida. She was obviously still suffering from the effects of the drug, but some colour had returned to her cheeks and she was able to walk.

When all five of us had been crammed into the Jeep, Cressida beside me, the driver engaged the gears and shot forward so abruptly that I was almost thrown off. 'Are you all right?' I murmured to Cressida.

She managed a smile. 'I'm fine.'

We were heading for the wooden structures under the mountain. The airstrip itself, I saw, had nothing much to mark it, just a few petrol drums indicating the line of the runway. And there was a fence of barbed wire, barely discernible amid tall grass. Beyond the wire some cattle were grazing.

As we passed between the sheltering arms of rock, I realized there were more buildings than I had been able to see from the plane; an overhang concealed them. There were also more people around. All men. One had a rifle slung on his shoulder. Another wore a gunbelt with a revolver. No one else was visibly armed. The sunset, reflected from the mountain, was turning red and the shadows in the valley were growing dark.

In a cloud of dust we drew up before the second of the two main windowed buildings. A small man, balding, with a deeply creased sun-browned face, stood on the veranda waiting for us. He wore a grubby white apron. Descending the three wooden steps, he greeted us—in an accent surprisingly, but unmistakably, Cockney.

''Ello, lady and gents,' he said. 'We been expecting you. I'm the 'ead cook an' bottle-washer. Not that I does much cookin' or bottle-washing. We got dagos for that. But I'm in charge, sort of. That your bag there? You ain't got much luggage, 'ave you?' He broke into rapid Portuguese, and one of our escorts extracted from the back of the Jeep the green canvas bag, which, I now noticed for the first time, must have been brought with us from the plane.

'Come along then, lady and gents. Let me show you to your rooms. Oh, I forgot to introduce meself. Charlie Bates is my name. That's me. At your service.'

'You're a long way from home,' I said.

'Ain't I though?'

I followed him. Cressida, beside me, was walking quite steadily now. Then came Surov, and, bringing up the rear, O'Malley's man carrying our bag. It was a weird parody of a normal arrival at a country house or hotel. We climbed the three steps into warm thickening darkness on the veranda. Bates pushed open a door and there was light, dim but electric.

'Own generator,' he said. 'It's a brute. Always going wrong. I kicks it. That's me remedy. A remedy for most things—engines, children, wives, too, if I 'ad one, which, thank God, I ain't.'

There were several bedrooms on both sides of the door. Bates allocated one to each of us in succession—Cressida, me, Surov. 'Strikes me,' he said, 'you ain't got very much in the way of gear. Now what might you be needing? Tell me, and I'll rustle up what I can.'

I said, 'Miss Lee and I are all right. Mr. Surov has nothing.'

'My needs are few,' said Surov, standing in the door of his room. 'I should like to wash. Soap perhaps and a towel?'

'I can do better than that,' said Bates. ''Old 'ard and I'll be back.'

O'Malley's man had dropped the bag in my room and disappeared. Bates now left us too. Cressida, Surov and I were, as far as we could see, alone in the building.

'What shall we do?' asked Cressida.

'Nothing,' I said, 'for the moment.'

Surov nodded. 'Exact. We wait. We shall see.'

'This is all my fault,' said Cressida. 'I'm sorry.'

'It's nobody's fault,' I replied. 'Or rather it's O'Malley's—with whom we have a score to settle.'

'I'm afraid he thinks he has a score to settle with us, and he's in a better position to do it.'

'For the moment. Things change.'

Surov looked at me speculatively. 'Good saying.'

We heard a footstep on the veranda, and stiffened. It was Bates, carrying towels, pyjamas, shirts and various minor items. 'A good 'otel we run 'ere,' he said. 'Everything provided.'

'Where are we?' I asked.

'That'd be telling. 'East o' the sun and west

102

o' the moon,' I've 'eard Mr. O'Malley say. A long ways from anywhere. You better ask 'im.'

'I shall.'

''E's expecting you for dinner. You'll be wanting to clean up first. I'll come an' fetch you in 'alf an hour. An' don't be trying anything silly in the meantime, will you, folks? There's men out there with guns. Not nice an' friendly like me.'

Grinning cheerfully, he strutted off.

'I would like to wash up,' said Cressida.

I asked Surov, who was picking what he wanted from the pile of things which Bates had left: 'Will your people come looking for us?'

'Will yours?' he replied.

'I don't know.'

'Mine will lodge an official protest. They will say I've been kidnapped. They would have said that anyway.'

'A lot of good that will do,' said Cressida.

'When Bates comes back,' I said, 'give me a moment alone with him. Perhaps I can learn something.'

'You mean Brit to Brit. He is English, isn't he?'

'Oh yes, he's English.' As the others withdrew to their rooms, I thought about Charlie Bates; and, since I had nothing else to work on, my mind strayed (typically, you may say) in a somewhat academic direction.

103

He was a Londoner all right; the accent was genuine. Even perhaps a little old-fashioned, as though he'd been away from England a long while. Accents are being constantly modified. Today's Cockney is quite different from the Cockney which Dickens knew. I suppose nobody now alive has heard that transposition of 'v' and 'w' which used to be the most characteristic feature. As when Sam Weller's father tells 'Samivel' to spell his name with a 'we' . . .

I stood looking out of the window; not that I could see much, since there was a mosquito screen across it and the night was now fully dark. But a pool of light came from an arc-lamp on a high pole, and beyond was a line of light which I guessed might mark the perimeter fence. I could hear a murmur of voices from one of the other buildings; just wooden huts, really. The whole place gave the impression of being a camp—a refugee camp, a prisoner-of-war camp—rather than anything more solid. Oh well, doubtless we should soon have some answers; but there was no use pretending that the situation was other than pretty nasty. A holiday camp this wasn't. O'Malley had not brought us here for our health. If Pedro had recovered from his knock on the head, he presumably would be looking for us. But even if he knew about this place—and, despite his vaunted sources of information, that seemed a long shot—what could he do about it at such a distance? Tell the police, presumably. But O'Malley didn't seem worried about that possibility. He was unpleasantly confident. Perhaps he had the police squared. More likely he was just confident that this hideaway really was secret. And, anyhow, poor Pedro might be in no condition to start a search. We didn't know how badly he was injured. Remembering Pedro's wife and the warmth of his home, I suddenly felt very angry with the man who had treated him, and talked about him, so ruthlessly. Yes, I should indeed like to settle that score. But what were our chances? I firmly suppressed that question; no point in theorizing, as Sherlock Holmes would say, ahead of the data. But, though the night was warm, I felt, undeniably, a metaphorical chill.

On a bare table stood an earthenware pitcher and an enamel bowl. I washed, using the towel which Bates had brought. He had also provided a shirt, but, observing its vivid green-and-yellow pattern, I decided not. Our canvas grip, which contained a spare shirt of my own, had been taken by Cressida into her room; inevitably most if its contents were hers. So I simply tidied myself as best I could.

My door was open, but, with a quaint formality, Cressida tapped on it. 'May I come in?'

She had changed out of the crumpled linen suit into black trousers and a white shirt; her glossy hair had been brushed and she was wearing lipstick. 'I'm frightened,' she said.

'Of course. But O'Malley wants us to be. So don't let him see it.'

'I'll try.' She came and stood beside me, and I put my arm around her. She said, 'I'm relying on you.'

I could think of no answer which would be both reassuring and honest. Surov's arrival saved me from having to reply.

Our conversation during the next quarter of an hour was desultory and circular. Where were we? What was O'Malley going to do? How should we respond? I explained to Surov what had happened in Tara's Hall after he left, and the reason for O'Malley's malevolence. Having listened calmly, he shrugged. 'I knew there would be risk today. This is a different risk, that's all. Not foreseen. Always there is something one does not foresee.'

As we talked, I kept an eye on the window and the area of light visible through the mosquito screen. Bates appeared. 'Come, Miss Lee,' said Surov. 'Let us leave the professor to interrogate this Englishman.' They slipped out of the room as Bates climbed the steps to the veranda. He had discarded the apron and was wearing a loose grey jacket.

'Ready?' he asked, poking his head into my room. 'Sorry I couldn't run to evening dress.'

'I'm ready. Is this going to be a formal occasion?'

Bates's monkey face creased in a grin. 'O'Malley likes to do things proper. You pinched 'is girl, I'm told. 'E won't 'ave found that comical. Oh dear, no. So if 'e invites you to dinner, I reckon 'e's got a party planned. An' I fancy you're goin' to be the entertainment.'

'Have you been with him for a long time?'

'Me? I've been in this godforsaken 'ole for a couple o' years. I don't know if you'd call that being with O'Malley. 'E only comes 'ere on special occasions. But once before we 'ad a dinner party like this. I remember 'ow that one ended.'

'How did it end?'

'You don't want to know. Might put you off your feed.'

'But you do work for him?'

'In a manner of speakin'. But come on now. 'E don't like being kept waiting.' He turned towards the other rooms. 'Come on, you two. Stop your titivating. Grub's up.'

They emerged instantly. 'Just waiting to be called, eh?' said Bates. Looking over his shoulder at me, he added, 'Nasty suspicious mind I got. I thought as maybe you was goin' to jump me. Be prepared, that's my motto.' He pulled aside his jacket to show the butt of a revolver in his waistband.

'I might have done,' I said, 'but what would be the point? What would we do next?'

'Good thinking. You're a reasonable man, I can see. Now, lady and gents . . .'

He conducted us out. I was going to say 'he led us out,' but in fact he didn't; he was careful not to turn his back on me. The night felt as warm and heavy as a blanket. Moths fluttered below the arc-lamp. In the distance, under the perimeter lights, I saw a figure move. A man with a rifle; a sentry, I presumed. From the adjacent building I could still hear voices; someone laughed. But Bates took us away, walking on hard-baked earth, deeper into the mountain cleft. I discerned the oblong of another lighted window, and, as we approached, I realized that it was in a little house, built close up against the rock wall.

The door opened before we reached it. Unlike everyone else I'd seen, the man who opened it was dressed quite elaborately, in a frilled white shirt and tightly cut embroidered trousers. Around his waist was a red sash. He held a silver candelabrum aloft. The house was lit entirely by candles.

The man appeared to be, or to be playing the part of, a species of servant. Without a word he ushered us—Bates had now dropped behind—through a miniature hall into the room with the lighted window. It contained a long table, elaborately laid with plates, cutlery and glasses, and candles down the middle. Against the wall, in the shadows, stood two more flunkeys, dressed like the one who had admitted us. And at the far end of the table sat O'Malley, in a white dinner-jacket.

'Ah, my guests,' he said, not rising. 'Cressy, come and sit by me.' He indicated the chair on his right. 'And since there are no other ladies, I'm afraid you two gentlemen will have to sit together.'

'What's this all about?' said Cressida. 'Why have you brought us here?'

'For dinner, of course?'

'You know perfectly well what I mean.'

'Now you wouldn't be wanting to spoil the evening before it's started. Sit, my dear. And you gentlemen. Wine?' He snapped his fingers, and one of the flunkeys—I call them that for want of a better name—filled our glasses.

Cressida tried another tack. 'Fernando,' she said, 'I'm sorry about the other night. I shouldn't have lost my temper—'

He stopped her. 'Don't apologize, my dear. We can discuss that in private, later.'

'It wasn't Professor Glowrey's fault,' she said in a very small voice.

'Sure, and he only behaved like any red-blooded man. But I insist. No business until after dinner. Isn't that the civilized way?

And you're all such civilized people. Not like me. I'm just a poor bog-Irishman. At least my father was. In my case I suppose it's the bogs of the Amazon.' He laughed.

'What is this place?'

'So the professor has an inquiring mind. All right, I'll tell you. My business interests aren't confined to Tara's Hall. Brazil's a big open country still, and there's lots of things which need helping on their way. Things and people. Drugs, for instance, and people whom the police, somewhere or other, would like to interview but who prefer not to be interviewed. Precious stones occasionally. But it's the drugs pay best. Cocaine. We do a bit of refining. So you might say it's a packing station, and a laboratory, and a staging post. And officially it's a cattle ranch. From the air it's a cattle ranch, I hope. The authorities on the ground, such as they are, have been—to put it delicately—squared. We're a long way from the nearest town.'

'Which is?'

'A long way. Now, tell me, what do you think of my chef?' He was a cook on a cruise liner who murdered one of his passengers for her jewels. He jumped ship in Rio. I got the cook and the jewels. He's quite an artist, wouldn't you say?'

Deplorable though it might be, and bizarre, and alarming, I couldn't help the thought that this was true. A cream soup had

110

been followed by some unidentified fish in a delicate pink sauce. My enjoyment was marred by the uncomfortable realization that O'Malley would scarcely have been so frank if he expected us to have the opportunity of passing on the information.

'And, Comrade Surov,' said O'Malley, 'how do you like the flesh-pots of the West?'

Surov studied him gravely. 'There are people like you in Russia. Not many, but some. We shoot them.'

'You'll never shoot them all,' replied O'Malley cheerfully. 'Free enterprise will always find a way, like water bubbling up. But I admit it's easier here, the saints be praised. I wonder what your countrymen would pay for you, Comrade Surov.'

'Are you holding us for ransom?' asked Surov. 'Is that your purpose?'

'It's not exactly my purpose, but I'm a businessman. I take a little profit on the side, when I can. But I shouldn't have raised the topic so soon. Not till coffee. Isn't that right?'

So the weird imitation of a dinner party continued. Conversational gambits were made and fizzled out. I tried, by several devious routes, to learn more about where we were, about the number of guards and so on, but O'Malley persisted in side-stepping those questions. Finally coffee came, in small cups of good china, and a bottle of Armagnac was left on the table. We had been served, throughout the meal, by the man who had let us in—he seemed to have the role of butler—and several others in the same uniform, who carried dishes through the room's only door. There were at least five of them altogether, and presumably a kitchen staff out of sight. Bates had disappeared. Now, the meal being over, the butler-man and the two who had acted as flunkeys originally did not withdraw but merely stood back discreetly in the shadows, the butler guarding the door.

Needlessly, since the conversation had again died, O'Malley tapped a spoon against his cup, as though calling for silence.

'Now,' he said, 'if everyone's happy, perhaps you'd like to be knowing my plans. There's no need for apprehension.' He patted Cressida's hand. She withdrew it sharply. 'I shan't do any of you the least harm in the world. Quite the contrary. Each of you's going to get just what I'm sure you most want. First, my dear Cressy'—he beamed at her—'will stay with me, where I shall take very good care of her. Oh yes, very good care indeed.' Medusa-like, she glared at him but made no comment.

He continued, 'Comrade Surov I'm going to help on his way. The only question is, which way? Home, where I dare say there's a warm welcome waiting for him? Or on, to wherever he was headed when we interrupted him? It doesn't matter to me. But I'm a kindly sort of fellow and I'm keen he should go where he'll be most appreciated. So I'll be making a few confidential inquiries, seeking offers, you might say. My guess is that it's his old comrades will be missing him most, but, if he tells me different, I'll get in touch with his new friends. Perhaps they can persuade me. We'll take our time. In the meanwhile, Comrade Surov, you'll be my guest here. All right?' Surov, looking into his coffee-cup said nothing.

'And now we come to the good professor.' Our eyes met. I hope I didn't show what I was feeling. 'You'll be telling me we have no quarrel, and nor we have. So I'll be letting you go, free as a bird. Aren't you relieved?'

'Continue,' I said.

'"Continue," is it? You're thinking there should be more? Well, that's the trouble. I can't spare anyone to go with you. Do you reckon you could find your own way home, Professor?'

'I'd need to know where I am first.'

'Why, you're here, Professor. That's where you are. You're a very clever man, I've no doubt, so you shouldn't have any difficulty in walking through about a thousand miles of rough country. It's true that some of the creatures out there aren't entirely well disposed. I never fancy the snakes myself. Then there's some Indians in the valley, with
113

whom I have an amicable arrangement. They know that I don't like my guests straying. But I'm sure you speak lots of languages, Professor, so you'll be able to tell them that you're the exception. You'll manage, won't you? And no one can ever say I've laid a finger on you.'

I drank the rest of my Armagnac in a gulp. 'I'll manage,' I said, 'and I'll be back.' Sheer bravado, but my immediate reaction had been largely unjustified relief. O'Malley wasn't going to murder me or even keep me prisoner. I was being given a chance to escape on my own, and I've always preferred to face problems on my own, to work things out for myself. Of course that initial reaction didn't last long: cold reality began to prick the pathetic balloon of my confidence.

'Bravely spoken, Professor. It'd be a pity if your little walk ended too soon, so we'll give you a picnic to take with you. Food and water. And a knife. How about a knife?'

'You can't send him out there alone,' said Cressida urgently. 'He wouldn't have a hope. He'll die.'

'Do you think so? The professor doesn't. He says he'll manage.'

'You've got me. That's what you wanted, isn't it? You can do what you like with me—'

'Oh, I shall, Cressy darling, I shall. When would it suit you to leave, Professor? Shall we say tomorrow night? Around sunset? It'll be more interesting for you in the dark, and—who knows?—the Indians may not spot you. We won't tell them that one of our guests is missing until the following day. O'Malley's promise. Scout's honour.'

The balloon was now wholly deflated. O'Malley meant me to die. He was simply playing with me. The chance I'd thought he was giving me was no chance at all. But at least I wouldn't give him the satisfaction of seeing that I knew it.

'This is your game,' I said. 'You make the rules.'

'So I do, so I do. Sunset it is then. We'll all come and wave you off. And that'll give you tomorrow in which to anticipate your journey. Charlie Bates will bring you your little bit of equipment. He might even find you some boots. Those shoes don't look as though they were made for the jungle. The snakes bite your ankles, you know. Mind you, there's other snakes in the trees. You need to keep one eye up and one eye down, like a picture by Picasso.' Still grinning, he surveyed the table. 'Well, it's been a good evening, wouldn't you say? Shall I convey your compliments to the chef?' He stood up. 'You'll be wanting a good night's sleep. Especially you, Professor. You may not get much sleep tomorrow night.'

I rose too. O'Malley noticed Cressida instinctively flinch a little away from him.

'Cressy darling,' he said, 'I'll be leaving you with your friends tonight. There'll be plenty of time for you and me to talk afterwards.' He spoke briefly in Portuguese to the flunkeys. 'My men will take you back to your quarters. And they'll keep watch outside. I wouldn't want you to be disturbed in the night—and I certainly won't want you disturbing me.'

'I despise you,' said Cressida, and walked, head high, to the door. Surov and I followed. The butler-person led the way, the two flunkeys brought up the rear. I wondered if they were armed. Probably.

'Good night,' O'Malley called mockingly after us.

The night was silent now, except for the noise of insects and, far off, the cry of some animal or bird. No one spoke until we had ascended the steps to the veranda, where our escort—or jailers—stopped, and entered my room. Cressida and Surov accompanied me without the suggestion being voiced; we all, obviously, wanted to talk. I crossed to the window, in order to make sure that the guards were out of earshot. They were. One sat on the steps, lighting a cigarette. Another leaned against the rail. The butler-person had gone.

'My God,' said Cressida, 'what a mess!'

Surov said, 'We might overpower those guards.'

I nodded. 'We might be able to. I'd

116

thought of it. But what then? We'd better wait. Something may turn up.'

'What could turn up?' asked Cressida bitterly. 'Nothing will turn up. And you know what's going to happen then.'

'We might be rescued. My friends in Rio must be looking for us. Surov's people must be looking for him.'

'You don't know O'Malley. I do. He'll have covered his tracks.'

'You have a saying, "While there's life, there's hope,"' observed Surov.

'I thought of that too,' I replied, 'but it seemed too much of a cliché. However, it's true. If O'Malley does what he said he's going to do, I may get away. I may find help somewhere. But, Cressida, I hate leaving you with him.'

'To a fate worse than death? Don't worry. It's not. You're the one—' She stopped, biting her lip.

'Let's sleep on it,' I said. 'He was right about one thing. I do need to get some rest.'

We talked for a little while longer without reaching any further conclusion. Then Cressida and Surov went to their rooms. I lay down, fully clothed, on the bed, hopes and fears chasing themselves through my mind. I must analyse the situation. But in fact I didn't. I fell asleep; a heavy sleep, perhaps what psychologists call a 'fugue,' an escape. Bates woke me, carrying three mugs of

117

coffee on a tray. He was wearing his apron again. 'Sorry, no tea,' he said. 'I believe in a nice cup of char meself, but they don't go in for it in these parts. 'Eavy night, was it? You ain't even took off your shoes.'

I could see bright sunshine beyond the veranda. The guards were gone. Recollection, equally clear and stark, flooded back.

'O'Malley said you might find me some boots.'

'Boots, eh?' His mischievous face turned grave. 'Yus, I 'eard what 'e was going to do. 'E's done it before, you know.'

'May I ask what happened when—when he did it before?'

'You still don't want to know.'

Taking the coffee, I looked at him, wondering if there was any help to be found in this quarter. Well, there was nothing to be lost by trying. 'Mr. Bates, I get the impression that you may not be absolutely whole-heartedly O'Malley's man.'

'I'm my own bloody man,' he replied. 'Make no mistake about that.'

'I don't doubt it. I only meant that I thought you might be willing—without doing anything that could get you into trouble—to tell me a few things which might be helpful.'

'Such as?'

'For a start, which way I should go when I leave here.'

'It won't make any difference.'

118

'Then telling me wouldn't matter.'

He cocked his head on one side. And after a moment said, 'All right. Why not? Let me deliver these 'ere other cups of coffee. I'll be back.'

By the time he returned, I'd splashed water on my face from the earthenware pitcher, smoothed my hair with my fingers and tightened my tie, which was all I could manage in the way of a morning toilet. I fancied that Cressida, even in these unpromising circumstances, would take considerably longer.

'The next thing,' said Bates, 'is breakfast. You come with me and we'll talk on the way. It'll look natural. Not that O'Malley 'ud care probably. 'E's got you marked down as a dead man. What dead men know don't do no 'arm.'

There was still some freshness in the air outside. It occurred to me that we might be quite high, although the mountains behind us were really not much more than rocky hills. The various wooden structures were, I could see now, cunningly dispersed among shade trees and beneath the overhang. The size and nature of the camp would not have been discernible except to someone coming close. The camp had begun to wake up; there were people moving about.

'Am I allowed to ask how you got here?' I said.

'Ask what you like. I don't mind tellin' you. 'Ow did I get 'ere? Same way as you—in O'Malley's aeroplane. Why's a longer story, but I'll cut it short. Me an' a couple of chums pulled off a big job, in London. My chums got caught. I didn't, an' I 'ad the cash. One way or another, I ended up in Rio, on account of because there ain't no extradition. That's when I met Mr. bloody O'Malley. For a sum of money which was somewhat less than 'alf what I'd still got—which was considerable—'e would transport me to the United States, an' see me set up there, nice and comfy, with a new identity, all proper. Much better than 'ere among the dagos. So I says "yus" an' puts meself in 'is 'ands, like; O'Malley being very plausible, as you may 'ave noticed.

'But—would you believe it?—somehow all my money vanished. Not O'Malley's doing. Oh no. "Not my fault," 'e says. "You 'as my sympathy. But facts is facts, an' 'ere you are without a brass farthing to your name. Suppose you come an' work for me. After a little while'—cash or credit, 'e didn't exactly specify—"you'll 'ave earned enough to pay your way, like under our previous arrangement. Otherwise," 'e said, "I wouldn't say as your future prospects looked good." So, reckoning I 'ad no choice, I said yes. I do one or two little jobs for 'im, an' I ends up 'ere. "I trust you," 'e says. "You're

120

very valuable to me," says 'e. I'm to 'elp 'im run this place. Kind of. The dagos do most of the work. An' they're the guards. Like I said, I'm just the 'ead cook an' bottle-washer. But I'm useful to 'im because I speaks English and can 'andle foreigners. Guess what, though? I don't get paid. Leastwise, not enough so it adds up to anything. "Next time I come," 'e says. "We'll talk about it then." You can imagine. I'm not 'appy, as you can also imagine. But what am I to do about it? Where can I go? Besides, by that time I've seen what 'appens to people who gets on the wrong side of Mr. O'Malley. So, the long an' the short of it is, I'm 'ere.'

We'd been walking under the trees, between the huts. The men we passed looked curiously at me. Bates waved at several of them.

'Later on,' he said, 'I'll give you the conducted tour.'

We entered a hut in which were the smells of coffee and cooking. A Chinese man and two dark-skinned Brazilian assistants were engaged around a large stove. (I assumed we were still in Brazil. My knowledge of South American geography, of distances and frontiers, was grossly inadequate.) 'Morning, Lee,' said Bates. Then to me: 'Lee Ong's our number-one cook. 'E used to be a number-one 'atchet-man, but 'e stuck 'is 'atchet in the wrong skull. 'E killed 'is own

Triad boss, an' you've got to run a long way to escape those fellows. But you're safe 'ere, aren't you, Lee?'

Lee grinned broadly. 'Me safe.' He brought the cleaver down, with an ominous *thunk*, across a side of bacon. 'But no fun. How about we go soon to bright lights?'

'I'm all for it, old son,' replied Bates. 'But right now let's be 'aving four breakfasts on a tray.'

Lee in fact provided two trays, each bearing large plates of fried bacon and eggs, bread and jam, and more coffee. As we carried them back to my room, Bates nodded towards a middle-aged man with horn-rimmed spectacles and a towel over his arm. 'That's Dino, 'E was a Mafia bagman. Carried their cash to be laundered. Then one day 'e carried it too far. That's another bunch you don't want on your trail. O'Malley picked 'im up an' whisked 'im off, an' whisked off the cash too. You see, a lot of interesting fellows we got around 'ere. All good honest villains, though. No terrorist rubbish. O'Malley don't like nutters. Unreliable, 'e says they are. So 'e passes them on quick.'

Bates's exposition had been so fascinating that I'd not got around to asking him the questions which mattered. However, there was time, and the more friendly I could make him, the better.

The four of us breakfasted together in my

122

room, Surov taciturn, Cressida alternating between nervous chatter and apprehensive silence, Bates and I conversing (I like to believe) almost normally. In the presence of the others he was less forthcoming. A prudent man, Charlie Bates. He didn't care what he said to me. I should be in no position to repeat it, and he probably enjoyed being able to talk frankly; but Cressida might carry tales to O'Malley and Surov was an unknown quantity.

When we'd eaten, he said, 'Right, Prof, let's get you kitted out.' We emerged again into the sunlight. Traces of mist, which earlier had veiled some parts of the landscape, had been burnt off; warmth was becoming heat. Bates halted at the bottom of the veranda steps and pointed down towards the distant mass of green tree-tops. 'See that bit o' smoke?' he asked. I did; a thin blue wisp, rising straight up. 'That's the Indians. O'Malley gives them things an' reckons they're friendly, though I wouldn't want to rely on that meself. Anyway, they're sort of an extra guard around this place. You'd better give 'em a wide berth if you can.'

'Is that the direction I should be heading?'

'Like I said, it won't make much difference. But if you mean is that the general direction of civilization, yes, it is. A long, long way off. Back of us lies rough country, mountainous like. There is a trail. The dope

123

goes along it, on mules. I don't exactly know where to. The customers come an' collect the stuff once a month. Maybe they just take it to another pick-up point. You could try that direction, but if there was any chance of you getting through, O'Malley wouldn't be letting you loose.'

'You're not much comfort.'

'Sorry, mate. That's 'ow it is. Best I can do is give you that knife, like O'Malley said you could 'ave, an' a pair of decent boots, an' a blanket for night-time, an' a box o' matches so you can light a fire, an' the biggest water-bottle I can find, an' I'll get Lee to stuff a knapsack with food.'

'You couldn't find me a gun, could you?' I said it tentatively, afraid of pushing him too far.

'No, I couldn't. For one thing, O'Malley may 'ave you searched at the gate, and if 'e finds anything you oughtn't to 'ave got, I'll be for it. Second thing, there ain't any guns, except the one 'e lets me carry in case of trouble. All the others is kept by the dago guards. An' they lives quite separate. Over in them far 'uts, by the airstrip.'

As though to change an awkward subject, he indicated a large windowless wooden building which we were passing. 'That's our laboratory, like. Where the snow gets refined. There's a Kraut called Fritz in charge. 'Ot stuff as a chemist, I'm told. 'E's quite a

124

decent bloke. 'Is father was a Nazi, escaped to this part o' the world after the war. Then those Jewish Nazi-'unters came after 'im. O'Malley said 'e could get 'im away, an' this is where 'e got 'im away to. Fritz and 'is dad. Now Fritz 'as to work for O'Malley, or O'Malley says 'e'll deliver 'is dad, all nicely parcelled up, for Yom Kippur. Personally I think they should leave the old gent alone, whatever 'e done in the war. I mean, after so many years. Don't you?'

'Actually I do.'

It struck me that, in a weird way, O'Malley's nefarious operations were kin to, or more accurately a mirror image of, what the Fishers did. Both groups smuggled people and valuables across frontiers. Both ignored, indeed were actively hostile to, the concepts of law and morality prescribed by governments. So how should one differentiate between them? Or were they really tarred with the same brush? No, of course they weren't. The simple answer was the one laid down, with such ringing conviction, in 'The Song of Roland': *'Les Chrétiens ont droit, les Païens ont tort.'* The Christians are right, the Pagans are wrong. But Gabriel wasn't a Christian. He was a Jew—though not a Nazi-hunter . . . I must have smiled at the thought of these moral complexities.

'Something funny?' asked Bates.

'Not really. In fact, not at all.'

'I like a bloke what can laugh when 'e's in your sort o' fix.' He pulled a bunch of keys from the pocket of his apron. ''Ere's my quarters,' he said, nodding towards a single hut, 'and 'ere's me stores.'

Unlocking and removing a padlock, he opened the door of a long shed adjacent to the hut. Inside, smelling musty, were piles of workclothes—shirts, jeans, overalls—tools and bulging sacks.

'That there gents' natty suiting of yours,' observed Bates, 'ain't exactly the right costume for a stroll through our part of the world. I reckon we better give you a few extra things.' Measuring me with his eye, he picked a dark-blue shirt and a pair of trousers made of dark, almost black, cotton. 'Choose a pair o' boots,' he said, indicating a line of footwear arrayed against the wall. 'The kind that comes up 'igh.'

While I was trying them on and finding that the leather was soft and surprisingly comfortable, he collected an army-type water canteen and a canvas knapsack, and added a leather belt to the shirt and trousers.

'I think we can stretch a point about the knife,' he said. 'A machete's more useful.' And he brought a gleaming hooked blade from the far end of the hut.

The pile of my new possessions seemed a pathetically small amount of equipment for the ordeal I was to confront, as, carrying

126

them (except for the boots, which I wore), we returned to the living quarters.

'Can't 'ang around all day,' said Bates. 'I got things to do.' There was, I thought, a trace of embarrassment in his voice; I believed he was genuinely sorry for me, ashamed even of what he was helping to perpetrate. No, 'ashamed' would be going too far, but we had established a kind of friendship. 'I'll send your lunch over, and the food for you to take with you. Then I'll be coming to fetch you meself at dusk.'

The rest of that day was extraordinary; terrifying, of course—it would be absurd to say I wasn't frightened—but, in a way, exhilarating too and highly charged emotionally. I was almost impatient for dusk, for the moment of setting out, with my fate again, at least to some degree, in my own hands. Meanwhile, there was Cressida.

Two Brazilians, who wouldn't speak, although Cressida tried talking to them in Portuguese, brought cold meat and a bottle of red wine for our lunch. They also brought, wrapped in white cloth, quite a large quantity of meat and bread, which I stuffed into the knapsack.

After lunch, Surov slipped away to his room, leaving me alone with Cressida. I can't really remember what we talked about during the next three hours; nothing very intimate, nothing of great consequence, and yet, in that

127

small sun-baked room, intimacy enclosed us and in the long run, I suppose, there were consequences. For the first time I saw Cressida with a layer of skin removed—or perhaps a layer of make-up would be a more accurate metaphor, since much of the personality she chose normally to exhibit was a carefully cultivated act. Now she was frightened—for me rather than herself, wanting to find words that might comfort and strengthen me; tender, at moments tearful, and yet practical and with a perceptible core of toughness. I value the memory of that afternoon.

The quality of the light had changed, was mellowing. 'Nearly sunset,' I observed. She squeezed my hand. And at that moment we heard footsteps on the veranda.

Bates came in, accompanied by the two flunkeys who had served at table the night before. Both now had rifles and cartridge-belts slung across their shoulders.

'This water's boiled,' said Bates, who was holding a bottle in each hand. 'Wiser, seeing you ain't used to ours. Better fill your canteen with it.'

I did. I'd already put on my new shirt, trousers and boots. Before doing so, about an hour earlier, I'd suggested to Cressida that she should leave while I changed my clothes. It was the only time that afternoon when she laughed aloud. Now I slid the machete through the leather belt, so it hung at my side, added the full canteen to the contents of the knapsack, which Cressida helped me adjust onto my back, and I was ready. Surov had emerged from his room and was standing in the corridor.

Stiffly, in procession—I first, with Cressida holding my arm, Bates a step behind, then Surov and, bringing up the rear, the two men who were obviously guards—we emerged into the evening light: a strange light, I remember, lurid, the sun having turned red as it began to vanish behind the mountains. At least I knew which direction was west, I thought. No one had offered me a compass. Perhaps I should have asked for one.

As we approached the main gate, I saw that quite a small crowd was awaiting us. There were several guards with rifles, and I recognized the Chinese cook, Lee Ong. In front of them stood O'Malley, wearing a gunbelt and pistol and a wide-brimmed hat.

He removed the hat with a flourish and bowed. 'I hope you've enjoyed our hospitality,' he said.

'It had its points,' I replied.

'And now, alas, comes the moment of parting.'

The gate itself was a crude structure of poles and barbed wire, some ten or twelve feet high, hinged to a thick post, with the wire fence running off in either direction. A rutted track led to the airstrip on the right. A footpath, barely visible amid rocks and stones, ran down the slope straight ahead. It vanished into thickening shadows; the great expanse of the tree-covered landscape beyond was already little more than a dark mass. One of the guards lifted a hook and swung the gate open.

'Bon voyage, Professor,' said O'Malley, 'I'd recommend you to get as far as you can before dawn. Take care.'

Deliberately not looking at him nor back at Cressida, I marched through the gate.

CHAPTER SIX

A DESPERATE GAMBLE

The moon shone above the distant hills like a silver coin, flooding the tree-tops with light and casting deep black shadows. I sat on a rock, trying to think calmly and rationally about my situation. When I'd left the camp, I'd marched straight ahead—'march to your front like a soldier,' said Kipling—down the track, until a clump of thick-leaved spiny bushes concealed me from the gate. Then I broke away to the left, across open but twilit ground, toward an outcrop of rocks, which seemed to be the beginning of the hillside flanking the camp. It was an instinctive decision. I wanted to get out of sight. I wanted time to think.

As I climbed, I kept turning to see if anyone had followed, but there was no sign of life except the rustling of insects and once, far off, the cry of a bird. Oddly, perhaps naïvely, I was inclined to believe what O'Malley had said. If only to protract my ordeal, he meant me to have a head start. No one would be hunting me until dawn. At least, not the Indians. But I had no idea what animals there might be. What sort of creatures were indigenous to Brazil? Some kind of panthers perhaps, jaguars, mountain lions? If so, did they hunt at night? I didn't know.

The twilight quickly turned to darkness, but then came the moon. Although I was following no track now, the going was quite easy; just a bare hillside with rocks and occasional bushes, and, on my left, a ridge between me and the camp. I climbed for the best part of an hour; then, more cautiously, veered towards the crest of the ridge, until I reached a point from which I could look down on the other side. My sense of direction had been accurate. An overhang blocked off most of the camp, but I could see the lights along the perimeter fence, and the gate, and the airstrip with the black shape of a single aeroplane still parked there.

I found a flat rock, and, after scrutinizing it

and the earth around for curled-up snakes or scorpions or tarantulas, I sat down and took a swig of water from the canteen. Only a couple of swallows; I didn't know how long it might have to last. My legs ached a little from the climb, but I wasn't tired. The adrenalin had done its work. I was keyed up, alert. So—think. Analyse the problem.

I was alone in a huge wild country of which I knew nothing. To reach safety I would have to cover hundreds, perhaps thousands, of miles. I didn't even know the right direction to go, except very roughly. There would be dangerous creatures, and, if O'Malley's threat was to be believed, hostile Indians. I had no map. I had enough food and water for perhaps two days. And I had a machete. That was the sum total of my assets.

Conclusion: I couldn't do it—or, at least, my chances of doing it were very slim indeed. Hence O'Malley's confidence that, by pushing me out into this terrible situation, he had, in effect, killed me. But I surely possessed one other asset. I refused to believe that I wasn't cleverer than O'Malley. I must out-think him.

What, then, were my options? I could set out, on my feet, through the forest, past the Indians, towards the coast. That was what O'Malley expected me to do, and he and I agreed that I should be unlikely to survive. I could try the opposite direction, farther inland, over the mountains, the way in which Bates had said the drugs went. I might reach a town or friendly Indians who would look after me. That sounded, marginally, a better chance; but O'Malley must know what lay in that direction, and must be confident that it offered no escape route.

Well, if I couldn't go anywhere safely, how about staying? Suppose I simply lay low among the rocks, waiting for help to come. Pedro or the Fishers must be looking for me. The Russians must be looking for Surov. But, again, O'Malley seemed confident that they wouldn't find us. And how long could I survive? A man skilled in survival techniques might last a long time, perhaps indefinitely, living off the country, but I had no such skills. Now another unpleasant idea occurred: if I began moving around in the daylight—searching for water—wouldn't I soon be spotted, by the Indians or by sharp eyes from the camp? I might already have left a trail which the Indians could follow . . .

All right, then. If I couldn't go and I couldn't stay, what was left? Nothing? Not quite nothing. One option remained.

The aeroplane was tantalizing but useless. Even if I could reach it, and if it wasn't guarded, and if it wasn't locked, and if there was fuel in the tank, I could do nothing with it, since I couldn't fly. But O'Malley didn't know I couldn't fly. Here was a chink in his planning: he should have found out. Even if the possibility of my stealing the plane seemed remote, perhaps he hadn't considered that I might break into the camp and hide there. Could I? Could Cressida and Surov conceal me in their hut? They might be able to, but not for long. Cressida, at least, was unlikely to be left peacefully to her own devices. O'Malley had other things in store for her.

That was another reason for going back if I could—to help Cressida. But at the moment I was in no position to help anybody. I was the one who needed help. What about Bates? He really could conceal me if he wanted to. Was that possible? Could he be bribed? From which point I began to speculate—wildly, but any course of action would be a desperate gamble—on a more ambitious scheme . . .

I waited. Sitting on the rock, I listened, not without apprehension, to the sounds of the night, the insects nearby and, far-off, occasionally the cry of some unidentified creature. I chewed a piece of meat from my knapsack, more for something to do than because I was hungry. The moon moved slowly across the sky. Periodically I consulted my watch, waiting until the camp below was really asleep.

I studied the movement of the sentries along the bit of the perimeter fence I could see. They didn't appear very systematic. And

I prowled around a little, studying my route. But it seemed wisest and safest not to move far. Eventually I just sat and meditated. I may even have dozed.

At last it was one o'clock, which was the starting-time I'd set myself. Climbing down to the camp would take, I'd reckoned, a full half-hour. In the event it took rather more. I wasn't going back the way I'd come. The route I'd surveyed was chosen because it looked quite an easy scramble and because rocks and scrub should hide me, for most of the way, from anybody in the camp who might happen to glance up at the mountainside; and it would bring me down behind the nearer huts, close to the point at which, I presumed, the fence ended against the cliff.

I moved steadily but cautiously, anxious not to kick a stone that might start a miniature avalanche and attract the attention of the sentries. The moon was almost down now, the shadows were longer. At some places I could step from rock to rock, as though I were descending a flight of stairs; at others I slithered; and there were stretches which merely sloped gently down. When I'd traversed about two-thirds of the way, I paused and examined the scene ahead. Directly below me was the roof of a hut which I thought might be the sentries' living quarters. And the fence did indeed seem to join the rock wall, at a point where the cliff became sheer behind it. The only human beings I could see were two sentries, with rifles slung over their shoulders, talking to each other beside the gate. The lights, on high poles, illumined most of the fence and parts of the camp but left considerable areas of darkness.

Now that I was in action, my nerves had settled. I simply concentrated on what was to be done. More carefully than ever I negotiated the final stage of the descent. I cannot pretend to have the instincts or skills of a countryman, but there was a gillie, when I was a boy, who taught me something about how to move on the hill. And when not to move. Keep absolutely still and you become almost invisible. I moved only when I was quite sure the sentries were not looking in my direction.

The two I'd seen before had remained together beside the gate. One of them was lighting a new cigarette from the stub of an old one. Crouching in the shadow of a rock, I studied the fence. Beyond the gate I could follow its line for perhaps two hundred yards, until the outline of another hut blocked it from my sight, and, as I watched, a third sentry strolled into view, walked to the gate and joined the other two. After a couple of minutes, he retraced his steps. One of the others, I guessed, should have been patrolling the fence in my direction, but neither of them showed any inclination to move.

So, finally, I did. I crawled, until I'd reached the cover of the nearest hut and the shadow it threw. Moving, after another pause, right up to the fence, I scrutinized the wire. The thought had occurred to me that it might be electrified, but I felt reasonably sure now that it wasn't; it consisted simply of barbed wire, twisted around, and stapled to, rough poles. Nor were the strands always very close together. As a barrier, whether against assault from outside or escape from inside, it seemed more symbolic than effective. The real barrier, I presumed, was not wire but distance—the remoteness of the place and the wildness of the country.

Using the machete as a lever, I prized up the lowest strand of wire until I was able to slide beneath it.

I was inside the camp, in the deep shadow between the fence and the back of the hut. I had already decided, while sitting on the rock, where I would go next. One option would have been to wake Surov and Cressida first, but there was nothing they could do yet, and, having embarked on my alternative plan, I didn't want to involve them in the immediate risk. Nor did I want any further delay. I would make the crucial throw at once.

As I threaded my way behind and then

between the huts, there was no sound of voices, no sign of anyone stirring. Although I kept as far as possible in the shadow, I could not avoid crossing a couple of open lighted spaces. I darted through the light and into the shadow again. Without mishap I reached the hut in which, I hoped, Bates was peacefully sleeping.

This was the first really dangerous point. Standing at his door, I would be fully exposed to sight. If it was locked, as it might well be, I could scarcely break it in. I should have to bang on the door and rouse him; and when he opened it, the moment he saw me, he might cry for help. Or he might come to the door, gun in hand.

The best thing was not to appear surreptitious. Boldly I stepped into the light, walked the few yards to the door and, very gently, tried the handle. The door yielded. It wasn't locked.

Inside, with the door drawn swiftly and silently shut behind me, there was enough light coming through a window to show the details of the room. A figure, presumably Bates, lay sleeping in a bed. I heard him snore. And—another bit of luck—his pistol hung in a holster on the wall beside him.

Stepping quietly across the small room, I extracted the pistol from its holster. Of course I wouldn't dare use it, except in a moment of desperation; a shot would rouse the camp. So

I transferred the gun to my left hand, and with my right, drew the machete, which had a razor-sharp blade. The top of Bates's head protruded from the single sheet and blanket which covered him.

I prodded the sleeping figure with the muzzle of his own revolver. He grunted, turned over and opened his eyes. For a moment, obviously, he didn't recognize me, though he stiffened at what must have been the alarming sight of a man standing over him with a raised machete. Then he did recognize me.

'Blimey,' he said, 'what are you doing 'ere?'

'I just couldn't keep away,' I said.

'The guards 'ad orders to shoot anyone they saw 'anging around the wire—meaning you.'

'They were otherwise occupied—gossiping.'

'I can believe it.' Bates was beginning to recover his poise. 'But that don't tell me why you're 'ere.'

'I'll tell you. But, first, have a look at this machete. You chose it for me, so you know it's sharp. I swear that, if you try to call out or do anything to alarm me, I'll cut your throat with it.'

'And that's my gun you're 'olding?'

'It is. And I've nothing to lose, remember. Which makes me dangerous.'

Bates grinned. 'Oh yes. A real Al Capone. So what do you want?'

'The first thing I want you to do is listen.' He pulled himself up in the bed, leaned back and looked at me quizzically. He was wearing striped pyjamas. For a moment I felt rather foolish brandishing the machete, but I knew it was my hesitation that was foolish. I didn't dare relax. But I lowered the blade.

'Mr. Bates,' I said, 'you know my problem. And I may be wrong, but I got the impression you weren't wholly unsympathetic. You also know the stakes are very high for me. I'm not fooling. So I want to make a deal with you.'

'A deal? You've got something to offer?'

'I've three possibilities to offer. You choose. The first, now that you've seen me, is that I put you out of action. I'll do it if I have to, believe me. The second is that you help me and my friends escape—we'll discuss what you can do—and you stay here. The third option is that you come with us. You don't want to spend the rest of your life in the back of beyond. You'd like to go home—to London. Well, I might be able to fix that. I know the Home Secretary—and the Director of Public Prosecutions.' (If you're going to shoot a line, I thought, you might as well shoot a big one.) 'I'm not without influence. I think they could be persuaded to drop the charges against you, in return for helping us now. At the very least they wouldn't press for

140

extradition. You could go anywhere, and be safe.'

That was the speech I'd prepared. In one sense, Bates was obviously a sophisticated man. 'Street-wise,' as it's called nowadays. But what can and cannot be done by Establishment string-pulling might well be outside his range. The tendency of outsiders is always to exaggerate what insiders can do. And I wasn't quite sure myself. Perhaps if Bates helped Surov defect, he really would have earned enough merit for extradition proceedings to be abandoned. As for the Home Secretary, I had met him once. He had dined in college. A most unimpressive man.

A long silence ensued. Bates was visibly thinking. At last he said, 'What did you 'ave in mind? What can I do?'

So far so good. 'You can bring proper supplies. You can help us leave the camp unobserved. And if you came with us, you could act as guide—couldn't you?'

'Me? Out in that bloody jungle? I'd be no better off than you.'

'But are you the only one who'd want to come? Mightn't some of the others join us? From what you told me, it sounded as though they were being kept here almost as slaves.'

He considered this idea. 'Could be. I dunno 'ow much that'd 'elp.'

'Isn't there anyone who knows the country? But there's another possibility. Is there

141

anyone who can fly a plane?'

He understood immediately. 'You mean—?' He paused. 'I believe Fritz can fly. 'E mentioned it once.'

'Would he come?'

''E might. You know, 'e just might.'

'Fuel? For the plane?'

'The plane's always kept ready. In case 'is nibs should need a quick getaway.'

'Well, then . . .'

'I gotta think about this. You ain't 'alf asking me to stick me neck out.'

'I'm afraid I can't give you much time to think. You've got to choose. But if you decide to come, perhaps you can hide me for a day while you talk to the others. But you'll have to be very careful. And, Mr. Bates, if anything goes wrong, I promise you this—I'll shoot you before they take me.'

He grinned, then shook his head. 'No, you wouldn't. I'd see you never 'ad the chance. But that won't do anyway. Them Indian trackers will be on to you tomorrow. They'll know you ain't gone in the direction you was supposed to go. And that girlie of yours. O'Malley's left 'er alone tonight, left 'er alone to think what's coming to 'er. But 'e won't leave 'er alone tomorrow. And since I reckon you wouldn't be willing to go without 'er, that won't do, will it? If we're going to go, we've got to go tonight.'

I glanced at my watch. 'It's past three now.

And it starts to get light—when?—seven? Could you find Fritz, could we be ready by then?'

'The more I think about it, the less ready I'm likely to be. But right now, Professor, you've near talked me into it. I'd give a good deal to see the smoke again. But supposin' we gets caught, an' supposin' you stay alive long enough to answer questions, will you back me up when I say you made me come along by pointing that there gun at me?'

'Yes.'

'Not that O'Malley will believe it, but I might talk 'im into 'aving enough doubts so 'e don't chop me the same time 'e chops you.'

'But you're going to have to persuade Fritz. He'll know.'

''E's a tight-lipped bastard. And we're chums. I don't think 'e'd give me away—whether 'e agrees to come or not.'

'So, is it a deal?'

Bates cocked his head on one side, grimaced and shrugged. 'What the 'ell? Sometimes you've got to take risks in this life. Yes, I reckon it's a deal. You can put that ugly great blade away.'

I slid the machete back into my belt. 'All right. I'll come with you to Fritz. After that, we'll wake my friends.'

'No, you'd better stick 'ere. The sentries might see us. Doesn't matter if they see me. And there's other people in Fritz's cabin.'

'If I let you out of my sight, why should I think I can trust you?'

Again he grinned. 'Suppose I give you the bullets for that shooter?' Feeling beneath his pillow, he produced a handful of cartridges. 'I'm not quite as green as I'm cabbage-looking. I didn't want anyone pinching my gun if I left it 'ere—or when I was asleep.'

Instead of taking the bullets, I handed him the gun. 'Load it,' I said. Embarrassed (I admit), I wanted to match his gesture, and, truth to tell, I had another motive—I wasn't sure I knew how to load a revolver without fumbling. He thumbed the cartridges into the cylinder and passed the gun back to me.

'No, I won't stay here,' I said. 'We've no time to waste. I'll go and rouse my friends.'

'As you like. But be careful, Professor. I don't care about your neck, but mine's going to be on the line as well.' As he spoke, he was pulling on trousers and shirt.

We parted at the door of the hut after making certain there was no one about. Bates walked confidently off; I slipped through the shadows, keeping close to the huts and outhouses. I could see the distant gate and the sentries, one of whom was now strolling idly along the perimeter fence. There was no visible guard on the verandaed hut where Cressida and Surov were presumably sleeping.

Cautiously I emerged from the shadows, mounted the steps and entered. The interior was warm and dark. I went into Cressida's room. She was lying on the bed, under a blanket, asleep. I remembered reading somewhere that, in order to wake a sleeping person without startling him, one should touch his feet; but I had little confidence in that method. Kneeling beside Cressida, I gently squeezed her shoulder, while keeping my other hand ready to clamp over her mouth if she started to scream. The precaution was unnecessary. Her eyes opened wide and she struggled to sit up, but I spoke before she could say anything: 'It's all right. Don't be frightened. It's me.'

'You came back,' she whispered.

'We're going to make a break for it. All together. Get dressed while I fetch Surov.'

Surov woke instantly at my touch, alert, watching me without apparent surprise. 'I've a plan,' I said. 'Get dressed and come.'

All the time I had one ear cocked for any sound outside. But there was nothing. Surov and I returned to Cressida's room. I looked out of the window, but there was still nothing. Had I been right to approach Bates? Had it been a gamble worth taking? I—who was not a gambling man? Well, we should soon know, and there was no point in rehashing a decision that had been made.

Turning back from the window, I told

Cressida and Surov briefly what I'd done and what I had in mind. 'I suppose you can't fly an aeroplane?' I asked Surov.

'No. If we cannot take the plane, we must walk. I am good at walking.'

'What about the jeep?' asked Cressida.

'From the look of the country,' I said, 'I don't think we'd get far in any vehicle. The jeep's probably just for use around the camp.'

'They must have brought it here.'

'True. But perhaps in a plane.'

I was at the window again, fingering the pistol. What would I do if Bates had betrayed us, and O'Malley came with a dozen armed men?

Minutes passed. Our desultory conversation dried up. Then, without warning, Bates appeared. And there was someone with him. More than one person. Crowding behind him on the veranda steps. In anger rather than fear, and without rational purpose, I raised the gun.

Bates saw me at the window. 'It's okay, okay,' he called in a low voice. 'These are me chums.'

There were, in fact, four men behind him. Before I could get more than a vague impression of them, they had crossed the veranda and were entering the hut. I swung round to cover the door.

Bates came first, hands raised as though to show that he was harmless. Since we had, of course, not switched on the light in the room, the others were still only dark shapes. 'This 'ere's Fritz,' he announced, 'And Dino. You saw 'im yesterday. 'E shared Fritz's cabin, and wants to come along too. So does these other two gents. I'll introduce you later. We couldn't get shooters, but they've all got knives and a couple of other things that may be useful. Are you lot ready?'

'We're ready,' I replied.

'I'd better lead the way. An' for Gawd's sake keep quiet.'

He was already moving back towards the veranda. I followed, with Cressida close at my elbow. I still could not be absolutely sure it wasn't a trap. My pistol was ready, but the four newcomers were close around me. Surov brought up the rear.

The moon was down by now but there was no light yet in the eastern sky. The only light came from the high arc-lamps and from the lights along the perimeter fence. The areas of shadow in between were dark enough to give reasonable cover. I suppose our movement would have been seen if anybody had been watching, but it didn't catch the sentries' eyes. There were three of them in view: one by the gate, one patrolling the fence on our side, the other walking away from us. They all had rifles slung over their shoulders and bandoliers of cartridges. Bates would know, presumably, if there were others out of sight.

When we were quite close to the fence and to the nearest sentry, Bates put out an arm to halt us, then gestured us into the dark between two huts. The man called Fritz was immediately in front of me. He was heavily built with fair hair. Bates was whispering to the two whose names I didn't know.

Like shadows, they slid away from us. Although they were so close, I hardly saw them go. And one of them seemed to disappear. The other—slim, not very tall—flickered from cover to cover, towards the nearest sentry.

He rose from the ground, and, in a single flowing action, pulled the sentry down. There was no noise at all. A minute later he was back with us, holding a rifle and a bandolier of cartridges.

I looked for the far sentry—and could no longer see him.

'Come when I beckon,' said Bates in a low voice. Before we could answer, he stepped out of the shadow and was strolling, hands in pockets, across the open space towards the gate. The sentry was leaning against one of the gateposts, smoking a cigarette and looking up at the sky. Bates was only about twenty yards away when the sentry noticed him. I heard Bates call a greeting, though I could distinguish no words. The sentry flipped an idle hand at him.

Approaching, Bates pulled something from

his pocket. Cigarettes. He extracted one, put it between his lips and leaned towards the sentry. Asking for a light. The sentry, heaving himself from the gatepost, offered his own lighted cigarette. Bates hit him on the side of the neck, and he collapsed. At a distance it looked very simple. Bates, turning in our direction, beckoned.

Fritz was off like a runner from the starting-block. Seizing Cressida's wrist, I pulled her with me. We were running across the open area, no longer worrying about cover. Bates stood in the light, with the sentry sprawled at his feet. But there was no alarm. Nobody had seen what happened. The only worthwhile precaution now, I thought, was to be quiet. We were running on baked earth; our footsteps made little sound.

Bates had unhooked a catch and was swinging the gate open. The man who had dealt with the third sentry joined him, as though from nowhere, also carrying a rifle and bandolier.

We pounded through the gateway. Still no alarm. Bates and Fritz were moving on ahead. The two men with rifles had waited by the gate, allowing us to pass, watching our rear. Now for the plane. It was perhaps five hundred yards away. Only the line of petrol drums, marking the start of the runway, divided us from it. Might there not, I wondered, be someone guarding the plane?

149

But no; if there were, Bates would not be leading us, pell-mell, towards it.

He and Fritz reached the plane together. Bates went first up the steps to the pilot's cabin. Did an aeroplane have an ignition key, like a motor car? What it did have, apparently, was a lock on the cabin door. Bates was stooping over it, working on the lock, as the rest of us panted up to the foot of the steps.

Then, from behind us, came a shot, and, immediately afterwards, the rapid tolling of a bell. That first shot may have been fired into the air as an alarm signal. The second definitely wasn't; it kicked up dust only a few feet away. And a third hit the plane's fuselage. I heard it.

The firing intensified. Our two men with the rifles were firing back. Everything happened so quickly that there was no time to think or be afraid. Instinctively I pulled Cressida down beside me. Surov had already thrown himself flat, and Dino was trying to take cover behind the wheels of the plane.

From above us, from the steps, someone—I realized it was Fritz—called out: 'They've hit the gas tank!'

He and Bates leaped down. 'Let's get away from here,' called Bates.

A bullet struck metal and ricocheted off with a whine. Fritz and Bates were running again, and we were close on their heels; away from the plane, away from the camp. We hadn't gone very far when the explosion came. Sounding as though someone had burst a giant paper bag, it knocked me off balance with a rush of hot air and a blaze of flame. We weren't hurt, just winded and rather stunned. We staggered on, the plane burning behind us.

I could imagine our figures as seen from the camp, running targets illumined by the flames. There was pungent smoke. And at last, blessedly, shadow; a slight ridge, and the ground sloping away. Bates and Fritz were crouching there. Cressida and I, and Surov and then Dino, joined them. Turning, I saw for the first time what had really happened.

The plane was still burning, like a blowtorch, casting a lurid glow across the whole area from the gate of the camp to the ridge that sheltered us. But no one was firing in our direction. There had been a gun battle. One of our two men was kneeling behind an oil drum, his rifle rested across it. The other lay on the ground; not, as I thought for a moment, dead or wounded, but in the classic firing position. They had clearly been very effective. Three bodies lay just outside the gate. The rest of O'Malley's men, if they had ever emerged, had withdrawn inside the fence. From the corner of the nearest hut, one of them snapped off a wild shot and then jerked back out of sight.

The man behind the oil drum was reloading his rifle. Having done so, he started backing towards us. The other man, scrambling to his feet, came too. They both kept their rifles pointed towards the camp: and, at a sign of movement, they fired simultaneously. They didn't hit anything, as far as I could see, but they were very successfully persuading O'Malley's men—and perhaps O'Malley himself by now—to keep their heads down.

We were all together, strung out behind the ridge. 'Well, that's torn it,' said Bates.

'We can't stay here,' said Fritz. His accent seemed as much American as German; not that I was thinking of such matters at that stage.

'They'll be talkin' things over,' said Bates. ''E'll be telling them to come on after us, and they'll be 'anging back.'

'Maybe they won't come until daylight,' said Fritz. 'You know what they're like.'

'Yeah, could be. They'll reckon there's no place we can go. Trouble is, they're right.'

I suddenly became aware that I was still holding the pistol and hadn't fired a shot. The range would, anyway, have been too great, but I felt that, in the moment of action, I'd been feeble. 'Better move than stay,' I said. 'If we work our way round up the hill, at least we'll be in a stronger position. We could stand off an attack for quite a while.'

'And then?' asked Bates. 'No, you're right, Professor. We'd better move, though Gawd knows what we do next.'

'We could do what I was supposed to do—march out. We're quite a strong party.'

'You just don't understand, do you?' he said with a touch of anger. 'You don't know what it's like.'

CHAPTER SEVEN

JUST LIKE XENOPHON

'He probably won't start after us until dawn,' said Fritz.

I looked at the eastern sky, wondering if the blue and the stars had already begun to grow pale. Not yet, not really—but soon.

'Think 'e'll come 'isself?' asked Bates.

'Yeah. He can't risk any of us getting away. And which of those deadbeats of his could he trust?'

''E don't like risks,' agreed Bates. 'Come to think of it, no more do I. I must 'ave been stark ravin' bonkers. 'Ow did you talk me into this, Professor?'

'I'm sorry,' I said. 'But you wanted to come.'

We were clustered about the very same rock on which I'd sat, waiting, earlier in the

153

evening. In fact I'd resumed my place on it. Bates sat beside me, on the ground, resting his back against the rock. Fritz stood, or paced up and down. Dino lay on his back, looking up at the sky. One of the men with rifles squatted near him; the other lay prone a few yards away, at a vantage point from which he could look down into the camp, watching what went on, without being noticeable to anyone who might chance to look up. Surov and Cressida sat together on my right.

'Without the plane,' I said, 'how's O'Malley going to get back to Rio?'

'No problem,' said Bates. ''E'll radio for another.'

'He's got a fleet of them?' I asked.

'In a way. 'E runs an air-freight business. No end useful. For all sorts of things.'

'But he won't go until he's sure of us,' said Fritz.

I looked up at him, silhouetted against the night sky. 'Bates told me,' I said, 'that the dope leaves here by mule, over the mountain. Do you know where it goes?'

'Not exactly. I believe it's picked up by helicopter.'

A wild idea crossed my mind that we might follow the mule train and hijack a helicopter. I was in better spirits than the others, no doubt partly, as Bates had suggested, through sheer ignorance but also because my situation

154

had been so bad when the night began that it didn't seem so much worse now. Indeed it was improved, to the extent that at least I had companions.

'How much ammunition have we got?' I asked.

'Not much,' said Fritz. 'We had the clips that were in the rifles, and the bandoliers. But they weren't full.'

'And your shooter,' said Bates. 'My shooter.'

I nodded. 'Any other weapons?'

'Felipe and Sebastian have got knives.' (So those were their names.) 'And we brought a couple of sticks of dynamite.'

'Well,' I said, 'I suppose you can never tell what may come in useful.'

'Ain't much, is it?' said Bates. 'Not enough. And we've no food.'

'Only what you gave me.'

Bates looked gloomier than ever. 'Maybe I can do something about that. I suppose I gotta try. Fritz, are you game to come with me? See what we can nick?'

'Back down there?'

'Yes.'

'Sure.'

'Do you think you can get in without being seen?' I asked. I looked up at the sky again. 'How long would it take?'

'We'll go in from this end. Same way you did, Professor. And if we're going, we better go now.'

'It'll be light in an hour or so.'

'When it is, they'll be running around like ants. And they won't be expecting a visit from us.'

'Let's get going,' said Fritz.

'Keep the 'ome fires burning,' said Bates to me. 'We'll be back. I 'ope.'

Pausing only to survey the camp and the way down, crouching for a moment beside Felipe or Sebastian (whichever it was who had been keeping watch), they slipped out of my sight, following the route I had taken a few hours earlier.

Cressida came and sat beside me. 'How bad a fix are we in?' she asked. 'Honestly?'

'Not good,' I said. 'But we're still in the game.'

'My Aunt Martha always did say I'd come to a bad end. That was when I wouldn't wear my white gloves to church.'

I put my arm around her shoulders. 'If Bates can bring us food and ammunition, we'll have a very fair chance. We'll fight our way home, like Xenophon.'

'Who's Xenophon?'

'He was a Greek. I suppose you might call him a gentleman adventurer. He was invited to go along, as a kind of civilian observer, with a mercenary force into Asia. Their sponsor died, leaving them far from home, surrounded by enemies. They started for

156

home, not really knowing the way or how far it was, though rough country full of hostile natives. And Xenophon himself gradually took command. So they marched and they fought, across deserts and mountains and rivers, for hundreds of miles, until one day Xenophon heard a tumult at the front of the column. He spurred his horse forward to the crest of the hill, and suddenly realized what his men were shouting. *"Thalassa, thalassa*—the sea, the sea!" And there it was, shining in front of them, the azure road back to Greece.'

'Do you really believe we can march to the sea?' asked Cressida.

'I'm pretty good at walking. I hope you are.'

'I doubt if your old Greeks had to walk through country as bad as this. Do you know there are poisonous spiders as big as your fist, and tree-frogs that can kill you if you just touch their skin, and jaguars, and piranha fish . . . ? I've heard about people who got lost, and when they were found—if they were found—there was nothing but a skeleton. And suppose we get sick? Fevers . . .'

'Now stop that,' I said. 'Stop imagining horrors. You can get run over by a bus in the middle of London. Or in the middle of Charleston, I dare say.'

'No. There aren't any buses in the middle of Charleston.'

'I'm glad to hear it. But the world's full of things to be frightened of. Remember, though, that most of them won't ever happen to you. You can't be stung to death by poisonous spiders *and* eaten by piranha fish. So there's no point in worrying about them both.'

She looked up at me and smiled. 'I'm not sure that's logical.'

The sky was definitely paler now. The stars were fading. Dino was talking, in a low voice, to Felipe (or Sebastian). Surov sat impassive and silent.

'Let's have a look down there,' I said. I walked over to where Sebastian (or Felipe) still lay prone. 'Anything?' I asked, though not knowing if he spoke English.

'Nothing,' he said.

There was indeed no sign of activity in the camp. From the airstrip beyond, a plume of black smoke drifted up from the wreckage of the plane. Beyond lay the carpet of tree-tops, dark but scored now with lines and pools of white mist. A thought struck me.

'Is that a river?' I asked, indicating a continuous long snake of mist.

'River? Sim, senhor,' he replied indifferently. 'Soon it will be morning. Then they come.'

Even as he spoke, a door must have been opened in the camp, followed immediately by another. The light pattern changed. I could see men moving about. But there was no sign of alarm, no shouts, no shots. Nobody running. Which there would have been, surely, if Bates and Fritz had been seen.

Unnoticed, Surov had approached behind me. His voice made me jump. 'If our friends do not return, we cannot wait for them. We shall have to go.'

'Yes, but it's worth waiting as long as we can.'

The daylight increased, and so did the activity in the camp. Men were assembling by the gate. A solitary figure joined them, walking briskly across the central open area. Even at that distance I recognized him. It was O'Malley, wearing a hat. They all stood talking for a while. Then a horse was led out from behind the further row of huts. O'Malley mounted, the men formed themselves into a rough platoon, the gate was pushed open, and, with O'Malley at their head, they issued forth. They were all, as far as I could see, carrying rifles slung across their backs. I tried to count them, but they were milling around too much; my guess was between twenty and thirty.

They disappeared from view between the rocks and down the slope, following the track which I'd been supposed to take and from which I'd broken away; a track which led heaven-knew-where but first, I assumed from what I'd been told, through the territory of

O'Malley's friends, the local Indians. He couldn't be sure which way we'd gone after the fight on the airstrip. What would he do now? He didn't seem to be hurrying. My guess was that he would talk to the Indians, ask them if we'd passed that way, and, if not, perhaps get them to cast around and follow our trail. I couldn't doubt that by one means or another he would soon discover, or deduce, the direction of our flight. But how soon? How much time had we?

I wished Bates were here to consult. At least I could talk to him; which I didn't feel I could to these men, complete strangers, who were with me now. I tried to visualize the landscape as I'd seen it from the gate of the camp and from the turn in the track. The sloping hillside had been virtually bare, I calculated, for at least a mile or a mile and a half; beyond which there seemed to be a belt of scrub before thick vegetation began. The Indians presumably lived in the shelter of the trees. Certainly no huts, and indeed no Indians, had been visible. To find them, therefore, O'Malley would need to travel two or three, perhaps four, miles, and then there would be talk. A minimum, altogether, of an hour and a half? Perhaps more. After which, they would still have to cast around for our trail.

We could afford to wait a little while longer yet. On the other hand, my reasoning was vulnerable. O'Malley might not be going to the Indians at all; or, even if that was his intention, he might, as he rode down the hill, come across indications—I couldn't imagine what, but it was obviously possible—that we'd gone left, up, not down, the mountainside. And he might follow us immediately. In which case, we had no time at all.

The minutes crawled by. The sun grew warm, the mist was dissolving from the tree-tops. I was aware of the others watching me, expecting me to make a decision. Dino had climbed a few yards higher, to a vantage point from which he could see most of the way down the far side of the ridge. The view wasn't perfect; I'd been up there myself to check. There were too many outcrops of rock, too many hollows. But I didn't think O'Malley's men could get very close to us without being observed; and most likely, considering what an undisciplined crew they were, we should be aware of them as soon as they started up the mountain. Indians, of course, might be a different proposition.

And when—if—no, when we did see them, what could we do? With so little fire-power, we could hardly fight. We should have to retreat further up the mountain. I looked upwards. The ground didn't seem too difficult, but there were ridges and peaks. I had no idea what lay beyond. O'Malley presumably knew.

I glanced again at my watch, learning only that another ten minutes had passed. I made up my mind. We'd better move to a higher position, and at least reconnoitre a line of retreat.

Just at that moment I heard a sound from below, from the slope leading down to the camp, and immediately afterwards Bates's voice: 'It's me. Don't get itchy trigger fingers.'

We all rushed to the edge of the slope, and a few minutes later, we were helping Bates up. And Fritz. And the Chinese cook, Lee Ong. Each of them had two rifles slung across his shoulders and a bulging knapsack.

'That's an 'ell of a climb,' gasped Bates, flopping onto the level ground. 'And I ain't as young as I used to be.'

'Well done,' I said, squatting beside him. 'Rest a minute. Then we must talk—and move.'

'Good,' said Dino, as Fritz handed him a rifle and some clips of ammunition.

'I come too,' said Lee Ong, grinning.

'You had no trouble?' I asked.

'Don't make it sound so bloody easy,' grumbled Bates. 'But if you mean was we spotted, no, we wasn't.'

'With these guns we're much better off, but I still think we ought to get out of here pretty quickly.'

162

'Can't be too soon for me.' He struggled to his feet.

'The question is, where to?'

'You're the guv'nor.'

'That's another thing,' I said. 'I know nothing about this country. Or about guns. You do, and Fritz does. Dino too, I suppose. If we're to get out of this, somebody should lead us out who knows what he's doing.'

'Meaning me or Fritz?' He shook his head. 'I've never been more than a mile from the camp. I'm a Cockney. I'm scared o' cows an' sheep. Fritz, 'e's bossy enough and 'e knows the country. But it wouldn't do, Professor. The boys wouldn't wear it. Now, you're an outsider and you're an educated man. They'll follow you.'

I must have hesitated perceptibly. Bates added, 'You got us into this. I'm goin' to sit back and watch you get us out. I 'ope. Oh Gawd, I 'ope.'

Cressida, putting her lips close to my ear, whispered, 'Remember Xenophon.'

I smiled. The prospect was far from funny, but I smiled; and I felt a curious thrill of—what?—pride?

'All right. Ask Fritz to come here.'

Fritz was helping to distribute the guns and ammunition. Bates called him over.

'Is there any way out,' I asked, 'that doesn't involve going past O'Malley and past those Indians?'

163

'Lots of ways. None of them going anywhere much. But we won't get ten miles before the Indians catch us up.'

'If they do, can we stand them off?'

'For a while, perhaps.'

'There seems to be a river cutting through the forest.' I gestured towards the general area across which that snake of mist had run. 'Could we reach that river without going past the Indians?'

'I guess so. Upstream.' He pointed behind him, over the next ridge of the mountain.

'Let's head in that direction.'

'It's quite a way.'

'So it's a race. And, if necessary, another battle. Shall we go?'

Bates and Fritz exchanged glances. Bates shrugged. 'Okay,' said Fritz. 'I guess that's as good a direction as any.'

'I want you to be in charge of the—er—military dispositions. Have one of those men keep an eye behind us. And another should take—point.' (I was rather pleased with that expression.)

'Yes, sir.' (An ironic 'sir'—but still . . .) 'You'll want this rifle. Unless the girl's a better shot.'

He handed me the gun—it was an old-fashioned bolt-action rifle—and three clips of ammunition. I loaded one, slipping the other two into my pocket. Bates and Fritz both moved away; Bates to have a word with

164

Lee Ong, who was standing beside the knapsacks which presumably contained food, Fritz to brief our front and rear guards. 'Sebastian!' he called, and the man who had lain watching the camp turned; so at least I now knew which was which.

I offered my pistol to Cressida. 'Do you think you could use this?' I said.

Slightly to my surprise, she took it without hesitation. 'I just point it and pull the trigger. Right?'

'Right, but be careful with it.'

'I've shot a gun before. We Southern belles aren't really so helpless. But why the river? What do we do when we reach it?'

'Follow it home, like the Greeks when they reached the sea.'

'But you don't know where it goes.'

'I know one thing about rivers in general. Small rivers flow into big rivers, and even the weariest river flows somewhere safe to sea. Perhaps we can make a raft. If not, we simply follow the river bank.'

She gazed at me. 'James Glowrey,' she said, 'you are an astonishing man.'

I suddenly realized that the talking had ceased. Everyone was waiting. Waiting for me to give them an order. I walked over to where Fritz and Sebastian were standing together.

'We need to keep out of sight from below,' I said. 'If we go up another hundred yards or so, then hook right through that dip in the crest there, and work our way down the other side, that should bring us to the river, shouldn't it?'

'Eventually,' agreed Fritz.

'Is there a better way?'

'No.'

'Very well. Let's go.'

Fritz touched Sebastian on the shoulder, and he loped ahead of us. I beckoned to the others. And our march began.

The sun had started to acquire real heat. Before we'd walked half a mile my shirt was damp with sweat. On that rocky mountainside I was grateful for the strong boots with which I'd been kitted out. Surov and Cressida were wearing ordinary shoes. However, once we were over the crest and on a downward slope, the going was easier; at the bottom I could see yellow grass, and, beyond, another immense vista of tree-tops. The flies, though, were a constant nuisance.

Felipe waited behind, sitting on the crest, from which, I hoped, he could see our pursuers when, inevitably, they appeared on our trail. I walked, for a while, with Bates. 'Tell me,' I said, 'about our companions. Who are they?'

'That ain't altogether a polite sort of question in my circles. Felipe and Sebastian, they're good with guns. You've seen that. And they're good with a knife too. Lee Ong 'ad the key to the food stores. In return 'e

166

wanted to come with us. There weren't no time to argue. We still 'ad to get the guns.'

'How did you get them?'

Bates chuckled. 'We were just going to break into the armoury. That's what O'Malley calls the 'ut where they're kept. Then along comes a group of those dago guards. With a key. They dished out rifles to themselves and went off jabbering. And—would you believe?—they left the door unlocked.'

'They are not the most efficient bunch, are they? But we mustn't underrate O'Malley.'

'I don't, Prof. Believe me, I don't. That one's a real mean bastard.'

'And Fritz. Can we rely on him?'

'Well, 'e's a Kraut, of course, but 'e's a pal of mine. And tough, which may come in useful. Knows a lot. They say 'e's the best cooking man in the business.'

'A cook? I thought that was Lee Ong's department.'

'Talk about bloody innocents abroad. Let me educate you, Prof. The cooking man's the one that turns the coca leaves into paste. I've watched 'im doing it, pouring in the acid and pouring out the liquid, until all 'e's got left is about a 'undred and fifty thousand nickers' worth of sludge.'

'I don't like drugs.'

'No more do I, Prof, no more do I. But Fritz ain't in the business for 'imself. 'E's a chemist, and O'Malley used 'im. No choice. 'E wouldn't 'ave been allowed to leave, not once 'e knew what was going on.'

We paused for a few minutes, and drank a little water. Not that I was really worried about water any more. We could get it from the river and boil it. I was concerned about Cressida, but she seemed to be bearing up pretty well, although her shoes were being cut to ribbons. 'I'll walk in bare feet when we hit the grass,' she said.

'Do you want to rest a bit longer?'

She smacked at a persistent fly. 'Yes, but I want even more to put distance between me and what's behind us.'

So we pressed on. I fell into step beside Fritz.

'I'd like to ask you something,' he said.

'Ask.'

'My old father is still back there in the camp.'

'Yes, Bates told me.'

'He was too frail for me to bring him. But if we get out of this, and I can fetch him later, could you find a place for him to go? Where he would be safe?'

'I could try.'

'You have influence.'

My famous influence—as passed on by Bates! The Fishers found safe places for people to go; that was their business. But I could hardly ask Gabriel, a Jew who had started by rescuing people from the Nazis, to find a refuge now for a Nazi war criminal. On the other hand, picturing Gabriel, I thought perhaps I could. Victor Gollancz, I remembered, had led a campaign to save Eichmann. If it would be wrong to underrate O'Malley's capacity for nastiness, it might be equally wrong to underrate Gabriel's capacity for goodness.

'I'll try. But it's a pity you couldn't have brought him. If we do get away and O'Malley goes back empty-handed . . .'

'I know. But we just might be able to stop that happening.'

'How—?' I began, but was interrupted by a shout from Felipe. His gestures conveyed the message all too clearly. The pursuers were in view. However, that presumably meant they were approaching the bottom of the hill on the far side of the ridge, which gave us twenty minutes or half an hour before they stood where Felipe was standing. Long enough, if we hurried, for us to reach the shelter of the scrub and trees below.

Felipe was already running down towards us. 'Come on! Fast!' I cried, and we were all racing, scrambling, slithering down. Fortunately we had already covered the steepest and most difficult part. Solid rock gave place, quite soon, to pebbles and crumbling dry soil; then, as the slope levelled out, to the long yellow grass, dotted with

169

thorn-bushes; then there were trees. I halted, panting.

Felipe had almost caught up with us. No pursuer had yet appeared on the hillside. A few yards more and we should be obscured from the crest of the hill by thickening vegetation; but our track through the grass would be plain. We could go on, we could cover more ground, but there would be no way to conceal the line of our flight.

Cressida was leaning against a tree, recovering her breath. Bates was looking at me with an expression at once rueful and quizzical, as though to inquire what the guv'nor proposed doing next.

We're told that, in moments of crisis, particularly moments of physical danger, our primeval instincts take over: adrenalin is pumped into the system and we become capable of surprising feats. And I think that must be true. I felt astonishingly alert and clear-minded.

Turning to Fritz, I said, 'We've got to slow them up. We can shoot from cover. They'll be in the open. If two of us stay behind, we can buy quite a lot of time for the others. I'll stay with whoever else is willing. With luck, we may be able to slip away when we've held them for a while. But I want you to take charge of the party—'

He interrupted me: 'Very brave, but silly. If anyone stays, it must be someone who can hit what he aims at. Can you do that? No, I thought not. I agree: we'll make an ambush. But it's not those peasants we need to shoot. It's O'Malley. If we kill him, the others will give up. They won't follow us on their own.'

I considered the proposition coolly. He was right.

'I'll do it,' he said. 'You go on.'

'But you'll need someone with you.'

He shook his head. 'If I can get one clear shot at him, that'll be enough. If I can't, two of us wouldn't be able to hold that lot for long. You'll be better off laying another ambush for O'Malley farther on.'

He was right again. 'We'll need you for that ambush. If you miss him, don't hang about. Good luck.'

While Fritz looked around for the best firing position, the rest of us hurried on towards the still distant river.

CHAPTER EIGHT

RIVER WAR

We heard the shots after about twenty minutes: first a single shot, then a fusillade. We hadn't covered as much ground as I'd hoped. The going had become steadily more difficult as the vegetation grew thicker, fronds

171

and looped tendrils, thorns and branches constantly hampering us. My machete was proving useful, indeed essential, but I was quickly exhausted from such unaccustomed labour. Sweat poured down my face, which made the flies and little biting insects even more of a nuisance.

Surov came up beside me. 'We take turns,' he said, and lifted the machete gently from my hand.

That was when we heard the shots. We were all bunched quite closely together. Now we all stopped, turning to look behind us. Of course there was nothing to see, except cut vines and broken branches showing the way we'd come.

The shooting diminished, became sporadic, died away. A flock of birds, which had whirred up above the trees, wheeled around and disappeared from view. The ordinary constant noises of the bush (if 'bush' is the right word; it was almost jungle now) resumed.

'What do you think?' asked Cressida.

'Can't tell,' I replied. 'He said one shot would be enough.'

'Do you want to wait 'ere and see?' asked Bates; a question, as the Latin grammar books say, expecting the answer no.

'No,' I said. 'We'll keep going. Will you ask Felipe, please, to drop back and see if he can find out what's happened? I'm not sure how well he understands me.'

'It must be your accent, Prof.'

'He needn't take too many risks, but I don't want us to be caught by surprise from the rear.'

Surov said, 'If they are still following, they will move quicker than us. In our tracks.'

'Unless they're afraid of being ambushed,' I said. 'Which I suppose they will be. That should slow them up.'

Bates said, 'I'll get Felipe started,' and moved away to brief him.

'And shall we make an ambush?' asked Surov.

'Later. If necessary. But let's try to cover a bit more ground first.'

So off we went again. Surov, without another word, took the lead, slashing at obstructive vegetation with my machete. Cressida, having thought better of walking in bare feet, had removed her unsuitable shoes and bound her feet and ankles with strips of material torn from her underclothes.

Our instinct now was to keep close together, while constantly looking behind. I fingered my rifle. What Surov had said was obviously right. If we were being pursued (and we probably were), it was inevitable that our pursuers were catching up. Felipe should warn us, though, unless they got him first, before he could even fire a shot. That was quite possible. A knife, an arrow, even (for all

I knew) a poisoned dart . . . Indeed, the same thing could happen to us. The Indians, for whom this was familiar territory, might be on either side of us or possibly ahead.

I shook such thoughts away, since there seemed no precautions I could take against that contingency. But the danger from the rear was both likelier and simpler. 'Bates,' I said, 'keep everyone moving. I'm going to scout back a bit.'

Holding my rifle at the ready, safety-catch off, my finger beside the trigger, I walked slowly back the way we'd come. After only a few paces, I was out of sight of the others. I realized, as I hadn't before, that, far from following a straight course, we'd been constantly veering left or right, avoiding obstacles and heading wherever movement seemed easiest. But always—I hoped—in roughly the right direction, towards the river.

Now, going back, I was uncomfortably aware that there could be a confrontation at every turn. I moved very cautiously. I listened; but there were a myriad sounds, and none that meant anything. None, at least, that I could interpret as meaning anything, although several times I wasn't sure, and halted, heart in mouth.

Then came a sound—I couldn't have said what it was—but different and close. Perhaps the snap of a twig or a kicked stone. I froze, but then, after a moment, took cover behind a tree, gun raised, waiting.

It might be Felipe. But it wasn't. Fritz came into sight, brushing past a bush, perhaps twelve yards away. As I stepped from behind the tree, his own gun muzzle swung up. Then he recognized me, and relaxed.

'You got him?' I asked.

'I did not. I got one of those poor wretches with him. I saw this guy wearing a hat. The only one who was. It was quite long range, but I had a clear shot. The hat came off as he fell. That bastard O'Malley must have made him wear it.'

I nodded. 'Sounds typical.'

'Then they all dived for cover and started blazing away. They hadn't spotted where I was, so they were just shooting wild. Trouble was, I didn't have a fix on O'Malley either. If I had, if I'd known which rock he was behind, I'd have waited and had another go. But I'll bet he was the last to move. And they were getting a bit close, so I thought it was time for a tactical retreat.'

'I'm glad you did.'

'I met Felipe. He's just hoping he can see them before they see him. He sure saw me first.'

'The only good thing is I imagine they'll be moving pretty slowly and cautiously now.'

'With O'Malley well to the rear. I told Felipe to put another shot over them if he could, and then get back to us fast. We can repeat the procedure. Slow them up anyway.'

'I was afraid we might be outflanked.'

'It's possible, but my guess is they'll take their time. They don't need to hurry.'

'Let's catch the others up,' I said.

That didn't take long. I was rather shocked to find how short a distance they'd covered. Dino had taken over the machete from Surov and was slashing vigorously at what looked like a solid screen of vegetation. Cressida clung to my arm while I told them briefly what had happened.

There was no alternative, as far as I could see, but to push on. Certainly nobody offered any other suggestion. I wished we had a compass; however, there was the sun to steer by, roughly. The trees weren't so tall as to block the sky.

And indeed the terrain suddenly improved. The vegetation thinned, leaving a broad strip of savannah rather than jungle. The grass was waist-high, dotted with bushes. We could cover the ground quite fast now, the disadvantage being that we were exposed to view from behind, from pursuers still unseen among the trees we'd left. But Felipe had brought no warning, had fired no shot. Perhaps they weren't yet very close.

I could see another belt of trees in the distance ahead of us, perhaps a mile away. If we could reach that, the positions would be reversed again: we should be invisible and our enemies exposed—unless they could move unobserved through the grass, which Indians might. Anyway, the quicker we reached the next lot of trees, the better. I urged my party on but hovered near the back myself, watching and listening. But there was nothing.

We reached the trees. They were quite widely spaced; it still wasn't jungle. 'The river isn't so far now,' said Fritz.

Just as we were about to move on, there came a shout and a shot behind us. A figure appeared, plunging out of the trees into the grass. It was Felipe. He had covered perhaps a third of the distance separating him from us when there were two more, almost simultaneous, shots. Felipe seemed to stumble, ran forward another step or two and fell, disappearing as though the sea of grass had sucked him down.

If I had been a hero—and a fool—I suppose I should have gone back for him at once. If I had been a complete coward or totally ruthless, I should have abandoned him without a qualm. As it was, I dithered; and, even as I hesitated, other men, O'Malley's men, appeared from the distant trees, walking cautiously in an extended line, advancing into the grass like timid bathers.

Raising his rifle, Fritz fired three shots. Whether or not he hit anyone I don't know; the line of men ducked, or fell, out of sight.

Others, who were still among the trees, opened fire. I heard a bullet slash through the leaves, above me and to the right.

'That'll hold them for a while,' said Fritz.

'Felipe—' I began.

'We cannot help him,' said Surov at my elbow.

Nor we could and, although the blind firing in our direction had stopped, there was nothing to be gained by staying in the target area. Our pursuers would move towards us through the grass: we wouldn't see them coming. Fritz loosed off a couple more shots, unaimed, I think, and then we all started off again at a trot. A clumsy trot, with sweat streaming into our eyes, but fear spurred us on. Dino kept in front, although the machete wasn't needed here. Fritz and I brought up the rear. That seemed, in this occasion, the right place from which to lead.

We emerged, unexpectedly, into a large cleared area, beyond which, wide, green and lazily swirling, flowed the river. Round the edges of the clearing stood a number of huts, not built European-style of cut timber, like those in O'Malley's camp, but roughly constructed of branches and leaves. The village, if you could call it that, was apparently deserted. Its occupants, having heard the shots and the noise of our approach, had probably run off. They might even be watching us now, but they weren't showing themselves.

And they had left us a precious legacy. A pair of long canoes, made from hollowed-out logs, had been pulled up onto the river bank. There were even paddles lying inside them.

I could hardly believe our luck. Here was salvation. As I sprinted towards the canoes, accelerating ahead of the others, I more than half expected their ferocious owners to burst out of the huts or wherever else they might be concealed, and rush at us, brandishing spears. But no one came. No spear thudded into the ground beside me. No arrow whizzed past me.

The canoes weren't even tethered. I tried to shove the nearer one into the water. It was heavy and wouldn't move, but Dino and Surov lent their weight and it began to slide. Fritz and Bates were hauling at the other one, Sebatsian and Lee Ong pushing from the back. Cressida bent beside me, grasping the wood with slim hands.

There was only a short muddy slope to be negotiated. The canoes slid easily into the water. The current must have been stronger than it looked, for we had to hang on firmly to prevent them swinging away. With no need of decision or orders, we scrambled on board, just as we were: Dino in the bows of my canoe, Surov behind him, then Cressida, then me; Bates at the front of the second canoe, then Sebastian and Lee Ong, and Fritz in the stern.

There were actually five paddles in my canoe, rather crudely carved but effective enough. A single thrust into the mud and we were away. The river gripped us, pulling our canoes out into the stream. They were much more stable than I'd thought. We swung wildly for a minute, but soon learned to control our course, paddling rhythmically.

The huts and the clearing fell behind us, and dwindled, still with no sign of life. The river was broad, perhaps three hundred yards across—nothing, of course, by Brazilian standards, and greenish-brown in colour. The far bank seemed to be a solid wall of vegetation. Something plopped on the surface. A fish, presumably. I wondered about piranhas. Did they really strip to the bone any living creature that fell among them? Would they bite off your fingers if you dipped them in the water? Or was that just a myth?

A patch of white foam ahead caught my attention. Rocks, with the water dividing around them. We must steer to the left. What orders should I give? Hard a-port? 'Dino,' I called, 'easy on your paddle.' And I bore down hard on mine. The canoe responded, but very little extra steering was needed. The current took us wide of the rocks. After that, we seemed to be floating more easily, in mid-stream.

I had time to look around, across the water to the trees and the distant mountains, at what seemed to be a flock of brightly coloured parrots and some other birds, vultures perhaps, wheeling high up. Once I saw something moving in the trees which I thought was a large snake. And basking on a mud-flat were several crocodiles, or, properly speaking, caymans.

We were using the paddles now more for steering than propulsion. The water simply carried us along, curving gently and sinuously but, overall, in an eastward direction; the mountain, looming above the tree-tops, gave me a point of reference. There was no sign of human life anywhere.

We were managing to keep the two canoes reasonably together. Mine was in the lead, but now Fritz steered his boat close, enabling Bates, in the bow, to lean forward and grasp our stern, pulling nearer. It was, I thought, rather like a bumping race at Oxford.

'Fritz wants to talk,' said Bates. Hand over hand, we pulled the two boats parallel.

Fritz, now beside me, said, 'In a little while more we'll come to the Indian village. Maybe five, six, miles. It's hard to tell with the river twisting so much. Not good for us.'

'O'Malley's friends?'

'Sometimes. He bargains with them.'

'Do you think they'll be waiting for us?'

'It's possible. He must know we got away

on the river.'

So the illusion of our tranquil voyage was unpleasantly shattered. But what were the options?'

'Well,' I said, 'either we risk it and go past the village, or else we leave the canoes and walk. Bypass the village. On the other bank.'

'I thought about that,' said Fritz. 'It wouldn't be easy. Thick jungle there and swamp.'

'Then it's your advice we should stick to the river?'

He shrugged. 'A little better chance. But it would be best in the dark. Why don't we rest soon until night? Perhaps we can slip by.'

That seemed to make sense. 'All right,' I agreed. 'We can probably all do with some rest and food anyway. Let's pull over to the far bank and find somewhere we can wait, in the shade and not too visible.'

Easing the canoes in towards the bank, we paddled along for another half-mile or so, until we came to a small inlet with overhanging trees. It was just wide enough for both canoes, side by side, and, though it narrowed almost at once, there was room for us to lie concealed, visible only to someone standing on precisely the opposite bank of the river. And, even if any such spectator had existed, drooping leaves and dappled shade must have camouflaged us. Insects were still a plague but we had grown almost accustomed to them.

Lee Ong, resuming his duties, distributed food from the knapsacks. Bates passed round the canteens of water. We didn't talk much. Everyone had his own thoughts, and I suppose we were all tired. Certainly I was. Chewing the bread and cold meat, I felt almost too drowsy to care about food.

'It ain't the Ritz,' observed Bates, 'but I've tasted worse. No breakfast, of course. I never did like doing without breakfast. I could use a pint of beer, though.'

The canoes were not quite long enough for us all to stretch out full length, but Dino and Fritz, having swung themselves up with the aid of a branch, were sitting on the bank. Cressida lay with her head on my shoulder. Looking up, I saw the brilliant blue sky through the green, and a big scarlet butterfly . . . and I slept.

When I woke, the brilliance of the blue and the dazzling sun were already muted. No one had moved. With their backs to a tree, Dino and Fritz were asleep. Surov was stretched out at the other end of my canoe.

'Are you awake?' asked Cressida softly.

'Yes.'

'I dreamt I was at home.'

'That was nice.'

'I'd like to go home. I didn't want to before. Now I would.'

'To Charleston?'

'Yes.'

A pause. Then: 'Are we going to get out of this?'

'I hope so.'

Another pause. 'And if we do . . . James, what do you want out of life?'

'That's a big question. To do what I'm good at, I suppose. To be with people I like.'

'That would be enough? Enough to make you happy?'

'Aristotle said that happiness consists in the unimpeded exercise of our highest faculties.'

'Then Aristotle was a pompous old bore. What is our highest faculty anyway?'

'He thought it was the ability to do philosophy.'

'You can tell Aristotle from me he didn't know what he was talking about.'

She fell silent again. It was an oddly companionable silence. 'To be with people I like,' I'd said. But how many of those were there in the world? I'm quite gregarious. I enjoyed the life of the common room and the club. But Cressida's question was pointed. Was it enough? An even more curious thought struck me. At this moment, in spite of everything, in spite of danger and physical discomfort and with a most uncertain prospect immediately ahead, I was actually rather happy.

During the next half-hour we talked a little more and dozed a little more, until I saw

Surov consulting his watch and I looked at mine.

The time had passed, for me, in an almost dreamlike way. Now the tropical dusk was thickening around us. 'We should go soon?' asked Surov.

'No, not yet. It's worth waiting a few more hours until they're asleep.'

The waiting, from then on, I found difficult. Fritz had already broken my tranquil mood by slapping a new clip of ammunition into his rifle. 'What's beyond the village?' I asked him.

'Just river and jungle. But I've not been very far.'

Lee Ong distributed more food, mainly, I think, for the sake of something to do. I remember Bates swearing as he tried, in vain, to knock the mosquitoes away. The dusk had become dark. The moon rose. I looked at my watch too often. And we waited. When I felt that we'd waited long enough, I forced myself to wait a little longer.

Eventually I gave the word, and we paddled out into mid-stream again; but only very briefly into mid-stream, since, after rounding the nearest bend, we hugged the left bank. Our two canoes were in line, the bow of the second just a few feet behind where I sat in the stern of the first. We didn't hurry, but the stream bore us on, faster than I might have wished, as impatience gave way to

185

apprehension—or, if not exactly apprehension, at least to an uncomfortable tenseness.

The vegetation formed a solid black wall on either side of the river. Above, the velvet sky was full of stars. The water glimmered with a kind of phosphorescence as our paddles dipped.

'Soon I think,' said Fritz. 'Maybe round this next curve.'

'No talking from here on,' I called—unnecessarily, since no one had been talking anyway. 'Quiet as we can.'

With two hard strokes of my paddle I nosed the canoe even closer to the left bank. Fritz's expectation proved correct. As the river curved, the black silhouette on our right changed, becoming more serrated and then dipping away altogether. There was a wide clear space on the bank of the river, and in the moonlight I could see huts and canoes pulled up on the mud; but no movement.

The forest is never silent but we had grown accustomed to the background susurration and the occasional cry of some nocturnal bird or beast. It was the splash of our paddles that seemed loud, gently though we tried to dip them. I strained my ears for any sound from the village, but heard none. It might have been as deserted as the much smaller group of huts from which we had taken our canoes. And yet surely it wasn't? The whole village would not have gone with O'Malley.

The angle of the moonlight across the river enabled us to keep, more or less, in shadow. We were gliding directly opposite the village now. I literally held my breath as we emerged into a bright patch of moonlit water. I didn't dare steer closer to the bank for fear of running aground. The shadow enfolded us again. We were leaving the last huts behind. The trees returned, reconstituting their wall. Twisting around, I watched the motionless village retreat and, quite soon, as the river continued to bend, fall out of sight.

'Made it,' said Fritz, answered by a general murmur of relief. The tension was gone, and so, after a few more minutes, any need for silence. Bates said something to Lee Ong, and they both laughed. We plunged our paddles into the water with renewed and careless vigour. Having rested for so much of the day, we weren't tired, and the most desirable thing now, by common unspoken consent, was to put as many miles as we could, as fast as we could, between us and the Indian village and O'Malley's camp.

The sensation of increased speed was gratifying, with the river sliding beneath us and the always changing, never changing, outline of trees unfolding on either side. Because the river turned constantly, doubling back on itself, the miles we covered were, to some extent, illusory; but the bulk of the mountains still provided a point of reference. They were, however gradually, receding.

After a while, our rate of paddling inevitably slowed, but, in our exhilaration at having got clean away, we didn't want to stop. The best plan, I decided, was to continue until daybreak, and then find another sheltered place where we could wait while the sun was hottest. Wait and consider what to do next. Not that there was really much choice. We must, surely, stick to the river. With guns and ammunition we could get food; and the danger from O'Malley seemed, with any luck, over—though it was possible he might follow us down river. Yes, that was indeed possible; we couldn't afford to relax too much. And, of course, since we knew so little about the geography, there could be other dangers—rocks, rapids, waterfalls. Nevertheless, my original thought remained valid. Rivers go somewhere, and a voyager on the river moves much faster than a traveller on land.

Dawn came, pearl-grey with mist on the river; but the mist vanished very quickly, and it was full daylight again. I began looking for a convenient spot in which we could have breakfast and then rest a while. Twice I was about to pull in towards the shore when a movement, or closer inspection of what seemed to be a log, deterred me. The river was well populated with crocodiles. At one point, too, I saw a snake swimming across.

Partly because I was looking at the shore and partly just because the stream drew us that way, we were quite close to the left-hand bank as the river curved in another wide sweep. The tug of the water increased. The river, I perceived, was narrowing, constricted on the left by a tumble of rocks and, on the right, by a broad spit of sand protruding from the shore. Swirls of white foam suggested that there might also be unseen rocks below the surface.

'Pull for the middle,' I called, exerting as much pressure as I could with my own oar.

What happened then was so unexpected, so stunning, that, for a moment, bewilderment almost blocked fear. A net rose out of the water in front of me. Before I could comprehend the phenomenon, the bow of the canoe was trapped, and the water swung us round broadside against the meshes. The second canoe, perhaps because Fritz or Bates was trying to avoid hitting us, struck the net at an angle and overturned. I don't know who cried out. Someone did. And there they were, bobbing and struggling in the water—Bates, Fritz, Lee Ong and Sebastian. Dino, in the bow of my canoe, had grasped the net itself to steady us.

The first wild shot kicked up water several yards away, but it drew my attention to the shore. Men were running out onto the sand spit.

The net, I realized, must have been floating on, or just below, the surface, and, as we approached, had been hauled erect. A bunch of brown-skinned Indians were tugging one end of it on the far side of the spit; the other end was among the rocks, and there too I could see a cluster of naked figures pulling. Some of the other men on the sand spit were Indians, holding spears and bows. But not all of them. The rest, holding rifles, were all too familiar—O'Malley's men. They loosed off several more shots. And an arrow thunked into the wood of the canoe.

I didn't know the depth of the river, but I thought it unlikely that one could cross without swimming. 'Head for the rocks!' I called, pointing towards them. Our four men from the capsized canoe were already struggling in that direction, Fritz and Sebastian swimming, Bates and Lee Ong hauling themselves along the net. Grasping Cressida's wrist, I pulled her with me over the side into the water, as something else—a bullet this time—hit the canoe.

We too were instantly washed against the net, but the force of the water proved not very strong. I kicked myself away from the net, swam a few strokes and found I could touch bottom. Cressida was close beside me.

But Fritz and Surov were first ashore. They had both kept hold of their rifles, and so, I

190

realized, had I—almost without thinking. I saw Fritz take cover among the rocks and fire. Surov, staggering from the water, steadied himself against a rock and fired too. There was a scream from the Indians and the net went slack.

I felt rock beneath my feet now. Cressida slipped, but regained her balance even as I put out my hand to her. Dino had joined Fritz and Surov. Glancing round, I saw that the remaining three of our party were still unscathed, dripping and spluttering but dragging themselves ashore. Arrows from the Indians on the sand pit were falling short, but a bullet ricocheted from the rocks with a whine.

Wondering if my rifle, which, although I'd tried to hold it aloft, had dipped below the surface a couple of times, would still fire, I thumbed off the safety-catch, pointed it towards the sand spit, without really aiming, and pressed the trigger. Somewhat to my surprise and gratification, it fired perfectly well. The bullet went high. I squeezed off another shot, more carefully, and it knocked one of O'Malley's men over. There was no cover for them on the sand spit. Several threw themselves down, a couple retreated hastily towards the bushes which had concealed their end of the net. The Indians loosed off more arrows and threw spears, but we were out of range.

Neither bullets nor arrows appeared to be coming from our side of the river. Two Indians lay sprawled across the rocks, where Fritz and Surov had shot them. The others had disappeared, presumably into the jungle beyond the rocks. Our abandoned canoes were floating down stream, beyond recovery. It occurred to me that there had been no sign of O'Malley himself.

Fritz, with Surov just behind him, had already clambered up to what was, in effect, a strong point among the rocks, a miniature cockpit, and, as the rest of us followed, they fired over our heads to discourage the men on the sand spit. Cressida and I slipped in beside them. We'd been very lucky so far. None of us had been hurt, we were safely ashore and the bulk of our enemies were on the far side of the river.

But, racking my mind for a sensible next move, I was seized by doubt. O'Malley, or, if he was not here in person, whoever had been in charge of the attack, must have envisaged the possibility that, when our boats were snared, some of us would get ashore on this bank. There must surely be more enemies waiting for us.

An arrow, whizzing from the bushes beyond and above the rocks, instantly confirmed my fear. It did no harm, and Fritz replied with a shot, which merely cut leaves. But how could we move out of the rocks, up into that menacing wall of green? And yet we'd have to. The canoes were gone.

I looked up and down the river—and was appalled. Perhaps a quarter of a mile upstream, just before the bend of the river would have concealed them totally from sight, two—no, three—crowded boats were nosing out from the far shore and being paddled by Indians towards our side. They contained not only the Indians, but white men in shirts and trousers. More of O'Malley's men. And among them, glimpsed for a moment before trees on this side of the river intervened, sat O'Malley himself. I might have snapped off a shot, but the chance was gone before I registered the possibility.

'Blimey!' said Bates, who had been looking in the same direction. 'That's torn it.'

We had only two options now, the simplest of all: run or fight. I should have much preferred to run but the odds flicked through my mind with the speed of a computer, and the conclusion seemed too much like inevitable disaster. This time we should have only a few minutes head start, and O'Malley already knew where we were. And he'd chosen this ground. We had nowhere to go and no idea of the country. The Indians we'd seen on this side of the river, the ones who'd been hauling on the net, might have fled but they had probably not gone far and were probably now alone. O'Malley, foreseeing that some of us would get ashore, must have been prepared to hunt us down . . .

The alternative was hardly better. We could make a stand here among the rocks, hugely outnumbered. The end would be no less inevitable, except that there was still just a chance that we could achieve what Fritz had proposed before. We might, if only with a lucky shot, kill or disable O'Malley. If that happened, and we could also inflict more casualties on his men, they might give up and let us go. Well, it was a chance.

Nobody, anyway, seemed keen to do the other thing. We were all trying, the discomfort of soaked and dripping clothes forgotten, to squeeze ourselves flat behind whatever rocky protuberances could deflect a bullet. Dino was wiping water from his rifle with a handkerchief. Fritz, his back to me, said something I couldn't hear to Sebastian. Bates and Lee Ong crouched, side by side, looking at me. Surov, raising his head cautiously, scrutinized the surrounding jungle.

'I dropped the gun,' said Cressida.

'Me too,' said Lee Ong. 'I lose gun.'

The rest of us all hung on to our weapons. I patted my pocket to make sure the spare clips of ammunition were still there. They were.

Fritz said, 'Has anyone a cigarette lighter? The matches are wet.'

''Ere,' said Bates, holding out a small red

lighter.

He took it, and Sebastian handed him what seemed to be a pair of candles. I wondered, then guessed, what they were. Dynamite. Fritz was adjusting a fuse.

'Don't blaze away,' I said. 'We're going to need every bullet we've got. And, remember, it's O'Malley we want.'

Nobody talked. There was no planning to be done. We just waited, everybody facing outwards now.

Although the sun was warm, the clamminess of my clothes felt unpleasant. And, as we lay there motionless, the flies became more persistent. Behind us, on the sand spit, no one was moving either: but of course they were still there. They might have boats; we knew they had guns. We mustn't expose ourselves from the rear.

It wasn't a long wait. 'Listen,' said Fritz.

We listened. 'I can't 'ear nothing,' said Bates.

'Exactly.'

He was right. The background noise of the forest had stopped. Then a flock of black-and-white birds rose squawking above the trees only about two hundred yards away.

'For what we are about to receive . . .' said Bates.

Another minute passed.

The fusillade, when it came, was so abrupt and shattering that it seemed to overwhelm

195

us. Shots crashed from every point in the semicircle of trees by which we were enfolded. Bullets splintered the rocks and ricocheted off them. Arrows clattered down as well.

I hadn't even fired back—there was nothing to aim at—when the noise ceased as sharply as it had begun. Instead, brown figures were leaping towards us from the trees. Without thinking or consciously aiming, I fired and dropped one of them. Others fell on either side of the man I'd hit. Emerging from the trees, more hesitantly, came the first of O'Malley's men. One of them fell immediately. I fired at another and missed. Weaponless, Cressida simply lay face down beside me, but the rest of our party were firing steadily and to good effect.

Only one of the Indians got as far as the rocks which sheltered us, a big fellow brandishing a spear. Dino shot him at point-blank range. O'Malley's men had all withdrawn again into the cover of the trees. Those Indians who were still on their feet seemed to be hesitating. Surov shot one of them in the chest. He spun round and collapsed. The remainder turned and ran. A couple more shots from the trees whirred over us. Then silence fell.

Miraculously, none of us had been hurt. Lifting her head, Cressida asked, 'Is it over?'

'For the moment,' I replied.

'Not for long,' said Fritz.

We'd done well, as the bodies littered between us and the trees, some still moving, grimly testified; but the target we wanted—O'Malley—had not presented himself, nor, I feared, was he likely to do so until the fight was over. And how many more attacks could we hope to repel?

Minutes passed with no further attack eventuating. The silence after so much clamour was eerie. It was broken by a single shot, which narrowly missed Sebastian, who, in shifting his position, must slightly have revealed himself. The echoes died away. Silence fell again. We couldn't return the fire, because there was nothing to shoot at.

A fresh thought had struck me, like a blow from a lead-filled boxing glove. There need not be another attack. Rather than risking the lives of any more of his men, let alone risking his own skin, O'Malley could simply sit us out, firing an occasional shot, like that one, if any of us dared even to move. How long could we last? What would be the end of such a siege? I deliberately stopped that train of thought.

Steam was rising from our wet clothes. My mouth felt dry. I allowed myself two substantial sips from my water bottle, which I then offered to Cressida. She drank.

'I wish I had a gun,' she said.

A spent arrow lying near her caught my

eye. The tip was stained brown. I remembered reading that, despite what we used to be told about 'deadly curare,' the poison painted on their hunting arrows by South American Indians was in fact fatal only to birds and small monkeys; but I wasn't anxious to test this theory. Unobtrusively I pushed the arrow away from Cressida with my foot.

And at that moment my second line of speculation was contradicted. The prudent course for O'Malley might indeed have been to leave us untouched until exposure and thirst delivered us to him, but he was not a patient man or scrupulous about the lives of his followers. Another volley of shots crashed and whined all around us. Again the Indians, reinforced this time with some of O'Malley's own men, were halfway towards us before we even realized what was happening. I snatched up my rifle. Surov and Dino were already firing. My first shot bowled over one of O'Malley's men.

The firing from the trees had stopped after the initial volley, because the charging men were between us and the guns. But I knew, in that instant, we couldn't hold them off. There were too many.

Fritz stood up and threw. A stick of dynamite arced above our assailants to fall among the nearest trees. The explosion was stunning. It slammed me back against the rocks, and it threw several of the Indians up into the air like rag dolls.

The charge in front of us had been very effectively broken. Those who still could scurried for cover. But, after only a brief pause, while smoke from the explosion still hung in the air, there was movement among the rocks and bushes on our right. Whether driven on by O'Malley's threats or by their own zeal, men were advancing again. Not a great number, though, and moving much more slowly. We could probably have picked them off with gunfire. But, following Fritz's example, Sebastian rose to throw a second stick of dynamite, and, in the act of throwing, was hit. As he fell, the dynamite was tossed forward only a few yards. With its fuse visibly spluttering, it rolled across a flat rock.

One of O'Malley's men was nearest to it. Popping from cover like a rabbit, he ran, and the others followed him. Transfixed by the burning fuse, none of us fired at them.

'I get,' said Lee Ong, jumping up. He dived across the rocks, and, hurling himself onto the dynamite, extinguished the fuse. He turned and smiled broadly at us, and a single shot from the trees hit him. He lay twitching and groaning.

Bates went to fetch him. Apparently without hesitation, he stepped out into the open, seized Lee Ong under the arms and began dragging him back. I thought he was going to get away with it. He had only another yard or so to go when an arrow bounced off the rock beside him and a second pierced his leg at the knee. He stumbled, and Lee Ong's weight carried him down.

Fritz leaned forward and grabbed Bates, while Surov and Dino blazed away at the trees. I joined in. Fritz managed to pull Bates back into the shelter of our cockpit. Lee Ong, out of reach, was lying still and silent now.

The shooting had stopped. But this was, I realized with terrible certainty, the last relief we should enjoy. Bates sat propped against a rock. When another attack had not immediately materialized, Fritz had yanked out the arrow and Cressida had bandaged the wound with another strip of cloth from her underwear. He was looking very pale but was quite conscious, with a rifle across his lap. Cressida had taken Sebastian's gun. Fritz had distributed more ammunition. There were fewer of us now; fewer of the enemy as well, of course, but surely too many. If they rushed us in force, we probably had more bullets than we would ever be able to use. And the alternative remained: they could keep us pinned down, sniping, eventually picking us off one by one. O'Malley could summon reinforcements from across the river . . .

A new and unfamiliar noise became perceptible, grew louder fast, grew very loud. It was approaching from the east, along the line of the river; a harsh clattering. A large helicopter came into sight, flying low above the tree-tops and the water.

'Rescue!' was my first thought. Here, at the crucial moment, was a Brazilian army or police helicopter. But there were no markings on it. This wasn't a military plane. And I remembered what Fritz had said—that the cocaine paste was collected by helicopter. The rendezvous should have been somewhere on the other side of O'Malley's camp and the mountains behind it, but perhaps he had summoned this formidable ally to help him track us down. Formidable? Conclusive. As the helicopter swept above us, I could see the open door in its grey flank and a machine-gun protruding.

There was no question that we'd been seen. The helicopter swung around and came back towards us, flying even lower. It passed, and almost immediately turned again. The noise became deafening. I could feel the wind of the rotor blades as it hovered above. Two ropes snaked down, one from either side: men were sliding down the ropes, carrying guns strapped across their chests.

This final blow had come so fast that none of us had said a word or raised a weapon to resist. A couple of shots were fired, however, not by us but from the trees. And not at us. The unseen gunner in the helicopter responded. And he wasn't firing at us either.

He was firing into the trees. A scythe of bullets slashed across the foliage.

The men from the helicopter—six of them—deployed in a highly professional manner as their feet hit the ground. They were wearing jungle-green battledress, and their guns, unclipped as they landed, were stubby automatic weapons. Already they were crouching behind the rocks along the perimeter of our cockpit, facing the trees, into which the heavy machine-gun in the helicopter sent another burst of fire.

But one of them, instead of taking immediate cover, walked coolly up to me. 'Hello, 'ello, 'ello,' he said. 'Spot of bother, what?' Just so did Blücher, arriving on the field of Waterloo, greet Wellington with the memorable words *'Quelle affaire!'* In neither case, I honestly believe, had the remark been rehearsed. Simplicity of very different kinds was natural to them both.

I hadn't recognized him at first. I knew I knew him, but in what context? When he spoke, though, everything clicked into place. This was Gabriel's chief of staff, Richard's friend, Jeremy Mitchell-Pearce, who had driven me home to Kensington from Belgravia, just a few weeks ago, which seemed like a hundred years.

'More than you led me to expect,' I replied tartly.

'What are we up against?' He nodded

towards the trees.

'Probably nothing you need worry about, with your kind of fire-power.' I told him briefly about O'Malley and the Indians and their weapone. There was, in fact, no sign of them, except for the dead and wounded. Jeremy had crouched down beside me, sheltered by the parapet of rock. Having asked one or two more questions, entirely practical, he waved at the helicopter. It ceased hovering and slid sideways across the river.

'This will be easier than hauling you up,' he said.

Amid a cloud of dust and dried leaves from the adjacent bank, the helicopter settled gently onto the sand spit.

'The natives over there aren't friendly,' I warned. But nor were they visible. Prudently they kept out of the way. One man jumped from the helicopter, and another passed something down to him, which proved to be an inflatable dinghy. While the second man stayed in the aircraft, presumably covering the whole operation with his machine-gun, the first embarked across the river.

Everything was done so efficiently that, although, when one thinks about it, any number of unassessable dangers could have developed, it all seemed quite easy and secure. Jeremy briskly examined our casualties. Lee Ong and Sebastian were dead.

Dino had a flesh-wound in the arm, to which Cressida, resuming her role of nurse, applied a temporary bandage. Bates couldn't walk but was quite cheerful. 'What's all this then?' he said. 'The U.S. bloody marines?'

'Friends of mine,' I said.

'You've certainly got some useful friends, Professor. You certainly 'ave.'

We moved around very carefully at first, exposing ourselves as little as possible, but gradually our confidence increased. O'Malley and his private army might still be lurking, but they seemed unlikely to renew their attack, now that we had been so powerfully reinforced.

Making a rapid calculation, Jeremy said, 'I think we can just about take everyone. But I'm afraid not those two of yours who were killed.'

'It seems heartless just to leave them lying here,' I said. The thought of crocodiles came unpleasantly to mind. The dinghy plainly couldn't convey all of us to the sand spit at once: there would have to be three or four trips. 'I'll do what I can. We'd better get Cressida out first.'

'The girl? Yes, all right.'

One of Jeremy's men shepherded Cressida, Surov, Dino and Fritz into the boat, and crossed with them himself. Bates would have to be carried. He watched what I was doing, 'Poor old Chinaman,' he said. I straightened them out and piled stones on top.

By the time I'd finished, the dinghy had returned. 'Ready?' asked Jeremy.

'Yes.'

He turned away to speak to the man who was holding the dinghy steady against the rocks. The others too were preparing to leave; they weren't watching the forest edge as carefully as before. So I was the only one who saw O'Malley.

He was standing in the shadows, between two large trees, dishevelled and with a look on his face of pure malignity. The distance can't have been more than about twenty yards. Our eyes met. As he saw that I'd seen him, he swung the rifle he was holding to point at me. I dived for the ground, putting a rock between us.

What he did then must have been quite deliberate. He shot Bates, who was in the process of struggling, one-legged, upright, in preparation for being helped to the dinghy.

Hit in the chest, Bates fell back. Very rarely in my life have I lost my temper; certainly never before had I been filled with a berserker rage, in which one's own safety becomes less important than one's anger and the desire for revenge. But some such emotion seized me then. I didn't think. I didn't plan. I suppose, after all we'd been through, I was far from normal. I simply hurled myself from behind the rocks and rushed, full-tilt, towards where O'Malley had been.

He'd gone from between the trees. As I raced up those few sloping yards, leaping across the cleft between one rock and another, I vaguely heard Jeremy, behind, shouting my name. I think he was calling me to stop. But I paid no attention.

The trees were on either side of me now. The bright sunshine had given way to green shade. A branch had been snapped off just ahead. And in that direction I could hear somebody moving, not stealthily but crashing through the undergrowth. I followed, and it was only when the noise ahead of me stopped that I paused. I won't say that my temper had wholly cooled down, but an element of caution entered. Watching for signs of my quarry—broken twigs, displaced leaves, bent grass, I moved forward slowly; but of course, not being a skilled tracker, I found such clues very scarce, more fancy than reality. However, there wasn't much choice. Tangled thickets with sharp thorns blocked most ways. I doubted if O'Malley could really have diverged very far, unless he was laying an ambush for me, as we had for him.

I didn't hesitate—my anger was still too strong for that—nor even pause to wonder if Jeremy was bringing support, but I advanced more slowly, scrutinizing each bush and tree.

Thinking I heard another movement

ahead, I halted, listened, then gradually moved on. Several times my heart jumped and my finger closed on the trigger, as I thought I'd seen or heard some sign of an ambush. Causes and consequences were still hardly registering; I was concerned wholly with the present, with the oncoming minutes.

O'Malley too must have been disoriented. Really, he was no more a woodsman or a forest fighter than me. He could have ambushed me. He could have been lucky. But he wasn't, and I was.

I'd gone perhaps a half a mile, keeping close to the river, heading downstream, when again I heard a noise, not an ordinary jungle noise, ahead of me. I decided to work my way round it.

I moved inland a little, carefully parting branches and stepping over twigs, in order to make the minimum of noise. Then I closed in to the right, towards the river, I'd got ahead of O'Malley. Another sound of movement made me certain, although it could have been one of his men, or one of the Indians; but I was so completely absorbed, concentrating so hard on the game of pursuit, that no other possibility occurred to me, any more than I thought now of snakes or animals.

Again a sound: and it was no illusion. Delicately I inched forward, towards it, until I caught a glimpse of something white between the branches. O'Malley's shirt. The ground had been sloping gradually up. He was standing on the brow of a small cliff, one hand resting on the trunk of a tree, looking back the way we'd come. The rifle was tucked beneath his other arm. His attitude told the complete story: he knew I'd followed him, expected me to be somewhere on his heels, somewhere among the trees and undergrowth and trailing vines, but he had in fact no clue to where I was.

I could have shot him. I could have told him to drop his gun, but I was in no mood for that kind of risk. And the berserker madness was still, to some extent, in possession of me. I can't rationalize what I did. From one point of view at least it was out of character. Ordinarily I hate to harm any living creature. I fish spiders from the bath and let flies out of the window.

I changed the grip on my rifle. Holding it by the barrel, I stepped from behind the tree, one pace forward, and, with all my strength, swung it like a club. The stock of the rifle caught O'Malley on the back of the neck. Without a sound, he went over the edge of the cliff.

Peering down, I saw his body for a moment spread-eagled on a rock, lapped by the river. But only for a moment. My apprehension about crocodiles had been justified. They'd been frightened away perhaps from the scene of our battle, but here they were waiting.

There was a swirling, an ugly snout moving very fast, and O'Malley's body disappeared, leaving only a brief patch of red on the brown water.

I scarcely remember walking back, though I know Jeremy and one of his men met me. Among the rocks again, I felt very tired and sat down abruptly. Then I was in the boat, being ferried across to the sand spit. Then I was being handed up into the helicopter. I was shivering as though it were cold. Cressida clung to me.

'Well,' I said, 'that's it. We seem to have pulled it off.'

'Yes,' she said, 'you have.'

The helicopter lifted beneath us. It should have been a moment of great exhilaration, but I was drained. And, as we flew away from that dreadful place, my last thought, before I fell asleep, was a pang of sorrow for a Cockney crook who had died so far from the sound of Bow bells.

CHAPTER NINE

'I'VE SEEN THAT MAN BEFORE'

The sidewalk was a checkerboard of white, black and red paving to represent Brazil's three main racial groups, and along it flowed

209

specimens of them all, chattering, flirting, showing off, planning deals, talking politics, talking sport, holding hands, waving their hands, busy with their own and each other's lives, just as they had been before O'Malley snatched us away and as they would still be long after I was back in Oxford. Nothing had changed, but I surely had. One can hardly emerge untouched from the kind of experience we had been through, and yet the memory of it already seemed curiously dreamlike.

Cressida, wearing a newly acquired dark-red frock, her glossy black hair as immaculately neat as when I first saw her, was animated and cheerful. Our ordeal seemed to have left no mark on her. Pedro was cheerful enough too, and talkative, but there was a bandage around his head; and here was Jeremy, elegant now in a light-weight grey suit, his presence the most vivid reminder of what had happened. I could picture him, of course, landing from the helicopter, holding his machine-gun, but it was indeed more like a picture than reality. And what of me, the gun I'd held in my hands, the blow I'd struck . . .? Had that been real? What ought I to feel about it? The fact was that I felt very little; certainly no remorse; to be honest, a kind of satisfaction; but no great relief. We had stepped out of our ordinary lives—been taken out of them—for a few days, but now everything was normal again, without danger or tension or any responsibility weighing on me, stretching me.

We sat at a table outside what Pedro had told us was one of his favourite cafés, with a big orange sunshade above us and coffee-cups and brandy glasses in front of us. Across the wide road and the beach, the sea sparkled, and Sugar Loaf Mountain, looking absurdly like a brightly coloured postcard, rose beside the entrance to the bay.

'You know,' Jeremy was saying, 'I actually remembered this time to test the bath water.'

'You don't trust our water?' asked Pedro. 'You going to drink it maybe?' He laughed, showing his gold tooth.

'No, no. Not the water itself. The way it goes down the plughole. You know, it's supposed to go round one way north of the equator and the other way when you're south.'

'Ah yes,' I said, 'I've always wondered about that. And is it true?'

'I'm afraid not. You can make it reverse direction with your finger.'

'But that may be cheating. It's the natural order of things we're concerned with; the effect, I suppose, of the earth's spin.'

'Quite right,' agreed Jeremy.

Of course, we'd long ago discussed the essential matters. Surov was in a safe house, guarded by two minders, all fixed by Pedro.

It was thought wiser that he should not be seen on the streets of Rio. He would be flown to London, I gathered, within the next twenty-four hours; I didn't ask the details. Nor did I inquire too closely about Pedro's arrangements with regard to O'Malley's camp—and the permanent absence of O'Malley. He assured me that everything had been arranged. 'I fix,' he said. 'I know people.' I'd asked Jeremy whether this really would be all right, and he'd said yes, there was nothing to worry about; the gist being that the Brazilian authorities were pleased enough to have the drug-running operation handed to them, and were not unduly disturbed that O'Malley should have been removed from the scene. Brazil is a very big country, in which many things happen; violent deaths do occur, bribes are paid, political pressures applied. Pedro knew what and whom to fix.

I did ask specifically what could be done for the remnants of my villainous little troop, for Dino and Fritz and Fritz's father; and again Pedro assured me that he would fix it, they would be looked after. 'And if you can't,' Jeremy had said, 'I'm sure we will. Gabriel's good at that sort of thing.' I believed him, although I made a mental note to ask again in a few days' time, just to make sure.

Pedro's fixing capacity had been proved by

the speed with which Jeremy was able to find and rescue us. If O'Malley had been as prudent as he was ruthless, he would have made sure that Pedro couldn't organize a pursuit; he could have gained a much longer interval before anyone came looking for us, or at least came looking in the right direction. Instead, Pedro had simply been coshed as he collected the van in which to pick us up at the hotel. He never even saw his assailant. He found himself lying in a doorway. When he had recovered enough to stagger to a telephone, he had called the hotel in the hope of warning me; but it was already too late: we'd gone. His first thought was that the Russians had intervened to prevent Surov's defection, but then he realized this was unlikely. They wouldn't have attacked him; they would simply have whisked Surov out of circulation. So then he guessed it was O'Malley. He immediately called Jeremy in London, who had said he would be on the next available plane. By the time Jeremy arrived, Pedro had already done a good deal of work.

He had established that Surov and I had left the conference together, and that Cressida had been waiting in the lobby, but no one had seen us leave the hotel or get into the van. He had his contacts, though, in Tara's Hall, and he tried them next.

'At first they don't talk,' he said. 'They're

frightened. But that's okay. I see they're frightened, so I know they know. So I do a bit of persuading, but still they don't talk. I go away to meet Senhor Jeremy, and, when we get back to my apartment—poof!—one of them is on the phone. I don't even have to pay him very much.'

'You must know how to twist arms,' said Jeremy.

'Oh, Senhor Jeremy, I did not touch him. But now he wants to talk. Maybe he likes me.' Pedro turned to Cressida. 'It was the croupier. You remember him? Leon. He work with O'Malley a long time.'

'Yes, of course I remember him. They were very thick.'

'Thick?'

'They talked a lot.'

'Exact. I reckon he maybe knows what O'Malley would be doing. O'Malley doesn't trust him, sure. O'Malley doesn't trust no one. But O'Malley likes to talk. And I'm right. Is true. He knows about the camp, and he guesses you've been taken there. I think maybe, in private heart, he's not so fond of O'Malley. He not mind if we clobber him. That's the word—"clobber"?'

'That's a very good word,' said Jeremy.

'What do you suppose will happen to Tara's Hall?' asked Cressida.

Pedro shrugged. 'Maybe Leon runs it. Maybe that's what he wanted.'

So they knew, more or less, the location of the camp; they knew that O'Malley was missing from Rio; and Pedro had known already that O'Malley, with a share in that air-freight firm, would have had an aircraft available. Putting these facts together, Jeremy decided it was the likeliest bet; whereupon Pedro did some more fixing. He arranged for the helicopter and a team of mercenaries and the guns. Pedro had wanted to go with them, but Jeremy insisted that he should stay in Rio. After all, he pointed out, they could still be wrong.

But of course, they weren't wrong. 'It was a wonderfully impressive rescue party,' I said.

Pedro spread his hands deprecatingly. 'In this country money buys everything. Senhor Jeremy gives me plenty money. So I buy plenty good men.'

'You're a good man,' I said.

'He is,' agreed Jeremy.

And suchlike nauseating guff. I suppose we were quite exhilarated and pleased with ourselves. Now, twenty-four hours later, we'd calmed down a bit. This was really in the nature of a farewell lunch, since prudence dictated—and Pedro had courteously hinted—that we should leave Brazil as soon as possible. Leave, and go our separate ways. Jeremy would accompany Surov to London.

'I've never asked you,' Jeremy had said to me earlier during lunch, 'what you feel about

215

Surov now. You marked him okay during the conference—and that's the assumption we're working on—but you've seen a lot more of him since then. So what's the verdict? Seal of purity still?'

I thought about that question. 'Oddly enough, I don't feel I'm any closer to him than before. Yes, I saw him in very different circumstances, but he left a curiously blank impression. He's a tightly closed man, which is probably natural. I've no reason to change my mind about him. But I never said I was absolutely sure.'

Jeremy nodded. 'We realize that.'

Although I didn't tell him, because there was nothing to tell, I had talked briefly with Surov the night before. He had been waiting in my hotel room while Pedro fetched the car in which to take him to the safe house. Jeremy was in another room, telephoning London. Cressida was in her room, having a bath.

'What are you planning to do in England?' I said. 'Are you going to resume an academic career?'

'I think I shall be busy for several months. There will be a price to pay for refuge.'

'Yes. Well. You must come and see us at Oxford when you can.'

'I should be honoured. I wish to say, Professor Glowrey, that I have very much admired your resourcefulness and your

216

leadership. You should have been a soldier.'

That was really all our conversation amounted to. But I was flattered, naturally. Dr. Johnson says that any man thinks more meanly of himself for never having been a soldier; and sedentary intellectuals, among whom professionally I must be numbered, are especially liable to such dreams.

While I was recalling that exchange, Pedro said, with a new edge to his voice, 'We speak of Russians. Over there, look—or maybe you better not look—is Kallinin.'

'Kallinin?' asked Jeremy.

'You mentioned him,' I said. 'He's the KGB Resident? Which is he?'

'The man in the tan suit with wavy silver hair. Just sitting down.'

'Does he know you?' I asked.

'Oh, sure. But not to worry. He comes here often.'

'It's lucky Surov's not with us,' observed Jeremy.

'I would not have brought you here if he was.'

'How have the Russians reacted to his disappearance?' I asked. 'How much do they know?'

'They ask questions, but I don't think they find much. They haven't so good contacts, like me.' Pedro grinned, showing a flash of gold.

'You disappeared from the conference at

the same time,' said Jeremy to me. 'And you must have been seen talking to him before. I think it's just as well you're not staying in this town much longer.'

As the implications sank in, I felt a distinct chill. Kallinin was reading a newspaper, not apparently paying any attention to us.

Cressida said, 'I've seen that man before.'

'Where?' asked Jeremy sharply.

'In Tara Hall?' I asked.

'I don't think so.' She frowned. 'But it was somewhere quite recently.' We waited. 'No, it won't come. It could have been anywhere. Perhaps just in a café, like this.'

There was nothing to be gained by pursuing the matter and it probably had no significance; but a certain damper had been put on our cheerfulness, without any very clear reason. Pedro paid the bill. As we left, I kept a surreptitious eye on Kallinin, but he never looked up from his newspaper.

The café wasn't far from the hotel; the same hotel where I'd stayed before. It had seemed such a safe and familiar haven when we'd returned to it. Now I wasn't so sure. I wasn't sure anywhere in Rio was safe because, of course, what Jeremy had said was perfectly true. If the Russians were looking for Surov—and they presumably were—they must have been given my name by Korbanov and Ilyin, those two constant and, I'd always thought, suspect companions. I hadn't bothered to ask Surov about them. Truth to tell, that whole aspect of the affair—my reason for being here in the first place—had been largely driven from my mind by the more urgent perils which had followed.

On the other hand, if the Russians really knew nothing about our kidnapping by O'Malley, they might reasonably assume that Surov was long gone, spirited out of the country by the British Secret Service or, more likely, the CIA. In which case, they were probably not interested in me. When we'd passed through so many real dangers, it was perhaps foolish now to be frightened of goblins.

At the entrance to the hotel, Jeremy and Pedro left us; they had a few final arrangements to complete. Cressida and I were supposed to remain in the hotel until we were collected later. I was to catch a plane for London that evening; a different flight, I gathered, perhaps a different route, from the one which Jeremy and Surov would be taking. My taste for travel and adventure having been somewhat exhausted, I had abandoned the idea of going anywhere else in South America; the grey towers and green fields of Oxford seemed nostalgically attractive. Cressida was booked on a flight next morning to Miami, and thence to Charleston.

'Could we walk a little?' she said. 'I'm

restless.'

In the middle of the afternoon, along the crowded beach front, I couldn't believe there was much danger. So we walked. Cressida was uncharacteristically silent.

'I shan't be sorry to leave Brazil,' I said. "Brazil where the nuts come from." You know that line from *Charley's Aunt?* The interesting thing is that the joke has completely changed. Originally it was a pun on the word "knuts" with a "k," meaning young men about town—as in "I'm Gilbert the Filbert, king of the knuts." No one remembers that now but, after a hundred years, audiences still invariably laugh.'

'They do?'

'I always used to say that *Charley's Aunt* was absolutely foolproof, the only one—out of heaven knows how many Victorian and Edwardian comedies—which not only survives but never fails. It would be a good question in an English exam to ask why. And then some idiot went and cast a drag artist in the lead, ruining the whole point—'

'Oh, shut up!' said Cressida. 'I'm scared.'

'What of? Now?'

'Going home.'

'I thought you wanted to?'

'I do in a way. But they say you can't really go home, don't they? Is that true, Professor?'

'Yes, I think it is. But that doesn't mean there's never anything to go back for. Isn't

220

there anyone in Charleston who'll be glad to see you—and whom you'll be glad to see?'

'There's my aunt and uncle, but I'm not sure how glad they'll be to see me.'

'You mentioned your aunt once before,' I said, 'but I thought you had no family.'

'Oh yes, there's Aunt Martha and Uncle Ted. They brought me up after my parents died.'

But when she had wanted to come with me to Chile, instead of returning to Charleston, she did give the impression, as I remembered, that she had no family. I was under no illusions about Cressida. Her notion of veracity was not, perhaps, the most rigorous.

'Well, I'm sure they'll be delighted to see you,' I said. 'The prodigal returned.'

'You don't know what they're like. They're awfully strict. They may turn me away.'

'Surely not.'

'They'll think I've disgraced them. I have disgraced them.' She looked at me. Her eyes were filled with tears. 'But oh, James, I've learned my lesson. I very much want to be good. I want to be the sort of person you'd approve of.'

'My approval doesn't matter. But you'll find that most people aren't as censorious as you imagine. Which of us can afford to be?'

'Aunt Martha can. Charleston's a very small town. Respectability's terribly important.' She put her hand on my arm.

221

'James, you wouldn't come with me, would you, and speak for me? They wouldn't be able to ignore an Oxford professor.'

I smiled, and shook my head. 'You'd be surprised. No, I don't think that's a good idea.'

'Please.'

'No, we must both go back to where we belong.'

'But I've—liked knowing you. I don't want us to lose touch.'

'We won't. We'll write.'

'Write!' She scorned the suggestion. 'Well, if you won't, you won't.' She turned on her heel, walking so quickly that it was almost a run. I followed as fast as my dignity would permit. She stormed into the hotel and straight up the stairs to her room on the first floor. I reached the end of the corridor just as she was putting her key in the door.

'You're a heartless brute!' she called, pushed open the door and slammed it behind her.

So that was that. But what else could I reasonably have said or done? Now I was the one to be restless. Instead of going to my room, I left the hotel again and marched along the sea front, quickly and angrily, then slowly and thoughtfully. Yes, I'd done the reasonable thing; Cressida was behaving outrageously. But . . . 'Reason has moons, but moons not hers, lie mirror'd on her sea . . .'

In just a few hours now my plane would take off, climb above the lighted city, I should look down on Mount Corcovado with the Christ-figure, and then there would only be the night sky and the sea and the rest of my life ahead. Everything that had happened here would become increasingly unreal. The widening gap of time would separate me, for ever . . .

I'd stopped altogether, oblivious of the crowd around me. Now I took a deep breath, turned and marched back to the hotel. Up the stairs I went and along the corridor, and knocked at Cressida's door.

'Who is it?' she called.

'Me. James.'

She opened the door. 'What do you want?'

'I want to come with you to Charleston,' I said. 'I've always had a fancy to see the Deep South.'

The look on her face was reward enough. 'The magnolias will be over,' she said, 'but the mint juleps are always in bloom.'

CHAPTER TEN

CAROLINA IN THE AFTERNOON

The plane was half-empty. Towards the rear clustered a small party of very young American sailors, new recruits, I gathered from their conversation, headed for the naval base. In front of us sat an elderly couple, brown and dry as walnuts, and across the aisle was a fat man in a string tie, endlessly working things out with a pocket computer. Cressida had insisted that I should sit by the window, so that I could see the countryside, but now, as the descent began, she leaned across me, peering down into the golden haze of a summer afternoon.

'It seems like forever,' she said, 'but everything looks just the way I remember it. That's what people always say when they come back to Charleston. Fort Sumter still in the bay. Hominy grits for breakfast. Everything just like it was a hundred years ago. I used to hate that. I felt I was being stifled.' She relaxed into her own seat. 'Now I think, perhaps, I'm beginning to understand.' She smiled at me. 'Could it be that I'm growing up?'

'Highly improbable,' I said.

'There must be some kind of magic which

pulls Charlestonians back. Do you know, I've got nearly thirty cousins here from one side of my family or the other?'

I looked at her in astonishment. 'Cressida,' I said, 'only a few days ago you told me you were alone in the world, with no relations whatever. Now you have, not only a perfectly good aunt and uncle, but thirty cousins.'

'Cousins don't count,' she said, fastening the seat-belt around her slim waist.

We were skimming low above trees and bushes. It had been a long flight, interrupted only by the tedium of transit lounges, and I was looking forward to the fresh air. She had warned me that, at this time of year, Charleston could be oppressively hot, although in the old days it was treated as a summer refuge from the mosquitoes and fevers of the plantations along the Ashley and Cooper rivers; but, according to the local paper at which we'd glanced while waiting in Atlanta, the temperature was only in the low seventies, less than we'd come from in Brazil.

As the plane bumped onto the tarmac Cressida put her hand on mine. I glanced at her profile, always worth looking at. Her eyes were shut. I could only guess at her feelings, indeed I couldn't guess them, beyond realizing that this was, for her, a moment of some emotional force. I wondered what her ferocious aunt and uncle were really like, and what they would think of me; I had been

225

rehearsing speeches in Cressida's defence, which was, after all, supposed to be my function.

After so many big impersonal airports—Heathrow, Rio, Atlanta—the modest white buildings which constituted Charleston's greeting to the modern world seemed almost cosily domestic. There were no formalities and not many people. Walking half a step ahead of me, looking cool and crisp in her cream linen suit, Cressida led the way to the place where our baggage should appear.

And there, waiting, peering eagerly towards us, were her dreaded aunt and uncle, Ted and Martha Lee. Aunt Martha, small, plump and white-haired, wearing an unfashionably long powder-blue dress, fluttered like a bird. Mr. Lee, in a crumpled grey flannel suit and with spectacles crooked on his nose, ran his fingers through sparse hair as he blinked around. One felt that he was the sort of person who would always be peering in the wrong direction. It was Martha who spotted us, and ran forward, arms outstretched, to enfold Cressida.

While they were clutched together, both talking at once, Mr. Lee extended his hand. 'Better introduce myself. They'll be chattering for an hour. I'm Ted Lee, Cressida's uncle.' His grip was firm, his eyes blue in a sunburnt face.

'Glowrey,' I said, 'James Glowrey.'

226

He inspected me quizzically but uncritically. 'So Cressy's telegram said. And a professor?'

'I'm sorry to impose myself—'

'Not a bit. Pleased to have you. And if you're the reason Cressy's come home, we're grateful. She's skittish, that girl. But you'll have found that out.'

He squinted at me over his spectacles. 'I'm beginning to,' I said.

'But she's a dear girl. You've never seen such a pretty little thing, when she was growing up.'

Detaching herself from Cressida, Aunt Martha turned to me. 'We haven't had a house guest since I don't know when. And Cressy home too. My, what a day! Now come along, you must be tired. And you're an Englishman. You'll want tea. I only hope we can make it properly. We've a tea service that my great-grandmama brought from England . . .'

While Aunt Martha chattered on, I caught Cressida's eye. She had the grace to blush.

Mr. Lee heaved Cressida's two bags into the boot, or, as he would have said, trunk, of a large American car, and I swung my suitcase on top of them. I sat beside him, the two women behind, as we drove into Charleston.

When I'd told Cressida that I had always wanted to see the Deep South, it was true.

Most of us find natural affiliations in history, no less, and sometimes with no more rationality, than in contemporary life. I mustered myself to the Confederate flag in the American Civil War as surely as I supported the Cavalier cause in our own.

Both represented, if nothing else, a lost civilization, crushed by advancing modernity; colour and courtesy against the levellers' drabness. I'd seen the films, like everyone else; the South, I knew, was beautiful, and Charleston surely would be the essence of the South. Wasn't it Rhett Butler's home port?

To anyone who has never been there—and Charleston is still a curiously secret place, belonging to Charlestonians and to an almost private group around the world who love her—I can only say that never was expectation more richly fulfilled. Charleston is an enchanted city and, unlike everywhere else, actually more beautiful that it used to be. After the Civil War, or 'the late unpleasantness,' as the Charlestonians prefer to call it, everybody was very poor. 'We were too poor to paint and too proud to whitewash,' they say, 'so we polished.' And they went on being poor, by American standards, for a long while. Old buildings were not pulled down. In New York office blocks and apartment blocks rise and fall as transiently as each season's daffodils: 'This site is being improved,' lie the notice-boards.

In Charleston no site was improved.

When, after the Second World War, there was a little money, the Charleston Preservation Society began buying old houses, restoring them and selling them, as far as possible, not to outsiders but to Charleston families. The heart of the city, therefore, a square mile or more, is perfect—and expanding, with hardly an anomalous thing. From the old guns facing out across the harbour, inward through the widening tongue of land, lies an ancient network of quiet streets, gardens and houses. And such houses! Warm Georgian brick, white pillars, iron railings and balconies, wooden galleries (which Charlestonians call 'piazzas'), painted shutters, 'earthquake bolts' (where metal rods were inserted to strengthen the building), every house different, but the most typical following a strange basic pattern—they are built end-on to the street so that the real front of the house, with its piazzas, can catch the cool wind on a summer evening blowing off the Ashley River, and in winter the warmth of the sun. Inside, there are polished wooden floors, and grandfather clocks, and china cabinets, and rather bad ancestral portraits, and four-poster beds. Many of the houses bear plaques with the name of the original owner—the Miles Brewton House, the Joseph Manigault House, the Daniel Ravenel House. Those

Charleston names fill the telephone book today as they have filled the pages of the city's history, so strife-torn and yet so tranquil now, almost since the first three small ships arrived from England in 1670.

The spine of the city is King Street, running straight down from South Battery. Flagstoned sidewalks invite a gentle stroll past painted doors with gleaming brass knobs, and casement windows, and red brick paths beside neat lawns and subtropical flowers. Even the fire hydrants are quaint, having been painted—by art students, I was told, some years ago—in red, white and blue, with arms outstretched and pointed caps, like little gnomes.

The Lees lived in King Street, in a proper Charleston 'single house'; that is, a house end-on to the street, one-room deep, with two rooms on each floor (as distinct from 'double houses,' which are square, with four rooms on each floor). There were three floors, each with its piazza, and, at the far end, a 'back house,' where the servants would have lived, not unlike the mews cottage behind a Belgravia mansion.

The street door, which Ted Lee unlocked, opened into the garden, where a flight of wooden steps led to the real front door, which was in the middle of the house. Pushing aside the mosquito screen, he ushered us into a hall between the two ground-floor rooms. I smelled the scented wood-polish, which, I was to discover, is so typical of Charleston (along with mildew and mothballs, cynical Charlestonians would say), and heard the gentle ticking of the old long-case clock, and felt a comforting coolness after the heat outside.

'You are *so* welcome,' said Aunt Martha. 'Now, Ted, if you'll just take Professor Glowrey to his room, I'll fix the tea. Oh, Cressy . . .' She hugged her again, and there were tears on her cheeks.

'Now, now, Aunt Martha,' said Cressida softly. 'But it is nice to be back.'

An immaculate white counterpane gleamed invitingly on the four-poster bed. French windows, mosquito-screened, opened onto the street. The house opposite was much grander, with a cobbled courtyard and a gas-lamp which burned night and day. Unpacking, I hung my clothes in a handsome old wardrobe, paused to examine the Audubon prints on the wall and then went down to join the others.

An elderly black woman in a flowered apron was helping Aunt Martha make her elaborate dispositions, which involved, not only a silver teapot and fine china cups, but a spirit lamp for keeping the water hot, a silver cream jug and a great array of biscuits and cakes.

'Betsy,' said Aunt Martha, 'this is Professor

231

Glowrey, all the way from England.'

'Welcome to Charleston, Professor,' said Betsy. 'I've seen English movies on television.'

'I just hope we can make him feel at home,' twittered Aunt Martha.

When Betsy had withdrawn, Ted said to me: 'Interesting woman, that. I knew her father. He was one of the last of the real old-style Nigras. Spoke Gullah. That's the local patois. And he'd tell you stories, wonderful stories. I can hear him now. They always began the same way. "A long time ago, befo' yestidy was bo'n, and befo' bygones was uster-bes."'

'Betsy has stories too,' said Cressida. 'I loved them when I was a little girl. "Fac' fo' fac' an' true fo' true, lak de L'od talk een de Gospel. Ah saw it wid ma own two eye."'

They all laughed. They were a family. And I was too enthralled even to be exasperated with Cressida.

'Do have another cookie,' said Aunt Martha.

'You'd better,' agreed Mr. Lee. 'I don't know if Cressy warned you, but mealtimes in Charleston aren't exactly the same as in most other places.'

'Dinner at three,' said Cressida.

'The young ones don't do it,' said Aunt Martha. 'They're always hurrying back to their offices. But I'm afraid we're rather old-fashioned.'

'Dinner at three and then a late supper,' explained Mr. Lee. 'I guess that was the eighteenth-century habit and we just kept on. Like a lot of things around here.' He grinned. 'But don't worry. There's drinks to fill the gap.'

When tea was over, I went to my room and rested for a while, until the cool of the evening began. Then there were indeed drinks. Ted Lee made mint juleps, as promised, although I discovered that this was something only done for visitors; Charlestonians by themselves were more inclined to drink whiskey. After dinner, or supper, Cressida and I strolled up King Street, through the warm darkness, to the Battery, where we could look out across a still sea to Fort Sumter, the starting-place of the Civil War.

'I've rarely met,' I said, 'two less alarming people than your aunt and uncle.'

'I'm sorry,' said Cressida in tones of ostensible contrition, 'but I did so much want you to come and see Charleston with me.'

'I noticed they were very tactfully not asking questions. What have you told them about Brazil?'

'A censored version. They're a bit shockable. You won't give me away?'

'No. For their sake, not yours, you wretched girl.'

'Thank you. Let's forget about Brazil, can we? Not how splendid you were—I won't ever forget that—but all the frightening part. You were going to have a holiday anyway. You like old things. There are lots of old things here, plenty I can show you.'

'Why not? You have an astonishing way of shaping people's lives to suit yourself. I might as well relax and enjoy it.'

'That's a good professor.'

So we began what I can only think of as an idyll out of time. During the next few days we walked, or drove, around Charleston, and then, venturing farther afield, traversed roads which were tunnels of live-oaks, dripping with Spanish moss, to visit plantation houses gently decaying amid lawns and venerable trees. Cressida knew everybody and everybody seemed happy to see her. I could have asked for no better guide. Here, at home, as the days passed, the slightly frenetic quality which had burned inside her when we first met smoothed itself away. She was confident and cheerful and surprisingly knowledgeable in answering my questions. Some of the history she had probably absorbed from her uncle, who proved to be a Civil War buff. He and I had long discussions about strategy and whether the South could possibly have won.

The time went by, seductively. Lying in that broad four-poster bed, the room softly lit by the glow of the gas-lamp in the cobbled yard across the street, I pondered the strange sequence of events that had brought me to this beautiful town, and felt, as I hadn't consciously felt for many years, that there was nowhere else in the world I should rather be.

I'd been in Charleston for a week when the first untoward thing occurred. By now we'd established an easy domestic routine, delightfully reminiscent to me of the small-town America which Hollywood used to depict in a more innocent age. Cressida and I usually went shopping in the morning.

When we emerged, Cressida and I were both carrying large brown paper bags into which the packer (why do British supermarkets not have packers?) had skilfully arranged our purchases. We walked across the road to where we'd parked the car.

That is, we started across the road. The sun was bright and warm. Out of the corner of my eye I caught the flash of sunlight reflected on a windscreen, and I heard the sudden roar of an accelerating engine. There was no time to think. I just caught Cressida's arm and pulled her sharply back. I could almost swear that the car brushed my jacket; I certainly felt the wind of its passage. It was a large mauve limousine, which had appeared from nowhere—from a side-street, I suppose—and was driven fast, straight down the middle of the road, straying indeed onto the wrong side altogether.

I couldn't see who was in it, although, thinking about the incident afterwards, I had a vague impression that there were two men in the front. By the time I'd recovered, it was almost out of sight, disappearing round a corner, too far away for me to read the number-plate. I wasn't hurt, merely shaken. Cressida had stumbled and half-fallen, spilling the contents of her brown bag onto the road. A squashed tomato lay red against the tarmac, while several cans were rolling in different directions.

'Are you all right?' I said to Cressida.

'Yes, I'm fine. That was a bit close, though. Some drivers!'

'And there's never a cop around when you want one.'

'Well, we're down one tomato,' observed Cressida, 'but otherwise I think we're intact. Lucky I didn't drop Uncle Ted's whiskey.'

'Lucky altogether,' I said. 'It could have been us instead of that tomato.'

'Ugh! Don't be so gruesome.'

Looking carefully up and down the road, on which there was now no moving vehicle except a horse-drawn tourist bus, we walked to the car. I had no reason to think that our near-miss had been other than an accident, and I gave it no more serious thought. At least, not much more thought. When we got home, Cressida told Ted and Martha what

236

had happened, and they responded with suitable expressions of outrage and concern.

It wasn't until after the second incident that I remembered the saying which Ian Fleming, in one of the James Bond books, attributes to Chicago gangsters: 'Once is happenstance; twice is coincidence; the third time, it's enemy action.'

Another day had passed, slipping by. It was early evening. Ted had gone to a committee meeting at the sailing club and Martha had not yet returned from a session of some ladies' group at which samples of their culinary skill—cakes and cookies, to be precise—were exhibited, compared and discussed. Cressida and I went for a walk, not, on this occasion, along the sea-wall, but downtown, simply for a change.

The shops were closed. The streets were not exactly deserted, but they weren't a seething mass of people either. We strolled, absorbed in our conversation. Somehow—I don't know how—I became aware that we were being followed.

Of course, to begin with, I wasn't sure; indeed, if it hadn't been for our melodramatic experiences in Brazil, I don't suppose the thought would have occurred to me. But there were undoubtedly two men, one black, one white; the black man, wearing a rather sharp, well-pressed blue suit, on the far side of the road, paying no attention to us, gazing in shop windows but keeping parallel; the white man, in an open-necked shirt and jeans, strolling about fifty yards behind us on our side of the road. They showed no sign of being together, and yet they held their stations like two ships manoeuvring. It must have been this pattern, this regularity, which caught my eye. They didn't fit. There was nothing apparently purposeful about them, and yet they had a purpose. And I became increasingly convinced that we were the purpose.

Before saying anything to Cressida, I deliberately varied our pace, dawdling beside a row of antique shops, then speeding up past a gents' outfitters and a shoe shop and a jeweller's. Then we crossed the road to look in the window of a paperback bookshop. The black man didn't hesitate. He walked on, and I thought for a moment that I must have been mistaken, but he halted some twenty yards ahead, poring over the menu outside a Vietnamese restaurant. And the white man, who was now almost parallel, started to fall back a little.

'Cressida,' I said, 'don't look round, and keep calm, but I think there are two men watching us.' And I described them.

'Do you think they're going to mug us, right here in the open? What should we do—run, scream for help? Or could we simply turn around and walk back?'

The dusk had thickened, and the street, I realized, was emptier than before. There was no one very close except the two men. They might be muggers, tracking casual victims, but somehow I doubted it. We could, as Cressida suggested, try walking boldly past them, but I didn't like the idea. I didn't like the way they held themselves, the black man with his hand in the pocket of his coat, the white man with his fists clenched.

We were passing a gateway beyond which was a red brick path flanked by bushes, leading to a white-walled church. A notice-board described the church's antiquity.

'Does that path go through?' I said. 'Into the next street?'

'I think so.'

'Come on.' Seizing Cressida's arm, I wheeled sharp left, and we ran. The two men dropped all pretence and came after us. Looking back, as we pounded across the uneven bricks, I saw that they both now held weapons, the black man a revolver, the white man a knife. There was no outcry from the street, no sign that anyone else had noticed. Probably no one had. As soon as we, and our pursuers, had turned in at the gateway, we must have been out of sight, except to someone standing directly opposite. And the daylight had almost gone. The path was illumined by a single, rather dim

239

lamp-standard near the gateway.

The church itself seemed to be deserted, its door shut. The path carried on, debouching through another gate onto the side-street, which looked even emptier than the street we'd left.

There was one point, just beyond the door of the church, where the path curved a little, skirting a large tree and a tombstone surrounded by an iron railing. Bushes obscured the curve. Our pursuers were still a fair distance behind as we ran past the church, and, for a few yards, the bushes lay between us and them. I pulled Cressida off the path and into the shelter of the bushes. There were tombstones and plenty of other bushes and trees, behind which we might have hidden and which offered intermittent cover. We began working our way towards the far side of the church. Another path, narrow and overgrown, seemed to go all the way around. We followed it, between scattered bushes and ancient graves, until, from the shadow, we were looking out again on to the illumined area beside the gate through which we'd entered. The light, however dim, made those few yards look horribly open and vulnerable.

I hesitated, then pulled Cressida to the ground near an old stone bench around which the grass and wild flowers had been allowed to grow knee-high. In daylight we should have been quite visible, but in the half-dark perhaps not.

'Keep your head down,' I said, 'and keep quiet.'

'As a little mouse,' she whispered.

I couldn't see the two men. They'd passed the church and were out of sight, probably peering up and down the side-street. They might conclude that we'd made a successful escape, or they might search for us behind the parked cars and in the gardens, which would give us our chance. But they didn't. I heard them talking in low voices as they came back. They hadn't followed us around the church. They were returning along the main path, looking on either side, behind bushes and the larger tombstones. I watched them through the grass, which smelled warm, almost cosy. Cressida's face was pressed to the ground.

'They're not here,' said the white man. 'I tell you we ought to have looked behind the cars. They'll have got away by now.'

'They didn't have time,' replied the black man. 'I think they're still here.' They both spoke standard American, without, to my ear, any perceptible accent. The black man's gun had acquired a bulbous end—a silencer. The white man, though he still had the knife, held it unobtrusively, pointing down beside the seam of his trousers.

'Well, if they are, I don't see them.'

'They could be anywhere. Take it easy,

man. We're in no hurry.'

He stepped off the path, walked a few paces more or less in our direction, halted, looked around and then advanced another few paces. I calculated our chances of making a dash for the gateway. We should take them by surprise; or perhaps that was just the kind of move which the black man was expecting us to make. And he would fire the moment we jumped up. He walked another couple of paces nearer to us. I began wondering if I could grab the gun before he had time to react. I might be able to do so, but the other man would immediately be on to us with his knife.

We should be like rabbits jumping up from the grass or wheat as the farmer approaches . . . But, as I braced myself to try, the tension was broken, suddenly, by cheerful voices. A group of teenagers, chattering among themselves, one with a portable radio blaring, had come through the gateway; not churchgoers, I presumed; they were simply taking a short cut.

The gun and the knife disappeared instantly. The two men, absorbed now in talk with each other, moved away, passing the teenagers, who paid no attention to them.

I rose, pulling Cressida to her feet as well. 'Put your arm around my waist,' I said. I put mine round her shoulders. Like an amorous couple, we followed in the wake of the noisy youngsters. I could almost feel eyes from behind, watching me. I forced myself not to turn round until we reached the gate into the side-street. Then I did glance back. There was no one in sight. I peered into the shadows but still saw no one.

Once out into the street, we kept warily close to the teenagers until we came to a bigger road. Again I scrutinized the shadows, thinking that the two men might have circled the block and be waiting for us. But I could see no sign of muggers or assassins. However, there were now quite a few people around, and an occasional car purring by, and another of those horse-drawn tourist buses.

'Which way home?' I asked.

'This way. Back to King Street.'

I felt reasonably sure we weren't being followed. 'James, who were they?' asked Cressida.

'Not your local villains?'

'Did you think they were?'

'Not really.' We walked on in silence.

As we turned into King Street she asked, 'Should we call the police?'

'I'd rather not. Yet.'

She accepted it. Two considerations weighed with me: I didn't want to talk about O'Malley and I didn't want to talk about Surov and the Fishers. And presumably, if those two men hadn't just been local muggers, they must be connected with what had happened in Brazil; which was an ominous, but perplexing, thought.

'Let's not tell Ted and Martha,' said Cressida. 'It would only worry them.'

'I agree.'

As we approached the house, I looked very carefully at the parked cars and into shadowy corners but there seemed to be nothing and no one suspicious. It was just a warm quiet night, peaceful and friendly, as I had come to expect of Charleston. I should have liked to forget those moments of fear in the churchyard, to believe they'd never happened; but, of course, I knew I couldn't, mustn't, daren't.

Ted was watching television, Martha was preparing dinner, or supper, in the kitchen. Cressida went to her room to change. She was uncharacteristically subdued, and I wondered if Ted might notice. He gave her, I fancied, a speculative glance, but said nothing. Perhaps he thought we'd quarrelled.

In my room, usefully, there was a telephone. Within a couple of minutes, I was dialling the number of Pedro's apartment in Rio. Luisa answered, recognized my name and said something, obviously friendly, in Portuguese. She was a sweet-natured woman. She held no grudge against me for the injury to her husband, of which I had been, indirectly, the cause.

Pedro came on the line. 'Hello, Professor.

All's good? You are having fun, you and the girl?'

'Quite fun. I called to make sure everything's all right your end. There's no trouble about O'Malley?'

'No trouble. Is like I tell you. Police are happy. Leon at Tara's Hall is happy. He runs the joint now. He'll make big money.'

'But somebody must surely have wondered where O'Malley's gone?'

'Me and the police spread a little story. We say that O'Malley was killed in big fight between drug-runners. The other men were trying to hijack his load. Okay story, no?'

'Sounds okay. So no one's been asking questions?'

I could almost see him shrug. 'Who would ask? Who wants O'Malley back?'

'And no one's been asking about me? Or about Cressida?'

'No one. Don't worry, my friend.'

'The Russians?'

'They're maybe a little bit cross, but it's not the first time. They'll try to find Surov in England. But I think Senhor Jeremy fix that, don't you?'

'Probably. Nothing for me to worry about anyway?'

'Nothing. Enjoy your holiday, Professor.'

With pledges of mutual esteem we hung up. For a moment my hand hovered above the telephone as I toyed with the idea of calling Gabriel or Jeremy: but I decided against it. What could they do? What should I tell them? Just to cry for help would be feeble—or, at any rate, premature.

The next move was up to me.

CHAPTER ELEVEN

THE HOUSE IN THE WOODS

'There's an old plantation house,' Cressida had told me, 'out along the river. I don't know when anybody last lived there, but it's still in the family. Spanish Oaks. I guess it's kind of eerie, with the marshes and the woods and all those empty rooms. Exciting, though. I used to like being taken out there when I was a child.'

'We might go and look at it,' I'd said.

'Why not? As a teenager, when I used to bicycle all over the place, I was forbidden to go to Spanish Oaks on my own. Too dangerous. I might have fallen through the rotting floorboards, or been bitten by a snake. Or the hants might have got me.'

'Hants?'

'Ghosts. Of course I did sneak out there once or twice. It was a bit scary. But I never saw a snake, let alone a hant. I made sure I away before sunset, though.'

246

It occurred to me now, remembering that conversation, that a trip to Spanish Oaks might serve my purpose. The day after our alarming experience in the churchyard we were very careful. Standing on the piazza outside my bedroom. I scrutinized King Street in either direction; and when, later, Cressida and I went out, I was alert and wary. The headrests in modern cars make it easy for someone, slumped in the front seat, to remain invisible until you're right beside the car. And all the time I was half-expecting trouble. But nothing could have been more peaceful. We deliberately didn't go far. We strolled under the trees, over the tabby—crushed oyster shells—of which the paths are made in White Point Gardens, and along East Battery, and back in front of the big galleried houses which face the sea. There were children and dogs and a few people fishing. As we returned to the Lees' house, I watched again for a trap. Still nothing.

Was I perhaps worrying needlessly? Those two men had been real, their weapons had been real, but they might, after all, have been ordinary muggers. They might but somehow I couldn't believe it. And if they weren't, if they were something else, then it seemed unlikely that they had simply gone away. The difficulty was that I couldn't imagine their motive. Revenge by associates of O'Malley? Possible, I supposed, but Pedro had not made it seem probable.

Cressida, sensing—and, no doubt, sharing—my concern, was unusually subdued. We went into the cool drawing room. I could hear Aunt Martha and Betsy talking in the kitchen.

'I want to try something,' I said to Cressida. 'If there are—unpleasant people—interested in us, I'll try to draw them out and have a look at them. That would be easier outside town.'

'You're not leaving me behind. Don't think it.'

'I had no such intention. I thought we might visit that old family house you mentioned, Spanish Oaks. I imagine the roads would be fairly empty? We could see if we were being followed?'

'I guess there's more traffic than there used to be, but, yes, they're country roads.'

'Shall we do it tomorrow?'

She nodded. 'If you like. Aunt Martha may want to come with us.'

'That won't do.'

'I'll make her think we want to be alone. She'll believe that.'

'Hm. Do you know if, by any chance, Ted has a gun?'

'He used to have a shotgun. He talked about hunting squirrels, though he never did. Aunt Martha wouldn't let him. He kept it in a cupboard in their bedroom.'

'If we borrow the car again tomorrow,' I said (Aunt Martha had her own smaller car), 'do you suppose that Ted's gun could somehow find its way onto the back seat?'

'If it's still in the cupboard, and the cupboard isn't locked . . . Or, rather, if the key's been left in the lock, which it always was . . .'

'And ammunition.'

'There used to be a box in the desk drawer.'

★ ★ ★

Nothing changes in Charleston. Nothing had changed in the Lees' house. 'It's in the car,' Cressida whispered to me as we prepared to set out next morning. 'Under the rug.'

Aunt Martha had packed lunch for us in a wicker basket; wine or beer or both we could pick up from a pleasant little shop, with which I had become familiar, on South Battery. As predicted, she thought it entirely natural that the young people—meaning, heaven help us, me—should enjoy a romantic day by themselves in the country.

'Be careful where you walk,' was Ted's advice. 'Hot weather brings the rattlers out.'

'They do say,' observed Aunt Martha, 'that there are panthers in the deep woods. But I never heard of anybody seeing one.

But it wasn't rattlesnakes and panthers that

249

worried me.

Cressida drove. She wore an open-necked white silk blouse and light-blue trousers. Her skin was golden-brown against the white of the silk. Having collected a jug of Californian wine and a six-pack of beer, we crossed the Ashley River Bridge, and I soon lost track of where we were.

'How far is it?' I asked.

'Fifteen, twenty miles.'

'Let's take the longest route. We might even stop for lunch somewhere else. The more circuitously we go, the better chance we'll have to spot anyone who's tailing us.'

'Everything seems so normal,' she said, 'and it's such a lovely day. Oh, why *can't* this just be a picnic in the country?'

'Perhaps it will be. It probably will be.'

Already we were on an almost empty road, with the branches of the live-oaks meeting above us. There was only one car visible behind.

'At least it's not mauve,' said Cressida, who must have noticed me glancing in the mirror. Actually the car was red.

'It wouldn't be, would it? If someone really was trying to run us down, they'd have used a stolen car. But that may simply have been an accident anyway, nothing to do with those two men.'

She turned off the main road, and the red car vanished from sight. A few minutes later she swung through rusted iron gates and followed a grass-grown drive past the front of a more-or-less Georgian house with all the windows shuttered. We parked beside the house in a field which had once been a lawn.

'Whose house is this?' I asked.

'It belongs to some cousins of mine,' said Cressida. 'They're in Europe at the moment. Not that they come out here much anyway. They live in town. There are a lot of houses like this around Charleston. People just open them once or twice a year for the Plantation Tour.'

We had our picnic beneath the trees, with the river barely visible beyond the remnants of an unkempt garden. The sun was warm. So inevitably, was the wine, but it didn't matter. Yellow butterflies fluttered among the wild flowers. Our conversation became intermittent. I dozed.

When I woke, I found Cressida asleep on the rug beside me. I looked at my watch. The time was five to four; we'd slept for well over an hour. What alarmed me was our vulnerability. Anybody could have come up to us—and done anything.

Eventually we were in the car again, resuming, belatedly, our journey to Spanish Oaks.

The main road was deserted as we drove back into it, and we met very few cars during the next half hour. The journey became dreamlike; the trees flowed past, the trelliswork of branches above us alternating with bright sunshine. Even conversation seemed too much effort.

'Almost there,' said Cressida.

Again we turned off the road, not now onto a formal drive, however derelict, but along an unmade road, deeply rutted in the baked mud. The dark tangle of trees and undergrowth, which at first flanked the track on either side, gave way suddenly to an open vista of bright green, of reeds rippling at a breath of wind. We were on a small plateau of firm ground narrowed into a wooden causeway. I could see water between the reeds.

'The marsh is rather beautiful, isn't it?' said Cressida. 'It's always changing, never still.'

Then the woods closed around us again, until, after perhaps another five minutes, we emerged into a cleared area. At least, it must once have been cleared; now the vegetation was creeping back, saplings and briers, like a stealthy besieging army. The object of their siege, and of our journey, stood in the middle, more resigned than defiant. It was an obviously very old, quite large house, built entirely of what seemed to be bare greyish wood. If the windows and the doors had ever been painted, the paint had long ago worn off. The windows stared blankly, with only a few broken panes of glass remaining. Shutters hung at crazy angles. The railing along the porch had collapsed at several points.

I understood why Cressida had called it eerie. The feeling of weirdness was heightened by the fact that, because we'd dallied so much on the way, the sun was only just visible above the tree-tops, casting long shadows.

She stopped the car on a patch of rank yellow grass near the porch. As I got out, the air felt oppressive and motionless; the breeze which had ruffled the marshes didn't penetrate here. And there was no sound. In the trees around us where we'd had our lunch all sorts of birds made a joyful noise. For some reason no birds sang here.

'If you still want to be safely away before sunset,' I said, 'we can't spend very long in the house.'

'We've got an hour or so.'

'Quite enough, I should think.'

The steps up to the porch felt soft beneath my feet, as though the wood were rotten and might break. The door yielded to Cressida's touch; any lock or catch had rusted away. As we stepped into the semi-darkness of the entrance hall, some small creature scurried into hiding.

'I didn't realize it was going to be as bad as this,' said Cressida. 'I wanted to show you the mouldings and the carved woodwork. They are rather nice, aren't they? Charleston had some wonderful craftsmen in the old days.

'Do you think the stairs are safe?' she asked.

'I doubt it. Keep near the side.'

The banister certainly felt as though it might collapse if one put any weight on it. However, we negotiated the stairs successfully and entered a bedroom, which still contained its four-poster bed, looking rather like Miss Havisham's room in *Great Expectations*. I walked across to the window. One shutter was in place, the other hung preariously from a single hinge.

The sound of an approaching car had scarcely registered before the vehicle itself appeared, bumping out from between the trees. It was a red saloon.

That I should have been so completely shocked was absurd. The possibility of such a thing was, after all, implicit in our whole expedition. But, during the last couple of hours, I'd almost forgotten the purpose of that day's journey. Now, sickeningly, I realized that my negligence might prove fatal. The red car had halted close to ours, and the same two men alighted.

'What is it?' asked Cressida. She hadn't heard the car, but saw that I was looking out of the window. And she must have seen my expression.

The black man stood beside the driver's

door of the car, holding and adjusting something in his hands. It was a pistol. He was screwing on a silencer. The white man held a weapon about which I'd read often enough but which I'd never seen—a sawn-off shotgun, an ugly stubby thing. He peered through the windows of our car. Ted's gun was on the back seat but concealed by the rug. The man didn't notice it; at least, he didn't open the door and take it. I cursed myself for not bringing it with me.

Cressida, having approached the window, gave a little gasp.

'Keep back,' I said, moving to one side.

'But they must know we're in the house.'

The two men were now walking, in a leisurely way, towards the porch. I wondered, for a moment, if, when they'd entered the house, we could escape through the window; but the idea hardly seemed practicable. There were no drain-pipes or creepers. We should have to drop onto the sloping—and decaying—roof of the porch. The odds were that we should fall straight through; and even if, by any chance, we didn't, the noise would inevitably attract the gunmen's attention.

'Is there another staircase?' I asked urgently. 'Any other way down?'

'I don't think so.'

The two men mounted the steps to the porch, and disappeared from view. I moved to the door of the bedroom. I could hear their quiet footsteps down below. They would go from room to room, and, when they didn't find us, come upstairs.

Cressida, at my elbow, whispered, 'I've just remembered. There may be another way.'

She slipped past me and along the gallery away from the main staircase. I followed. Keeping close to the wall, we couldn't be seen from below. The gallery turned, at the corner, into a short passage with two more rooms leading off it. Cressida ignored them, going instead to a bookcase at the end; the shelves, surprisingly, still contained books. Or rather they didn't. The books were false. Cressida ran her fingers up the side, pulled, and the whole bookcase swung open.

She took my hand and drew me in. It was dark, but I could just make out a flight of stairs.

'Better pull the door shut,' she said.

'Can you manage in the dark?'

'If the treads aren't broken.'

The bookcase door was another beautiful piece of craftsmanship, swinging smoothly at a touch. The blackness then seemed to me complete, but Cressida led us down. We went cautiously. The stairs felt firm enough, though; better, perhaps because they were narrower or had been kept drier, than the main staircase. They were very steep. As my eyes became accustomed to the dark, I perceived daylight at the bottom. The outline of a door.

'They put these hidden staircases in,' said Cressida, 'so the slaves could come and go without being seen by the family. The door leads to the slave quarters at the back.'

My mind was racing between the horns of a dilemma. Should we make a run for it through the door or should we wait here, in the comforting concealing dark, until the gunmen gave up their search and left? They knew we must be somewhere in the house; perhaps they also knew about hidden staircases? Or would they conclude that we'd seen them coming, had slipped out through a window and taken refuge in the woods?

The dilemma solved itself. Looking back, up the stairs, I saw dimly the outline of the bookcase door through which we'd come, and a thicker line of light down the side. Although I'd pulled it shut, I hadn't done whatever was necessary to engage the catch, and it must have swung slightly open again. The gunmen would notice it sooner or later, and probably sooner.

Momentarily I'd restrained Cressida, but now I let her go on. She lifted a latch—I heard it click—and pushed the door open. We were outside, thank God. A row of dilapidated outhouses stretched off to the right. The edge of the woods beckoned temptingly about a hundred yards straight ahead. My choice would have been to sprint across and take cover among the trees.

But Cressida didn't wait. She was moving left, hugging the wall of the house. I had no option but to follow. She reached the corner and ran. I ran after her, over the grass, in front of the house, to the car. She was already in the driver's seat, turning the ignition, when I dived in beside her. The engine started at once. She engaged the clutch with a jerk and slewed the wheel round. We actually scraped the gunmen's car.

Something zipped through the roof with a curious, unmistakable noise and punched a hole in the windscreen between Cressida and me. But, if there were any more shots, they didn't hit the car. We were accelerating fast. The trees closed around us and we were sheltered from the house.

There was a limit, though, to the speed which was possible. Cressida wrestled with the wheel, manoeuvring the car over rough ground and away from a ditch which ran beside the track and away from fallen branches. The fading light was dangerously deceptive; a red glow through the trees.

I heard, or thought I heard, the gunmen's car behind us. Twisting and stretching over the back of the seat, I pulled Ted's shotgun out from under the rug. Awkwardly I broke it open across my knee. A yellow cardboard box of shells was in the glove compartment, concealed by a pile of folded maps. I opened the box.

In it were three golf balls, a pipe, a packet of pipe-cleaners, a cube of billiard chalk and a clasp-knife.

'Bloody hell!' I exclaimed.

Glancing sideways, Cressida saw the contents of the box and wailed, 'Oh God, I never thought to look. I just assumed they were cartridges.'

'So much for our armament,' I said. 'Do you think you can shake them off?'

She didn't answer. The answer was only too clear. The red car had become visible behind us; not yet very near, merely glimpsed through the trees as the track curved, but closing on us.

We were out of the trees now, onto the causeway across the marsh. The reeds were bending and rippling, and I realized that the sulphurous light was caused not by sunset but by an impending storm. Huge clouds were piling up. Cressida had to slow down slightly for fear of slipping off the causeway. And the red car was out of the trees too, only about three hundred yards behind us. I could see the black man driving. As I looked, the white man leaned out of the window, holding the sawn-off shotgun in both hands, lining it up, waiting until he was near enough to fire.

We were off the causeway, onto the plateau of firmer ground. And then, without a word, Cressida did an astonishing thing. She slewed the car right round in a circle and stamped hard on the accelerator. Before I could grasp what was happening, we were almost back on the causeway, hurtling into a head-on crash with the red car.

The black man must have been equally taken by surprise. He had no time for evasive action. The white man fired but the blast went wide.

Whether by luck or superb skill, Cressida used our car as a missile, aiming it as accurately as a billiard player using the cue-ball to clip another into the pocket. We didn't hit the red car head-on. Not quite. We smashed obliquely into its side. The impact threw me forward. I hit my head on the windscreen but not severely. Recovering, I saw the wheels of the red car coming up, the underside of the car exposed and then the whole vehicle tip over sideways into the marsh. For those few seconds I watched a slow-motion scene. Then it was finished. The red car was gone.

As Cressida wrenched the wheel and jammed on the brake, our own car almost went the same way. We ended diagonally across the causeway, the right front wheel protruding over the bank. Cressida gave a sigh and rested her head on her hands.

I wasn't sure what condition our car was in, whether the engine had been damaged, how long it would take, even if the engine wasn't damaged, to get us back on the road. And what condition were the gunmen in? They might already be clambering out of the marsh . . .

Ted's shotgun was the only weapon I had. I could at least wield it as a club. So I took it with me as I climbed, rather shakily, from the car, and walked to the edge of the causeway. I peered over.

There was nothing, or only a turbulence among the reeds. Then I could just make out a darker shape, the oblong of a car roof, which faded and disappeared as I looked. I could scarcely believe it.

Cressida, behind me, said very quietly, 'This always was the most dangerous place. We were warned about it as children. The marsh swallows everything up.'

She was standing beside the car, her face very pale. Our eyes met but we were both at a loss for words.

The first fat drops of rain began to fall, making little rings on the water of the marsh. A flicker of sheet lightning was followed by a rumble of thunder.

'I suppose there's nothing we should do?' I said, more to myself than to her. 'For them?'

She shook her head. The rain intensified, battering the reeds. Cressida got back into the car. The engine started without difficul   I guided her as she backed away from th╱ and off the causeway. When I'd clim

261

beside her, she turned the car and, without once looking back, drove very slowly away from the marsh and through the woods towards the main road.

The thunder seemed almost continuous now. Rain poured down in torrents and dripped in through the hole which the bullet had made.

After about five minutes Cressida spoke. What she said was terrible and memorable. 'You and I,' she said, 'are even now. The same thing on both our consciences.'

'I can live with it,' I said. 'You must.'

'I will,' she said.

We drove on in silence. I was wondering what we should tell the police; presumably now we should have to go to them.

She said, 'Do you mind if we make a detour?'

'No, of course not.'

The car, with its crumpled fender, must have looked a mess. But the roads, lightly used before, were quite empty in the storm. I don't think we passed a single other vehicle. The gunmen had been clever to follow us all day without our noticing them latterly; or perhaps it was simply my carelessness, and if I'd been more alert, I should have noticed them. Or could they have known where we were going or were likely to go? Hardly. My impression, increasingly, was that these were professional hit men, brought in from outside

262

to do a job.

No one had known our destination except Ted and Martha, and even in a world of mysterious motives and treachery I couldn't suspect them. They'd have to be told what had happened, though. At least they'd have to be told some story. The state of the car made that unavoidable.

We'd turned off the main road again and were negotiating another unmade side-road, which the heavy rain had transformed into mud. When Cressida halted the car, I realized where we were. Amid the dripping trees stood the small family church or chapel—Mulberry Hill, it was called—which she had shown me, a few days before, when we were doing the tourist round of Charleston and its environs.

'Wait for me, please,' she said. 'I won't be long.'

She ran down the short path between ancient graves and disappeared into the church. No light went on. There probably was no light.

I put my head back against the rest and closed my eyes. A vision of the red car sinking into the marsh merged with memories of Brazil. I wasn't trying to engage in systematic thought. My mind drifted; but the effect was like a kaleidoscope. The pieces fell into a pattern. Their sudden clarity shook me wide awake. Now I did start thinking systematically. Did it make sense, did it make better sense than anything else? Yes, it did.

Thunder still rumbled, but the rain was slackening. The door of the church opened, and Cressida returned, walking quite slowly, damp hair plastered across her forehead. She slid into the seat beside me.

'Thank you,' she said.

As we drove back the way we'd come, and then turned towards Charleston, I said, 'Are you all right?'

'I'm fine,' she said.

'What you did was absolutely self-defence. No one can deny that. And if the police bring up the car, they'll find the guns.'

'I know.'

'That would be the proper thing to do, the safest in one way, the safest for you—to tell the police everything.'

'All right.'

'Do you trust me?'

'You know I do.'

I looked at her. She was pale but quite calm. 'The trouble is, we haven't got time. If we go to the police now, we shouldn't be able to leave Charleston for days, perhaps weeks.'

'Does that matter?'

'Yes, it does. Those gunmen weren't here by accident, and there may be others. We're in danger; even Ted and Martha may be in danger.'

'Then surely we should ask for police

protection?'

'There's too much at stake. Not just us. If you really trust me, please don't ask me to explain at this stage. I will in a day or two, when . . . Cressida, I want you to come with me to England.'

'That would be nice.'

'Tomorrow.'

'Tomorrow!'

'We can come back later and square things with the police. They're not likely to find the car in the meanwhile, and if those gunmen were out-of-town hit men—as I think they were—no one's going to report them missing.'

'I probably should argue, but I'm beyond arguing. You're the professor. Whatever you say.'

The skies had cleared, leaving a pale sunset glow, as we crossed the bridge into Charleston. The danger, as I'd warned Cressida, wasn't over but we surely had a respite. It wouldn't be renewed for a day or so. And by then, I believed, we might have disposed of it. Keeping a wary eye had become a habit, but I should have been very surprised if we were still being followed or if the house in King Street was still being watched.

I told Cressida to drive the car straight into the garage beside the house, and then to distract Aunt Martha for a few minutes while

I had a word with her uncle.

Martha was, predictably, in the kitchen. I heard her exclaim, 'You're soaked!'

Ted, in the drawing room, looked up from his book. 'Can we talk quietly for a minute?' I said. 'There are some things I want to tell you.'

'Figured you might,' he said.

I'd already come to the conclusion that my original assessment of Ted Lee had been wide of the mark. He had cultivated a role which suited Martha, to whom he was obviously devoted, and the easygoing community in which he had lived all his life, except for a spell in the army, and which he found comfortable, observing the world with an ironic eye that few people ever noticed. The cracker-barrel exterior concealed a shrewd, as wall as a thoroughly decent, man.

So I told him, not quite everything, but most of the story.

'Now I'm afraid I've made you an accessory,' I said. 'I'm hoping you'll agree to conceal a crime, several crimes.'

'What crimes?' he said, fussing with his pipe. 'Cressy didn't commit one. That was self-defence. And those gunmen didn't. They may have tried to but they didn't.'

'I doubt if the police would be quite so amiable about it.'

'There was an automobile accident. I guess you should have reported that. But people often forget.'

'What can we do about the car? There's a bullet hole in the roof, as well as a crushed fender.'

'No problem. I'll enlarge the bullet hole a bit, so it'll just be a hole. And I'll take the car to our friendly neighbourhood mechanic. He'll believe what I tell him about a minor accident. Why shouldn't he? Incidentally, we'd better tell Martha the same story.'

We did, and she responded with a great deal of 'Oh my!' 'How terrible!' 'You poor things!' She fluttered even more when I told her that a sudden college crisis required my presence in Oxford and that Cressida was coming with me. But Ted soothed her as expertly as a cowboy gentling a nervous mare.

Cressida had a bath and changed but refused the suggestion that she should go straight to bed. She wouldn't be able to sleep, she said. After supper, the women went upstairs, leaving me to finish my whiskey-and-water and Ted to lock up.

'The important thing is,' he said, as he wound the grandfather clock, 'to fight a good war without hating your enemy. After Appomattox, there was a band playing on the lawn outside the White House. A message was sent to the President, asking him what he'd like the band to play. 'I'd like to hear them play "Dixie,"' Lincoln replied. It's hard not to have a soft spot for that kind of

267

feller, don't you think?'

CHAPTER TWELVE

ENGLAND, HOME AND BEAUTY

The magic ships of the Phaeacians, in *The Odyssey*, could bear one home in a single night, no matter how far the journey. Jet aeroplanes do much the same for us, it is a kind of magic. Food and wine, and blankets so that the passengers shouldn't feel cold, were brought aboard the Phaeacians' ships, Homer tells us, by 'lordly young men.' Not many airline stewards would qualify under that heading, but the food and wine and blankets are provided. The chief disadvantage—not suffered by Odysseus, who, by that time, was travelling alone—are one's fellow passengers. The Duke of Wellington was quite right in fearing that railways would encourage the wrong people to travel. Aeroplanes encourage them to travel further—businessmen, who insist on taking off half their clothes, babies who cry and appalling children who run up and down the aisles. Massed mankind on the move is not an attractive spectacle.

However, on this occasion I had other things to think about, good and bad. The good was that I looked forward to introducing Cressida to England. The bad was the reason for our hurried journey, the harm that might already have been done; but even on that score, I had to confess a certain excitement, the feeling of a hunter when the quarry is almost in sight. Anyway, the most compelling reason for the journey was that it seemed the only way we could be safe. The matter had to be cleared up once and for all.

Cressida slept in the seat beside me, snuggled in her blanket. I drowsed, thinking of Rio and Charleston and ahead to Oxford, drifting and dreaming as peacefully as though I were indeed in the safe care of the Phaeacians.

When the cabin lights came on, I leaned across and half-raised the blind, letting in the morning sun. Cressida's eyes opened and she smiled at me. Not many women still look beautiful after a night in an aeroplane. She did.

Before leaving Charleston, I had telephoned the contact number in London with which Gabriel provided me when I first set out. The phone was answered by an anonymous woman. I asked for Gabriel or Jeremy but was told that neither was available; so I left a message, giving my flight number and saying that we needed to talk urgently. I wondered if anyone would meet us.

Inevitably it took Cressida a few minutes to clear immigration while I waited for her beyond the barrier; but our luggage arrived on the carousel quite quickly. We went through the green channel—and Jeremy appeared at our side as though from nowhere, immaculate in a charcoal-grey suit with a small rose in the buttonhole.

'Welcome to England, home and beauty,' he said. 'That's all your luggage?' He scooped up Cressida's elegant suitcase. 'The car's outside. Have no fear—not mine. Gabriel's Daimler.'

Amazingly, the sun shone and the air smelt fresh; it was very much what a summer day in England ought to be. 'Where are we going?' I asked, as Jeremy expertly manoeuvred the handsome old car into the traffic on the road to London.

'Richard's flat. More suitable, we thought, for the reception of ladies than my bachelor pad.'

'You never receive ladies there?' asked Cressida drily.

'Well, hardly ever. Anyway, Richard's place is where we all confabulated before shooting James off to Brazil; so it seemed appropriate that we should meet there again. Gabriel likes patterns.'

'Who is Richard?'

'Very decent fellow. Old friend.' Then, to me: 'You didn't tell her about him?'

'Not by name.'

'You may not have noticed,' said Cressida, 'but, like the Scotsman he is, he rations the things he tells you. Or, at least, tells me.'

'I've noticed,' said Jeremy.

The journey from Heathrow into London is by no means a scenic route, but the white pillars and balconies of Belgravia gleamed handsomely.

Jeremy pressed the bell. Richard, wearing a tweed jacket and grey flannel trousers, came down the stairs to meet us and help with the luggage. Diana was waiting in the doorway of the flat. As I introduced her to Cressida, I though the two women made a poignant—and pleasing—contrast, the one fair-haired and manifestly English, the other with glossy black hair and a touch of strangeness, even though I knew so much about her now.

Gabriel rose from a chair beside the window. He shook hands solemnly, not only with Cressida but with me. 'I think,' he said, 'we owe you many apologies. I believed it was a small thing we were asking you to do. I'm sorry it turned out differently.'

'We're alive and well,' I said. 'So I honestly don't know if I'm sorry.'

'Come along,' said Diana to Cressida, 'you'll be wanting to clean up,' and whisked her away, without giving her a chance to refuse.

Gabriel said to me in a low voice, 'Before

271

we talk—how much can we trust her?'

'I trust her absolutely.'

He looked at me for a moment, then nodded. 'This is your meeting.'

'Where's Surov now?' I asked.

'He's in a safe house. Not ours. He's being looked after by a government department which is run by an old friend—sometimes an old adversary—of mine.'

'I think perhaps you should warn your friend, straight away, that Surov may not, after all, be what he's supposed to be.'

'You've learned something more?'

'In a way. That's what I'm here to explain. And I may still be wrong. But it would be prudent to assume I'm not.'

'I agree.' Gabriel went to the telephone, an ivory instrument with touch-buttons on a half-table against the wall. I heard him say, 'Sir Arthur Blaise,' whom I'd never met, but I knew the name and I knew what department he headed. After a slight pause, Gabriel was evidently put through. He began to relay my warning about Surov, but was interrupted. He listened. Then said: 'I see. I'll call you back.'

Gabriel turned to me. 'Surov disappeared last night. There were two men guarding him. One was knocked out, the other was tricked somehow. My friend thought Surov had been kidnapped. But you think perhaps he wanted to go?'

'Perhaps. He, or the people running him, may have decided that the game was up and he should be got out.'

'Because of you?'

Before I could reply, Diana and Cressida returned; Diana carrying a tray with a coffee-pot and cups, Cressida with a plate of biscuits. Richard and Jeremy, who had been listening to, without interrupting, my conversation with Gabriel, rose and adjusted furniture, until we were all seated in a circle with the coffee on a low table between us.

'Should I withdraw,' asked Diana, 'if you want to talk business?'

'Of course not, my dear,' said Gabriel. 'When you married Richard, you became part of our business.'

'I like to think so,' she said.

'Can I be part of it too?' asked Cressida.

'Unfortunately,' I said, 'you already are very much part of it, now, in this affair.' Nobody else spoke, and I realized that I had the floor. A slight breeze ruffled the curtains, and there was an ordinary hum of traffic outside. Talking about such things here, in the pleasant normality of a London drawing room, semed in some respects more bizarre than any adventure in far-off places.

'When we were in Charleston,' I said, 'we were attacked twice, Cressida and I. I'll tell you the details later—you may be able to help us—but, for the moment, take my word for it: they were serious attacks, by professionals. The question is—why? Why should anyone want to kill us, if that is what they wanted, and I think it was?

'I'm sure Jeremy will have told you what happened in Brazil.' Gabriel nodded. 'So, I wondered, could it be O'Malley's men, wanting revenge on me? But I talked to Pedro Ramirez, and that seems most unlikely. O'Malley didn't have that sort of organization, and, once he was gone, I very much doubt if anybody else would have been interested. If not O'Malley, could it be to do with Surov? The KGB is, no doubt, quite capable of arranging such things, but again, why? Revenge on me for having helped Surov to escape? Surely not.

'Then I tried it another way. Suppose we were wrong. Suppose Surov, or the man we called Surov, wasn't a genuine defector but was—as we always knew to be possible—an enemy agent. But that still made no sense. The last thing the Russians would want, surely, would be to call attention to the fact that something was wrong by murdering me. Unless they thought I knew some dangerous fact, something that would expose him. But I didn't. On the contrary, I was the man who'd authenticated him.

'So I tried again. Was it possible that I knew, or they believed I knew, something I hadn't understood? Reviewing our experiences in that light, a couple of oddities did occur to me. The first happened early on. When Cressida ran away from O'Malley's night-club, his men almost caught us. But someone—coming from nowhere, passers-by perhaps—rescued us. I wondered at the time if they were your men, if you'd been keeping an eye on us. But they weren't, were they?'

'No,' said Gabriel, 'they were not ours.'

'We ought all to have given more consideration to that incident. But too many things happened too soon afterwards, and I forgot about it. The second oddity—well, really, it scarcely was an oddity, unless you link it up in this way—was implicit in Pedro's account of how he found us, after we'd been taken from outside the hotel. His contacts among O'Malley's staff wouldn't talk at first, he said, and then, a few hours later, they did, without his having to offer much of a bribe or exert any special pressure. Otherwise Jeremy wouldn't have reached us in time.

'Twice, then, we were helped to survive at crucial moments. And it seems to have been very powerful, clandestine help. It didn't come from the Fishers. So who else, out there in Brazil, would want us to survive? And why? I didn't have any special friends; but I was there to do a job. For whom was it important that the job should be completed, that I should survive to identify Surov, and that Surov should survive to defect? The

275

Fishers—but, as you've told me, it wasn't the Fishers. MI6? Why should the British secret service behave in such a devious manner? Either they were co-operating with you or they weren't. But it could be the Russians, if they were trying to plant Surov on us. That made sense. They might have wanted to help us behind the scenes. And they could have put pressure on O'Malley's men to talk.'

The room was very silent; I could hear the clock on the chimney-piece tick. I was certainly holding my audience. No one even offered a comment.

'What still didn't make sense,' I went on, 'is that they should have tried to kill me afterwards, although I could very well believe that the gunmen in Charleston were the kind of professionals they might use. I racked my brain to see if I could remember anything I might have heard or seen which could be dangerous to the Surov plan; dangerous enough to justify such a risk. But I couldn't think of anything.'

Jeremy suggested: 'Might it have been something Surov let slip when you were in the jungle?'

'It might, but I'm sure it wasn't. The only remarkable thing about him was how little he said.'

'Could it,' asked Gabriel, 'have been something he said, not to you, but to—?'

'To Cressida. Quite so.'

'But I'm sure he didn't,' said Cressida. 'You're right; he talked very little.'

'Yes, I agree. I don't think it was anything Surov said. But I do think it was you, not me, that those gunmen in Charleston wanted to kill.'

'Oh,' she said, and then in a very small voice, 'but why?'

'You told us, when we were lunching at that café in Rio, that you'd seen Kallinin before. Kallinin,' I explained to the others, 'is the KGB station chief.'

'She might have seen him with Surov?' asked Gabriel.

'Apparently not. She'd have remembered that. Somewhere else. But she can't recall where.'

'Where could it have been,' asked Jeremy,' that would be so dangerous to them?

'I did try to remember,' said Cressida, 'but it won't come.'

'I suppose,' said Richard, 'that it might have nothing to do with the Surov business at all. She might have seen him making some other contact . . .'

'That's possible, of course,' I said, 'but I doubt it. One shouldn't multiply the entities unnecessarily—good old principle. I've an idea what Cressida may have seen.'

'What?' she asked. 'What did I see?'

'I don't want to put pictures in your mind. I want to unlock what's there.'

'And how do you propose to do that?'
asked Gabriel.

'By taking her to where we specialize in
liberating what's in young minds. Cressida
and I are going to Oxford.'

CHAPTER THIRTEEN

THE SPIRES OF DR. CALIGARI

We went to Oxford by train. When I see the
familiar grey towers, I remember Cardinal
Newman's sad recollection of how he left the
college, with the snapdragon on the wall,
where he had expected to spend the rest of his
life: 'I have never seen Oxford since,
excepting its spires, as they are seen from the
railway.' Oxford station used, as Max
Beerbohm said, to whisper the last
enchantments of the Middle Age, but is now
a horrid modern place, matched, at one stage,
by a poster saying 'Welcome to Oxford,
Home of Pressed Steel.' I loathe almost every
new building in Oxford, I have little regard
for most of the dons, modern undergraduates
often depress me. And yet, and yet . . . The
old magic insidiously returns: it pours from
the soft flaking stone, drifts into one's heart
with the mellow disagreement of the bells.

Since we lost the Mitre, there is no worthy

hotel, but I put Cressida into the Randolph. When she'd unpacked, we walked to my own college and had tea in my rooms. Did Robby, the porter, raise an eyebrow as we passed his lodge? Not literally, of course, but implicitly. If so, I could scarcely blame him. It struck me as odd, too, seeing her there, vivacious and—by Oxford standards—exotic, against the background of my books, her bright red dress against the peeling brown leather of the armchair.

After tea we began our perambulation of Oxford. Out of term it never seems to me quite right. The dons in *Zuleika Dobson* may not have noticed the absence of all the undergraduates who had drowned themselves, but I miss the young. Undergraduate generations arc very fleeting, but their constant renewal, the renewal of hope, is very much the point of Oxford. Now some of the leaves already had a tinge of brown. Some of the dons were back. The long vacation was moving towards its end; which meant that the New Year would soon begin, for the real New Year in England, I've always thought, doesn't happen on an arbitrary date soon after Christmas. It comes in September, when schools and colleges reassemble, and London clubs open again, and the world starts up. That, for me, is when the sap rises.

I tried to say some of these things to

Cressida, but I doubt if she understood. Why should she? I launched, instead, into the classic anecdotes of Oxford. I showed her the gates in Balliol, on which—if your imagination is adequately vivid—you can see the scorch marks from the fire in which the martyrs were burned. I talked to her about *Brideshead* and *Gaudy Night*, about an Oxford accent, about Oxford bags, about Oxford marmalade and about Oxford philosophy. I enjoyed myself. I hope she did. She seemed to.

Finally, we came to a college. We went through the open gate into a garden quadrangle, in which slightly tired flower-beds ringed an immaculate lawn. We sat down on a wooden seat.

I wasn't sure what to do next: flush the coverts in some way, I supposed. The odds, obviously, were against immediate success; but things occasionally happen against the odds. In the event I had no need to do anything more at all. My quarry walked into view.

The quad had been deserted. Now the door of the Old Common Room opened, and half a dozen people emerged, perhaps thirty feet away from us, wearing gowns. It was a coincidence, of course, but not a complete coincidence. The only reason I'd thought it worth coming to Oxford at all, during the vacation, was that I knew a succession of committee meetings had been scheduled. My quarry was, characteristically, an earnest member, far too conscientious to miss a meeting, let along the whole series.

They strolled along the path, talking. I let my guide's commentary to Cressida tail off into silence. She glanced casually at the dons.

I felt her stiffen. 'James,' she said, 'that's the one. That's who I saw with Kallinin. In the lobby of the hotel.'

At the same moment Emily Bryant looked over towards us. The evening sun glinted on her spectacles. I nodded an acknowledgement. She offered a chilly smile, which froze on her face. I doubt if she recognized Cressida, although she might have done, but she realized that something was wrong. Cressida's expression probably revealed it; or perhaps it was just my presence, which she may have considered, in the circumstances, odd. She hesitated, for a fraction of a second, as though she might have come over to us, but then turned back to her companion, resuming her conversation and her walk to the gate.

'Who is she?' asked Cressida. 'It was her, wasn't it?'

'Yes,' I said, 'it was. She's a don, here in this college. They have women now, although it's a men's college. I always did say that was a mistake.'

'But I don't understand. Why was she with

Kallinin?'

I shrugged. 'Your guess is as good as mine.'

'And that's why you brought me here? So I could see her? How did you know?'

Emily had disappeared through the gate. I rose. 'Come on. I'll tell you as we go.'

The quad was deserted again. We walked back to the gate. There was no one in the lodge either. Emily must have left the college; but there was no sign of her in the street outside, although two of the dons were standing on the pavement, chatting. Cressida and I retraced our steps towards the Randolph.

She repeated her question: 'How did you know?'

'"Know" is putting it rather too strongly. I asked myself what you could have seen that was so potentially damaging. You ought, as it were, to have seen Kallinin with Surov. But you didn't. Suppose you'd seen him with one of O'Malley's men; would that matter? Surely not catastrophically, particularly not after you'd left Rio. And if you'd seen him with some absolute stranger, it was most unlikely you'd ever have made the connection. But suppose it had been with one of us, with somebody from the conference, somebody from Britain, where Surov was going, and where, since you and I were together, you might also come. Well, that description narrowed the field. There were only five or six people from Britain at the conference. There were three of us from Oxford, one from Cambridge and a couple from provincial universities.'

I paused as we negotiated the traffic in the Broad. Most undergraduates still being away, there was a lack of bicycles, but cumbersome tourist buses were more offensive.

I gestured towards Balliol. 'One of us came from there. Very left-wing. I should have enjoyed suspecting him.'

'But you didn't? Or the ones from the other universities?'

'I didn't rule them out, but the next question was—where would you have been most likely to see such a meeting? It might have been anywhere; but the thought came to me that there was one, and only one, occasion when you could easily have seen anybody attending the conference.'

'While I was waiting for you.'

'Exactly. While you were waiting for me, in the lobby of the hotel, on the morning of Surov's defection. I remember that morning rather vividly; and, thinking back on it, I was pretty sure that only one British person came into the conference hall after I left you and before Surov and I made our run. That was Emily Bryant. Of course, one of the others could have come into the lobby and gone away again—'

Cressida interrupted: 'She came through the main entrance almost immediately after you'd gone up in the elevator. I remember thinking that such a plain dowdy woman was probably going to the conference. Kallinin must have been in the lobby already. He sort of appeared beside her. I think they were together only for a minute or so, but I wasn't really paying attention. I had plenty on my mind. But when I saw her again just now, I did remember. Quite clearly. Like a photograph.'

'I know. Everything's in the memory somewhere. It's just the retrieval system which lets us down.'

We crossed the road again, beside the Martyrs' Memorial.

'I still don't understand,' said Cressida. 'What was their meeting about? How does that woman fit in?'

'Now you're asking me to speculate. I don't know why they took the risk of meeting, at that time and place. Indeed, I don't know what she is. But my guess, in reply to your second question, is that our Miss Bryant is a long-term Soviet agent. A recruiter, here in the university.'

'You mean a recruiter of young people to be spies?'

'Something of the kind, although they may not regard themselves in that light. Not at first, anyway. It's a phenomenon of which

284

we've had some experience in Britain.'

Outside the sombre Gothic front of the Randolph, I glanced at my watch. 'Suppose we meet again in an hour. We'll have a drink in my room and then go out to dinner.'

'Sure. But come up now and wait while I change. I might have a shower too, but I won't be long.'

'No, if you don't mind, I'll go back to the college. There are one or two things I want to do. I'd better call Gabriel, for instance. Can you find your way, or shall I come and pick you up?'

'Didn't I tell you?' said Cressida. 'I used to be a Girl Scout. I'll come to your rooms.' She touched her fingers to her lips and then to mine, and went cheerfully into the hotel.

As I walked back to college, a queer feeling came over me. I'd been thinking about Emily Bryant, wondering about her motives, wondering what she was doing now. She didn't, I knew, live in college. She had a room there, of course, but I'd looked her up in the telephone directory and learned that she had a house, or a flat, in the Banbury Road. When our eyes had met, for an instant, in the quadrangle just now, a flash of compact, complex communication had passed between us. She knew I knew—something. And there was emotion—surprise, hatred, fear—on her face, wiped off again in a split second. What would her next move be? That would depend on too many questions to which I had no answer.

In theory I wasn't surprised to find a spy in Oxford. As I'd observed to Cressida, the situation was notoriously familiar. Nor was I surprised that Emily Bryant should be the spy. She was a classic type: clever but unloved and unlovable, therefore vulnerable. But in real life such a discovery is a shock nevertheless. It erodes the solid furniture of one's life, making everything and everybody doubtful. So, as I walked in the twilight through the friendly streets of Oxford, the college walls and towers and turrets began to seem weird and menacing, like the distorted streets and houses in *The Cabinet of Caligari*.

I thrust the mood away. There was a car parked outside my college, an ordinary blue saloon; nothing peculiar about it at all, except that the plump man sitting behind the wheel, reading a magazine, struck a tiny chord at the back of my mind. Like Cressida with Kallinin, I felt that I'd seen him before but, like Cressida, I couldn't remember where.

Before I could pursue this casual thought, which anyway was probably another illusion, I was accosted at the gate by one of my colleagues, fat old Giles Hanbury.

'James!' he said. 'Back at the grindstone already?'

'I don't propose to do much grinding,' I said. We exchanged pleasantries for a while.

I'm fond of Giles. He's idle and jovial, his erudition floating lightly on a sea of port; an epitome of the old, unworldly, celibate Oxford which the modern zealots—including Emily Bryant—have been trying, for at least a generation, to sweep away.

The conversation had cheered me up. I climbed the worn stairs to my rooms in an altogether happier frame of mind. My door wasn't locked; it's a new idea in Oxford that one might need to lock one's door. I pushed it open.

In the leather armchair sat Emily Bryant. On the sofa was Surov. Raising a small automatic pistol from her lap and pointing it at me, Emily Bryant said, 'Come in and shut the door behind you.'

'I wish that I could say I was happy to see you again, Professor Glowrey,' said Surov. 'Believe me, I desire you no harm. We have experienced much together, have we not?'

'Where's the girl?' asked Miss Bryant.

Without replying, I went over to my desk and sat down, conscious of her pistol following me.

'What do you want?' I asked.

'We were hoping,' said Surov, 'that we might persuade you to keep quiet, for just a little while. You and Miss Lee. We can offer several sorts of persuasion, nice or nasty. I should much prefer to offer the nice ones. Are you interested in money, Professor

287

Glowrey? Quite a lot of money.'

'Not your money,' I said.

'That is what I thought. Then how about Miss Lee's safety? I think you are interested in that.'

'You haven't got Miss Lee,' I said.

'We can find her.'

'You're too late. I telephoned my friends from her room.'

'Her hotel room?' asked Emily Bryant.

'I didn't say she was in a hotel. But it makes no difference. My friends knew why we came to Oxford. If anything happens to me, or to her, they'll know where to look. The mole's unearthed; your time's up. You've nothing to gain by hurting us.'

'I don't believe you,' she said.

Surov leaned towards her and said something in a low voice; not that I could have understood it anyway.

'You speak Russian?' I said to Miss Bryant. 'How conscientious. But of course you do. You wrote an article in *The Journal of Hellenic Studies* about classical scholarship in the Soviet Union.'

She ignored me, and replied in Russian to Surov; but her eyes, and her pistol, never strayed. 'Come to think of it,' I went on, 'and it did occur to me when I started to be suspicious of you, that was a little mistake you made at the conference. You never spoke to Surov. You deliberately kept away from him. That wasn't natural.'

Surov stood up. 'Professor Glowrey,' he said, 'I never doubted you were a clever man. You may be lying when you say that you have already talked to your friends tonight. But I cannot take the risk. My first responsibility is not to be caught and questioned. Miss Bryant will keep you here for a small time.' He smiled. 'Thank you for your help. I regret that I must leave. We could have had interesting conversations.'

And he was gone. Through the door, which he left slightly ajar, I could hear his footsteps echo on the stairs.

'Now it's just us,' I said. 'How long do we have to stay here like this?'

'Not long,' said Emily Bryant. 'I don't believe you've told anyone else about me yet. If you had, it wouldn't have been you who came this afternoon. At least, that's the chance I'm going to take. I'm afraid I shall have to kill you, and then I'm going to find the girl—I think she's in one of the Oxford hotels, there aren't many—and put her out of the way too.'

I could scarcely believe what I was hearing, or I should have been more frightened. But there was hatred in her eyes, quite different from the quizzical impassivity that marked Surov.

'Don't be absurd,' I answered. 'Whatever else you may be, you're a rational woman.

You can't kill two people in these circumstances, and think that it wouldn't very quickly be traced to you.'

'I know that. But my duty is the same as his.' (She meant Surov.) 'I mustn't be caught, and I don't intend to be. I've some papers to destroy and some people to warn. I need a little time.' She sat back in the chair, but with the pistol still pointed unwaveringly at me. 'I wonder. I wonder if I could put them on a false trail. Suppose I left a note suggesting I'd killed you because I was jealous. Do you think that might be believed?'

'Frankly, no,' I said.

It was a mistake. The hatred flashed out like a striking cobra.

'No, you wouldn't. Men like you never really think that people like me are human. I'm going to enjoy killing you, James Glowrey. You represent everything I detest in Oxford and in this society. You're exactly why I've done what I've done.'

'Oh dear. I never thought I represented anything except myself.' My mind was desperately thrashing about, seeking a way of escape. I remembered one of my pupils, a girl, who had been cornered by a rapist who broke into her flat. 'I said to myself,' she had told me afterwards, 'Wyatt Earp says. "If you keep them talking, they never pull the trigger"' And she had kept him talking, until she managed to slip into another room and out of the window. It seemed as good a principle as any.

'On the subject of what you've done,' I said, 'would you mind telling me—just as a matter of intellectual curiosity—why you had that meeting with Kallinin at the hotel in Rio? That's what gave you away, you know.'

'The girl saw us together. Yes, I know. It was Kallinin's fault. He'd grown careless. When you arrived to check Surov's credentials, which is what I suppose you were doing, Kallinin was worried. You weren't part of the original plan. So he wanted to find out about you. He had you followed, but that wasn't enough. He needed to know that you were what you seemed to be, and not a British agent leading Surov into a trap. And he needed to know quickly. There was no one he could ask except me. Apparently he tried to telephone but I was out of my room. So he came in person. He was a fool and I told him so, even though I didn't think, then, that we'd been seen. Does that satisfy your intellectual curiosity?'

'Yes. But there's a bigger question, to which I'd very much like to know the answer. Is Surov really Surov? Is he the scholar whose work you and I have read?'

'You mean the great professor couldn't tell? If he can't, how should a mere woman, with none of your social or academic advantages, be expected to do better?'

'I thought you might have inside information.'

'I'm really not that interested in what you thought. And I know what you're doing. You're trying to spin this conversation out. Well, we've come to the end of it. Surov should be clear away by now.' She rose from the chair, and, still facing me, stepped back to the door. 'This gun won't make much noise, but I'd better just shut the door to muffle the sound.'

I tensed myself. I'd have to try to jump, dive for her legs perhaps.

But, as she felt behind her for the door-handle, the door was pushed open hard, knocking her off balance. I leaped towards her. The gun went off, the bullet flying wide. She eluded my grasp, but her attention was now divided.

Cressida was in the room, and, without a moment's hesitation, grabbing a bottle from the cluster that stood on a shelf of the book case beside the door, she hit Emily Bryant hard on the side of the head. The blow must have been hard because the bottle shattered and Miss Bryant slid to the floor.

I was pleased to see that Cressida had chosen, not the good stuff, but a bottle of South African sherry which I keep purely to annoy liberal visitors.

CHAPTER FOURTEEN

PERIL CONFRONTED

Cressida had arrived at my rooms earlier than expected, which probably saved my life, because, rather than undertake an arduous quarter-mile walk through the streets of Oxford, the dear girl had decided to take a taxi. Hearing a woman's voice, she had tiptoed up the stairs, grasped the situation and plunged in. Subsequently she was able to exercise her Girl Scout training on Emily Bryant, whose straw-coloured hair was dramatically stained with blood.

While Cressida administered first aid, I telephoned Gabriel in London. This time I got through to him at once, and told him what had happened. He listened without interrupting, then said, 'Jeremy will be with you as soon as possible. Knowing how he drives, I should say that will be very soon.'

Emily Bryant, her head sponged and bandaged, had recovered consciousness and was sitting in the leather armchair; but she wasn't talking.

'What are we going to do with her?' asked Cressida. 'She ought to go to the hospital.'

'God knows where she ought to go,' I replied, 'and I'd rather not play God. Can she walk?'

'I can walk,' said Miss Bryant, and pushed herself up from the chair onto her feet.

'You're not just going to let her go?' protested Cressida.

'She's committed no crime,' I said, 'as far as we know—except shooting at me. And I won't complain about that.'

Without saying a word or even looking at us, Emily Bryant walked shakily towards the door. 'Your handbag,' I said, and gave it to her. 'We'll keep the gun.' She took the handbag and went slowly down the stairs.

'You're a soft touch,' said Cressida.

'Maybe. Gabriel will tell the right people about her. I doubt if she'll be prosecuted, but her fangs will be drawn.'

Actually it wasn't as simple as that. She'd spoken of destroying papers and warning contacts. I probably should have held her, at least until Jeremy came, but the idea of keeping her in my room, like a trapped animal, revolted me. I wanted her gone. Arthur Blaise and all the powers of government could pursue her if they thought it necessary.

While we waited for Jeremy, we cleaned up the broken glass and the South African sherry, fortified outselves with something rather better and found the spent bullet, which had lodged in an unimportant chapter of the third volume of the *Cambridge Ancient*

History. I did also take the precaution of going downstairs, having a casual word with Robby the porter, and glancing out into the street. There was no one hanging about. The blue saloon, I noticed, had gone.

Jeremy must have come bounding down the motorway in his appalling sports car. He tapped at my door less than ninety minutes after I'd spoken to Gabriel. I opened the door with Miss Bryant's automatic in my hand. But Jeremy's exuberant presence then filled the room. He took charge and there was nothing more for us to do.

Indeed, in a public sense, that was for me the end of the affair. A polite young man from the department headed by Sir Arthur Blaise did come to see me the following day, and I told him all I knew about Surov and Emily Bryant. Nobody criticized me for having let her go, and the police were apparently not brought into it. I talked a couple of times to Gabriel on the telephone.

Cressida said she would like to stay in Oxford for a few days, and be shown around 'without an ulterior motive.' So we did all the proper things: visited the Ashmolean and the Botanic Garden, walked through the fields to the Perch and the Trout, saw a play at the New Theatre and made an expedition to Stratford. We had tea on the college lawn and were lunched and dined by one or two friends. I realized, to my own astonishment, that I was enjoying a holiday; something I hadn't done for years. And Cressida simulated interest even in things which I cannot believe interested her.

Neither of us talked about the future. I did ask Cressida once whether she had any plans, but she joked the question aside. Then came a day when we were scheduled to go punting on the Cherwell; she called it 'polling.' As I went to pick her up, I met Giles Hanbury.

'Whither away, so summery?' he asked.

'I'm taking Cressida on the river,' I said.

'Have a care, Professor. Your bachelorhood is in peril.'

'Nonsense,' I said.

But, as I walked on, his remark had started an alarming train of thought. Was it nonsense? Need it be nonsense? Did I want it to be nonsense? Questions about the future couldn't be evaded indefinitely; it was no use pretending that nothing in my life had changed. But that was no reason to make a fool of oneself. Least of all here in Oxford. Rio had been a place for romantic adventure, Charleston the most seductive setting in which to mellow a relationship; but in Oxford the cynical observation of one's colleagues, and the portraits of one's predecessors, and the ghost of one's own youth, all alike demanded honesty. We were supposed, were we not, to be fearless seekers, following the truth wherever it leads? And what could be more important than the truth about oneself? More important—or more difficult? An old fool and what Dr. Johnson would have called 'a wretched unidea'd girl'; was that our case?

Thus musing, I arrived at the Randolph, where Cressida was waiting for me, brown arms bare, in a summer frock.

I'd booked one of the college punts. The effete habit, now, is to use an aluminium pole, but the boatman, knowing I prefer it, keeps one of the old heavy wooden ones for me. We glided out into the stream.

'Don't you get your sleeves wet?' asked Cressida, lying back against the cushions.

'Not if you know what you're doing,' I said. 'The secret lies in a rotatory twist combined with the upward flick.'

'Very impressive,' she said with a hint of laughter. All right, so I was showing off; but I am quite good in a punt. With firm strokes I propelled us over the quiet water. We seemed to have the river more or less to ourselves.

'This is a bit different from our other river trip, isn't it?' said Cressida.

'We've come a long way,' I said.

'Life's peculiar, isn't it? Without Surov you and I would never have met.'

'Life is very peculiar.'

'James, what was it all about? Surov, I mean. Why was he pretending to be a defector?'

'I've discussed that with Gabriel. He thinks

there were two motives. The first, and probably the less important, was to learn how the Fishers' pipeline works. They've slipped quite a lot of people out from behind the Iron Curtain, you know. The other motive, the main one, was the interrogation he'd have had when he reached this country. I told you, didn't I, that he was cypher expert? He'd have been asked all sorts of technical questions. The debriefing would have gone on for weeks. And from what they asked him he'd have discovered, or hoped to discovered, how much they knew.'

'And then he'd have re-defected to Moscow?'

'Exactly.'

I slid the punt in beneath the willows. 'Shall we pause here for lunch?' I said. 'We should really have been trailing the wine behind us to cool it, but I always think that's a bit hazardous, unless one's very sure of one's knots.'

'I'm sure of my knots. I used to be—'

'I know. A Girl Scout.' We laughed. 'By the way, I've remembered who the man in the blue saloon was. Or I think I have.'

'Oh, who?'

'The very first day I met Gabriel, with Richard—I think I told you. I was walking the dogs in Kensington Gardens, and there was this man sitting on a bench. I believe he was watching us. Watching Gabriel or

Richard, I suppose, because that's when Surov had just made contact. The London end of the Fishers was being kept under observation to see how they responded and whom they got in touch with.'

'And they got in touch with you; which was very wise of them. And that's how it all began.'

'If I'm right, if it was the same man, he was probably waiting in the car for Surov. I've been thinking about that aspect. I suppose when Surov escaped, or was removed, from the safe house, he came to Emily Bryant because she was the resident agent he knew. In which case, she may have been more than just a recruiter.'

'Dogs,' said Cressida. 'We must have dogs.'

'Dogs?' I replied in some confusion. 'Why dogs? I agree, one should have dogs. But have I missed a link in this conversation?'

'I was just thinking. You like dogs. I like dogs. We get along pretty well together.'

I'd secured the punt, and was now sitting opposite her, corkscrew in hand. Yes, we do.' A tiny breeze ruffled the surface of the river and seemed to make my skin tingle.

Cressida gazed at me, then leaned over the side of the punt and drew circles in the water with her finger. 'You realize,' she said, 'that I intend to marry you?'

'I hadn't realized anything of the sort,' I

protested. 'But—'

'I know you're a confirmed bachelor, whatever that means, and don't think you want to marry anyone at all, let alone me. But you need someone.'

'My dear Cressida, I don't need anyone, in that sense—'

'It's no use arguing. I'm prepared to wait. Maybe for years, but I'll convince you sooner or later. We Girl Scouts are very determined . . .'

'Cressida, will you be quiet?' I said. 'I'm trying to tell you, if only you'd listen, that I should like to marry you very much indeed.'

'You would?'

'Yes. At this moment, more than anything in the world.'

'Oh. Well, that's all right then.'

And it was. And is.

Photoset, printed and bound in Great Britain by
REDWOOD BURN LIMITED, Trowbridge, Wiltshire